A Winged Embrace

A Winged Embrace

TONI MOBLEY

ISBN: 979-8-88785-052-8 (Paperback)
ISBN: 979-8-88785-053-5 (Hardcover)

Library of Congress Control Number: 2025944194

Any references to historical events, real people, or real places are used fictitiously. Names, characters, and places are products of the author's imagination.

FMP book design by Allison Chernutan.
Cover illustration by Prashant Bisht.
Original cover design by Moonshot Covers.
Original interior design by SSB Covers and Design.
Edited by Swish Design and Editing, Emily Kudeviz.
Copy edited by Carol Kudeviz.

Printed in the United States of America.

Second printing edition 2025.

emily@fracturedmirrorpublishing.com
Fractured Mirror Publishing
Knoxville, Tennessee

www.fracturedmirrorpublishing.com

To my mother,
who loves aliens
as much as I do.

Chapter 1

ALTHOUGH THE SUN HAD FALLEN LONG AGO, THE SKIES were alive with the twinkling of the firmament spread across the heavens like ribbons sprinkled with glitter. It was my favorite sight, and tonight, in less than an hour, it would supposedly become the best I had ever seen.

My college friends and students from the rest of the dormitories scrambled for the best spots atop the roof. Everywhere we looked, people were gathered with blankets, pillows, and snacks like the night sky was our own personal movie theater. The janitorial staff had long given up corralling us off the roofs. I even recognized some of them at the other end of the roof, entranced by the display above.

Here and there, small streaks, so tiny they were barely perceivable, raced across the sky, disappearing as fast as they had appeared. I'd previously seen a meteor shower when I lived in Australia. The skies in the middle of nowhere there were clearer than here.

Somewhere nearby, instrumental piano music rose on the gentle breeze, filling the void of silence left by people who paused to listen. Every key resonated within me. Oh, how I envied the person who had a piano at their disposal at this very moment. Listening to Debussy being played with such heart and perfection under the twinkling sky was surreal.

"There!" someone cried out.

Everyone on the roof turned to stare upward, desperate to see the first meteor. If only I could tell them meteor showers often lasted days, and this one would be no exception. The news reported this shower would be bigger and brighter than the Perseids, Orionids, or even the Leonids, which were famous for their once-a-decade extravaganza. I'd only seen those once in my life, and I was too young to remember the details.

"I can't see anything," complained my roommate, Theresa, while she pouted.

Osman, a man who lived across from us, patted her on the back. "Don't worry. You won't miss anything." His accent was as thick as his beard, but his charm was undeniable.

When she was certain Osman wasn't looking, she raised her eyebrows at me, biting her lower lip. I gave her a wink.

She had been vying for Osman's affection since the beginning of the semester, and this was the first time he'd touched her.

"How can you be so sure?" she asked, batting her eyelids at him.

Osman flashed her a brilliant smile. "Do you not trust me, *güzelim* <beautiful>? I would never lie to you." His tone was adamant.

"What does that mean?" She sounded unsure as if he would suddenly go from endearment to outright insult.

"*Güzelim?*" He purred for emphasis. "My beautiful." He gave her another wink, sealing the deal.

Theresa nestled closer to him, and he squeezed her shoulder.

Although I wasn't against public displays of affection and overly cute things, I put some distance between them and me when I was certain their attention was elsewhere.

I'd hit an all-time low in the love department. My high school sweetheart decided my spending a year at a university in Austria instead of attending a local college in Australia with him was unforgivable. I cringed, remembering our very last conversation.

Young Emilia was so naïve.

"*When will I ever get a chance like this again? I'm eighteen…*" My voice was low that day, dejected, knowing even though I stood before him in the frilly pink dress he loved so much, the outcome would be the same.

"*Can't you think of me, Emilia? It's always you, you, you! I can't go to Austria.*" He wore a baggy band shirt and jeans that were a size too small. He insisted it was the style, but I knew it was because he refused to accept the fact he couldn't fit into the jeans he'd worn since he was sixteen.

"*It's just for a year.*" For a single moment in time, I thought perhaps I was being selfish, maybe even unreasonable.

I remembered his next reaction as if it had happened yesterday, not three years ago.

"*Really? You'd risk our relationship for what? Music? Dancing? You don't even know what you want to major in.*"

"*That's not fair, Alex. You know very well I want to work in film.*" Or the theater, hell—even as an extra in the background singing or dancing or even writing the music. I wanted it all, a slice of every pie.

"Why waste it on a role behind the scenes?" He'd asked that a few times, and my answer was always the same.

"Because that's what I want to do."

I should've seen the signs earlier. But when you're eighteen, in your first real relationship, the world is so very small. The only experience you have is the bubble you've put yourself in. I'd like to say I knew better now at twenty, but I'd be lying to myself.

Theresa tried to break the curse that had befallen me, and I'd let her try, but so far, Emilia Bauer was as single as they got.

So, of course, I said fuck it and decided to complete my Bachelor of Arts degree for dance in Austria. Which, admittedly, was easy enough because my parents were Austrian and had dual citizenship. But I was glad for the choices young Emilia had made because they led me to have the happiest memories and most amazing experiences of my life. If I was given the opportunity to go back in time and try again, I was confident I wouldn't change a thing. *Maybe dump Alex earlier?*

"Regardé!" <Look!> someone nearby shouted in French.

I turned to survey the rooftop, where everyone had fallen deathly silent. Even the piano had gone cold. In the silence, ribbons of blindingly bright green and blue streaked across the sky. Some were close, and some were far, but they all shared the same path. They rose over the fortress of Hohensalzburg to the north and disappeared over the taller roofs behind us.

"Mira!" <Look!> another person, closer this time, said in Spanish. He held his girlfriend on his shoulders, her wide eyes on the heavens above.

The meteors came faster and much, much closer together. If I hadn't known this was a meteor shower, I was certain I'd think I was in the middle of a warzone or on the foreshore during an Australia Day celebration. The flashes were insanely bright like someone had detonated an explosion above our heads. It moved like a meteor should, or at least, what my limited knowledge of meteors told me it should look like, but they were so close and bright.

One trailed directly over our heads, and an odd sensation rippled over me. For a single fear-gripping moment, I thought maybe it was a rocket before it followed the course of its companions, disappearing behind the apartments in the distance.

"That one was close," someone whispered in English, and I recognized a hint of fear in her voice.

"It's a meteor. You'll be all right," a man replied.

I turned to see the couple snuggled under a checkered blanket. "What if it hits us?" Her voice reminded me of a child hiding under the blankets from the monster that lived under her bed. I knew that well—that was me a little more than a decade ago.

The guy laughed. "The odds of that happening are basically zero."

The girl stopped fidgeting, and once again, the rooftop went silent. There were occasional bursts of oohs and aahs, but for the most part, it was easy to let nature's own fireworks display fill my mind. My mind had little room for anything but streaks of light and a soft explosion.

"W-what…" The voice of the English girl tore me from my reverie.

That was an explosion.

One of the meteors had flown so low I thought I could feel the flash of heat from it spiraling overhead. It disappeared over the town, and I shielded my eyes from the impossibly bright flash that followed. A moment later, the ground beneath us shook so lightly I was sure I had made it up.

"Did that…"

"*Mein Gott…*" <My God…>

That meteor hit something.

Dust gathered on the other side of the apartments, rising over its gray stone walls into the sky. Before we could react to one, another fireball careened overhead, colliding with the building itself.

"No!" There were so many cries it was hard to distinguish one from the other.

There was a moment of mute horror as our brains collectively scrambled to acknowledge what had happened, but I seemed to recover much faster than anyone else. I wanted answers, yet I knew if it happened once, it'd happen again. I needed to find my friends, and we needed to get off the roof. But in the crowd that had formed, I had no idea where I had left them.

"Theresa," I called, pushing past the crowd of terrified statues. Not a single person made a move, and I only prayed with the next hit, they would realize they weren't safe.

"Emi?" I heard Theresa call above the startled cries of others as yet another meteor hit. This one was closer and lit the roofs with an eerie green glow.

Shit, where was she?

I was in the vague area I had left them, close to the stairwell. "Theresa, where are you?"

"Emi!" Theresa ran into my arms, Osman right behind her.

"What is it?" he asked, watching an orange hue ignite along the ridge.

I kept Theresa close as I whispered, "The meteors...they're hitting the ground."

I felt so stupid explaining it that way, but words escaped me.

"Is that normal?" Theresa murmured.

"No," someone piped up next to us, a boy not much older than us. "If I were you, I'd be leaving."

He gathered his blanket and pillow, ushering the guy who sat there to follow him.

"Good idea," I muttered, pushing Theresa toward the stairwell. Osman followed behind us, not saying a word.

The guy in front of us tossed the door open as another meteor hit.

"This isn't right...whatever is happening with those meteors," Osman mumbled.

That's what the other guy on the roof had said. I couldn't fault Osman for thinking out loud. The situation was surreal.

"Meteorite," the guy in front of us said.

"Pardon?" The confusion was evident in Osman's voice.

"When meteors hit the ground, they're called meteorites," he replied, eerily calm.

I mean, thanks for the science lesson, but now is not the right time.

On the fourth-floor landing, the door to the floor flew open, and a terrified older woman emerged, tumbling into us. The men in front of us caught her, steadying her.

"What is it? What's going on?" The guy put his hands on the trembling woman's shoulders, trying to steady her. But whatever she had seen or heard, she was in no state to share.

She shook her head, shrinking from his touch before dashing down the stairs.

Our building had only four levels, but the flights down felt like twenty. My thighs burned, and my calves ached. I silently told myself I'd join the gym if I didn't die from a meteorite impact.

By the time we made it to the ground floor, the woman had long disappeared. We could hear the chaos in the rooms around us and from the stairwell we had exited. The ground had shaken half a dozen more times since we started our descent and once more as we stood in the hall, torn between returning to our rooms or leaving.

"What should we do?" Theresa ran her hands through her hair, her chest rising and falling. She was on the verge of hyperventilating.

I gathered her into my arms and pressed my lips against the top of her head.

The stranger turned to us, dangling keys in front of our faces. "I don't know what plans you guys have, but we're getting the hell out of here if you want to join us."

The parking lot was filled with honking cars and screaming people. With Theresa's hand gripped in mine, I pulled her after the two men from the roof, Osman following close behind. People shoved one another out of the way, screaming obscenities and, once or twice, even spitting at one another. It was utter chaos.

"Over here," the guy in front called out, leading us through the throng.

More than once, I received an unnecessarily hard shove as someone desperately tried to get past me. They could do whatever they liked, so long as I managed to get Theresa to safety. She was a ballerina in stature and demeanor, and the purest, most innocent, nicest person I had ever met. She only ever saw the good in the world, and I wouldn't let someone take advantage of that.

"Watch out!" Osman cried out from behind, but whatever he wanted to warn me about, it was too late.

The entire parking lot was enveloped in a hot, green light before a wall of dust swelled around us. I choked on particles that cut into my flesh and forced my eyes to shutter. My shoulders shook with the effort to draw in a single breath, my lungs burning. My hands went to my face, desperate to shield myself from the debris. I could feel the others beside me, coughing and spluttering.

Someone moved beside me, and a hand gripped my shoulder. "It's safe to open your eyes now."

The man stood over me, clutched his keys, and surveyed the lot. Osman and Theresa appeared at my side, their eyes roaming the debris that had flattened cars and broken posts. We moved toward the crater, where puffs of grayish smoke curled into the air. When the dust around us cleared faster than I anticipated, it revealed a rather small but certainly not shallow crater, with something oddly shaped sitting within.

"*Was ist das?*"<What is that?> An older man dressed in pajamas took a few steps toward the crater.

I followed the crowd that gathered around it. Theresa's nails bit into the flesh of my upper arm, Osman was on my tail, and the two men who had helped us were not far behind. We pressed into the crowd. Some had abandoned their vehicles, others their rooms, but all huddled around the hole in the middle of the asphalt, deep enough that crawling out without help would not be an option. I subtly pressed my hand against Theresa, corralling her behind me. If anyone fell in, I wouldn't let it be her.

As we neared the crumbling lip, a soft gasp escaped those who had reached it ahead of us. I steeled myself for what I was about to see, but it wasn't nearly as exciting as I'd hoped. It was just as I imagined—a hole filled with debris and a definitive center. A dark, near obsidian spherical ball sat in the center, nestled within the mass of dirt, rock, and what I strongly suspected used to be a car.

Please tell me that car was empty.

The man with the keys appeared at my side, a frown marring his face. "That doesn't look like a meteorite."

"How can you be so sure?" I don't know what made me doubt him, but I wanted to question everything, including the fact as we stood there, more and more meteors—*meteorites*—were falling from the sky.

"I work for the Aerospace Defense Bureau in Vienna."

"What are you doing here?" Theresa asked quietly. Why he was here didn't matter, but she probably asked to distract herself.

He pointed his thumb over his shoulder at the man who had silently followed him from the roof. "He goes to the university here." His companion, who I strongly suspected was his boyfriend by the tight grip of their hands, silently nodded.

"*Was ist es?*" <What is it?> asked the man who had reached the crater first, leaning over the edge.

The smoke had completely cleared, giving us an unobstructed view of the weird orb within. Yet, I would have preferred the smoke because I wasn't prepared for what happened next.

It *moved.*

I rubbed my eyes, positive the slight shimmer along its surface, like the ripple in water after you skip a rock, was all in my head. My adrenaline had begun to fade, and with it, I felt exhaustion tug at the edges of my mind.

That's all it was. I'm sure of it.

And I was. Until it happened again and again, and suddenly, the entire orb undulated like a barrel of oily eels. My hand shot to my mouth, stifling the gasp others around me could not control. The meteorite began to pulse with a soft, thudding noise that beat in rhythm to the ripples across its surface.

"We should leave," the guy said quietly, pulling his companion from the edge.

Osman took Theresa's hand, guiding her from the edge, clearly with the same mindset. But something had me glued to the spot. I couldn't move, even if I wanted to. I was transfixed, mesmerized, like a bull to a matador's cape. I couldn't look away. Even as the humming stopped, the rippling ceased, and the once shiny surface of the orb faltered. For all intents and purposes, it looked as if it were *melting.*

Globs of the darkened orb dripped off the surface, hitting the ground like water droplets. But the viscosity reminded me more of tar than anything else, and an odd feeling lifted the hair on my arms. A lump formed in my throat, and a pit in my stomach, as I watched in horror. The orb, although never moving from its cozy nook in the crater, seemed *alive.* It writhed and writhed, more and more droplets splattering to the ground until I finally understood what was happening.

The orb was disintegrating.

It continued to weep the sticky goo-like substance until enough had gathered around the orb to reveal a hollowness within. But even from there, I could see that, though it was hollow, it certainly wasn't empty. The crowd murmured in horror as the dripping accelerated, peeling away from whatever sat inside.

The man at the edge of the crater closest to the orb teetered on a wide pipe extended over the cavity, vying for a closer look. Liquid dribbled from the pipe and mixed with the tar. But it was akin to mixing oil and water—the tar practically repelled the steady stream. A woman called out in French, but the man ignored her and stood at the very edge.

The hollow widened. Strands of the tarry substance stretched across the concave surface like a spiderweb, and now, without a shadow of a doubt, I could see what lay within. My heart lurched inside my chest, and I suddenly forgot how to breathe. A vaguely humanoid *thing* was huddled beneath the webbing. It turned onto its back, raised its arms, and tore the webbing apart. The first thing I noticed was the grayish skin and bright crimson eyes that roamed over those watching it. When those eyes roamed over me, I couldn't control the shiver that ran up my spine.

Long, ebony hair, as slick and shiny as the tar surrounding it, cascaded across broad, muscular shoulders that shimmered with oddly glowing ivory tattoos. The tattoos reminded me of the symbols you'd see on runestones in Scandinavia, but those did not glow, not like this. It was as if the tattoos themselves were just as alive as the creature they were tattooed across. *Creature.* It was then the full realization dawned on me. This was a creature from space.

An alien.

I took a few tentative steps back, my usual surefootedness escaping me as my ankles wobbled with every step. I was *petrified,* for good reason. The creature stood from within the hollow, exposing its glory. From the streetlights illuminating the lot, I could see the creature was clad in hellish black armor from waist to toe. The forearms were adorned with bracers and the hands with gloves.

The man balancing on the pipe called out. "Welcome to Earth!"

The creature's head whipped around, those deadly crimson eyes narrowing. Something moved behind it, and horror filled my entire being as long wings emerged from the alien's back. But they weren't really wings. They weren't feathered like a bird's wings or joined with leathery membranes like a bat's. Oh no, these wings had nothing connecting them. Instead, the more accurate description of what emerged from its back was sharply pointed limbs, like spider legs.

"I said hello," the man shouted, oblivious to the creepy appendages sprouting from the creature's back. He took another step forward to the very edge and waved at the alien before the creature leaped and drove those pointed limbs through his chest.

Chapter 2

IF I THOUGHT THE PARKING LOT WAS CHAOTIC BEFORE, it was infinitely worse after. I didn't bother to glance behind me.

I ran and ran to catch up with my friends. "Run! Don't look back. Just go. *Go!*" I hollered as I got closer to them.

They did as I said and nearly toppled me in their mad dash to flee. I don't know if they saw what I saw, but I didn't have the breath to ask, and it didn't matter. A pod crashed into a parking lot, an alien emerged from it, and then it murdered a guy. I had all the answers I needed.

We followed a surge of people who climbed through the bushes bordering a road filled with honking cars. When the drivers noticed our panic and the sureness of our desperation to escape, they abandoned their vehicles and joined the throng. The intersection had turned into an enclave of stampeding humans, desperate to escape. I knew many had no idea what they were running from, only that they should run.

We easily broke off from the crowd, following the sidewalk down a side street.

The buildings were closer together here, separated by thin wooden fences overlooked by trees far older than I was. They provided enough cover for us to slip into an alley between two houses and catch our breath. Once we were sure no one would pass out, the questions started.

The guy who had offered us a seat in his car turned to me. "What is it?"

"What's going on?" Osman asked.

"Emilia?" Theresa said my name, yet I couldn't connect it was me she was talking to.

They talked so fast and over one another their words blurred together. I knew they all wanted the same thing, but I didn't have the words to convey what I had seen.

A warm hand gripped my shoulder, and I looked up at the man who had originally offered us a ride out of there. If we had acted sooner, maybe I wouldn't have the image of that guy with blood dribbling from his mouth and an alien's limbs embedded in his chest stuck in my mind.

"Felis." He offered me a tight smile before nodding at his companion. "My boyfriend, Oliver."

Oliver nodded, still as silent as before.

"I'm Theresa," my best friend said before pointing to me. "My bestie, Emilia."

"And I'm Osman. I live across the hall from these two."

Felis nodded before turning his attention back to me. "Sorry to be abrupt like this, Emilia. But I really have to know what you saw."

My eyes snapped to Theresa. *Fuck.* I'd sound absolutely mad if I told them the truth, but what else could I say?

"I-I don't know what I saw," I finally said. It wasn't a lie. Part of me hoped this was some sort of morbid nightmare concocted by a fretful night of cramming for tests and fueled by two full pots of coffee. I'd know because I had done it before. But previously, the worst that had happened was I'd developed a lack of depth perception and believed the toilet was a nice place to nap.

Felis ran a hand through his hair, trying not to reveal his agitation. "Please, Emilia. Tell me what you saw."

Theresa squeezed my hand for reassurance, but it did little to soothe me.

"You work…" I highly doubted there'd be a job to return to after this. "*Worked* for an aerospace agency. What do you know about this?"

He shook his head. "The Bureau doesn't know those sorts of things…or, at least, I don't think they do? And even if they did, that's way above my pay grade. I work in communications, you know, translating."

"Translating what?" Osman peeked around the corner and nearly lost his head to a couple who careened past on bicycles with little care for others.

"*Pislik!*" he called after them, and I blanched. I'd never heard Osman swear before, and although I didn't know what he said, his tone told me it wasn't nice.

"Uh, programs. Software. Hardware. I helped the IT Department with German and English translations from other departments."

"*So?*" Osman pressed.

"So, nothing like…whatever she just saw."

There was no escaping this. Felis knew I had seen something that sent hundreds of people scrambling into the darkness of the night like rodents, shadowed the lines of my face, and haunted my eyes.

"I don't even know what I saw," I said again, exasperation causing my voice to rise.

Theresa laid her head against my shoulder, peering up at me with soft green eyes. "Please, Emilia. If something bad happened, you need to tell us."

Damn her for using the puppy-dog look. She knew I hated it because I could not say no.

"Fine. I just…it's not safe. We need to get out of the city."

Felis nodded. "I agree. But why?"

Overhead, through the scattered branches of the tree that sheltered us, another meteor flew across the sky. Its eerie, hellish green hue lit up the alley we hid in. I could hear the commotion of people frantically packing bags and yelling at one another to move faster or leave something behind in the building we hid next to. It made me wonder if the news was now reporting what had happened.

"Something…emerged from the meteorite. It…" I swallowed, trying not to mentally replay the scene, but it was on a loop. I saw the expression on the stranger's face as he was impaled over and over again. "It killed a man."

Their faces were equal mixtures of horror and confusion.

"Phones…does anyone have their phone on them?" Felis snapped his fingers.

Oliver waved his smartphone, Osman procured an old flip phone from his pocket, and Theresa begrudgingly pulled her smartphone from her pocket.

Felis looked at me. "You?"

I shook my head. I regretted not bringing my phone with me to the rooftop. I thought enjoying the show without the urge to take a video or dozens of photos would improve the experience. *Ugh.*

"Call 112," Felis said, his phone already to his ear. Everyone did as he said, and almost instantly, a loud beeping sounded through their phones, followed by a feminine voice in German.

They pulled their phones from their ears, staring at the blinking number.

"All emergency services are currently busy. Please try again," Osman whispered in horror.

"*Scheisse!*" <Shit!> Felis swore, shoving his phone back into his pocket.

Not a minute later, a godawful shriek filled the air, and dread rippled across my skin, leaving goose bumps in its wake.

"The emergency sirens," I whispered. I'd heard them before. The city sometimes tested its emergency warning system.

"Better late than never, I guess." Felis rested his head against the wall, staring up at a speaker on a nearby telephone pole.

Theresa's hands went to cup her ears, and we stood there, waiting. The tone was undulated, and we looked at each other with wide eyes. Orientation was very specific about what that siren tone meant.

An attack.

Like clockwork, the sirens faded after three minutes, and we were once again surrounded by silence.

Felis spoke first. "How many meteors do you think fell?"

"I-I'm not sure…" After we went down the stairwell, and one hit the parking lot, I wasn't really counting. "Three?

Probably more…"

My eyes strayed north toward the town. Many had fallen in that direction.

"Then we'd better leave now," Felis murmured.

Osman took another peek around the fence. I don't know if he was looking for the creature he hadn't seen or a route out of this madness that wouldn't lead to us being run over by bicyclists, flattened by maddened drivers, or trampled by stampeding crowds.

I let out a sigh. "We don't have anything, though. No car, food, water…"

Theresa whimpered.

Oliver finally spoke, his voice deep and gravelly. "We can worry about that later."

"He's right," Osman said from his post. "Let's continue down the alley. It doesn't look very friendly this way."

Nodding, we left the main road behind and journeyed through the alleys.

Although smothered in the silence afforded by our concrete walls, we could still hear the cries of people scampering to flee. Occasionally, shadows moved in the windows, or we heard the echoing cries of a child or the incessant barking of a dog. I tried not to think about the animals that were about to be abandoned to their fates. Maybe we could come back later to help them.

The alley we traversed widened, a bush weighed heavily by a bounty of crimson flowers plucked at our clothes, and I shivered. The crimson color reminded me of blood. At the end of the alley, we could make out the distinct shape of cars abandoned in gridlock.

The streetlights were out, and it was hard to determine

whether the moving shapes in the darkness were humans or monstrous creatures.

We emerged at another intersection, but this one I knew very well. A burger shop sat at the corner of the intersection opposite us. We had sat in disarray at those tables many times, with the sun warming our backs. Tables were toppled, chairs were sideways, and something small and transparent glittered on the floor. I realized a moment later they were shards of glass, and the closer we got, the easier it was to understand what had happened or what was still happening.

The lights of the burger shop were as dead as the streetlights around it, and the darkness allowed us to see the flashlights streaking across the counters and tiled walls within. People were growling at one another in threatening voices that rose and rose.

"W-what are they doing?" Theresa squeaked.

I frowned, pushing her to move forward. "Raiding the burger joint."

"But why?"

It was Felis who answered. "When humans are desperate, they do weird things."

Indeed, they do.

Leaving the looters behind, we continued along the main road. Goose bumps pebbled my flesh as an uncomfortableness settled around us. The area here was open and wide. Not even the trees that reached toward the skies could shelter us. Fewer meteors flew overhead. Instead of hundreds painting the sky an eerie neon green, only dozens rained above now. But every so often, we heard and felt the thunderous boom of one landing nearby. It only quickened our mad dash through the city.

"Where are we going?" I called out once we had left the intersection behind.

Every passing second seemed to fill the roads and pathways with more people. Many were shouting, shoving, and generally letting their panic seize control.

It surprised me when our group managed to navigate the crowds unscathed and intact. More than one burning car littered our path when we found our way into the old part of Salzburg. There, the walls were made of crumbling, ancient stone, and the façades of the buildings called back to a simpler time. I knew many renovations had been carried out to restore these landmarks over the years, but in the spotty lights, the stark contrast of the freshly painted sections of façade beside their ancient counterparts gave the entire world a haunted look. I felt like we were the first humans to enter this area in a long time, even as I watched people flee it.

"There's a hunting store up ahead. I hope there's something left for us," Felis commented out of the blue.

The aesthetic of Old Town had been likened to Shakespearean times in every marketing pamphlet and tourism ad I'd seen for Salzburg. Even under the circumstances, I couldn't help but marvel at the beautiful baroque architecture, ornate gilded metal signs, and strategically placed laurel wreaths. The beauty of it reminded me of better times when meteorites didn't herald aliens that went on murderous rampages.

Sadly, not even a beautiful place like this could be immune to plundering. I was not unaware of the irony we were on our way to loot as well. But unlike the savages who tore apart mannequins, upended tables, and shattered every vase, glass, and statue in sight, we were only here for supplies to survive.

The bell tower at the town hall nearby chimed, welcoming the new hour. I squinted at the watch on my wrist, barely making out it was one in the morning. Exhaustion tugged at my senses, and I wished more than anything I was in my room, huddled under the patchwork quilt my grandmother had handsewn for me. So, I distracted myself with the stones and wooden window frames of the Getreidegasse, the most famous and busiest shopping street in all of Salzburg. But its claim to fame was not the rich architecture or the brand-named shops that belonged to a single canary yellow building in the center.

The bright yellow façade of Mozart's birthplace screamed at us, and it pained me to see such a historical monument was not spared by people taking advantage of the chaos. The famous iron doors, with their intricate carvings, hung from their hinges, and I made out the forms of several laughing teenagers within.

Tearing my eyes from the carnage, I focused on Felis and Oliver. They led us down a side street, blocked by a single car parked sideways. Ignoring the pit in my stomach, I followed Felis and Oliver's lead and climbed over the hood. When I was over, I held my hand out for Theresa, helping her. Osman climbed over effortlessly, and we continued into the courtyard beyond. The ravages of looters seemed to have bypassed this area entirely.

"There!" Felis pointed to a store with a dark stone entryway and a hanging basket of bright, bold flowers hanging from the sign.

Huddling under the striped awning, Felis reached for the doorknob and gave it a twist. The door swung open on silent hinges, a hint of lilac drifting toward us. Something in my gut told me we should leave now—that the car and the open door were related. But before I could say a word, Oliver darted to a nearby rack with winter coats, and Felis made a beeline for an endcap decorated with lanterns and flashlights. Ignoring the overwhelming desire to push my friends back onto the street, I stepped inside. The lights worked here, but only the display ones that lit the underside of shelves were on. It gave us more than enough light to move around, and Theresa and Osman immediately scattered.

"Anything in particular we should look for?" I asked, eyeing a wall of backpacks.

"General survival stuff. Warm clothes, snacks, canteens, matches. You know," Felis called back. I watched him gather a lantern under his arm and stride across the room to where Oliver seemed stuck choosing between a cream or dark green jacket.

I took a backpack from a hook, noting the oddly plastic feeling of it. Then, I went from aisle to aisle, shoveling whatever I thought would be useful into it—boxes of matches, a lighter, a flashlight, a pack of AA batteries, a metal canteen, and a few trail bars Felis had missed.

Theresa appeared at my side, a basket swinging from her arm.

"I grabbed these for you." She passed me a pair of jeans, a shirt, a long-sleeved shirt, socks, a scarf, and a pair of gloves. I rolled them, neatly stacking them at the bottom of the backpack.

I gave her a look, my eyes straying to the rest of the clothing in the basket. "Matching?"

She gave me a wink. "Of course."

"There are backpacks on the wall. You should grab one. Don't focus on clothing only."

Theresa waved off my concerns, prancing toward the backpacks. "I know, I know."

A small smile lit my face, and it brought me tremendous joy to know I could still smile after what had happened.

Glancing around the store, I noticed Felis by a door behind the register. No doubt it led to a storage room of some sort. Osman and Oliver made their way toward us, backpacks slung across their shoulders, obviously filled.

"Felis, ready to go?" I called to him, pulling a coat from the rack. It was thick and heavy, perfect for repelling snow or rain. I donned the coat, knowing I had no idea where we were headed after this, but the chill in the autumn air easily bit through my cardigan. I noticed Theresa had done the same, except she was wearing the coat. We'd left our room wearing jeans, shirts, cardigans, and sneakers—your typical twenty-something get-up.

"*Scheisse!*" <Shit!> Felis swore.

I looked up to see him back out of the supposed storage room with his hands held high.

"*Geht.*" <Leave.> A voice came from the darkness, followed by the unmistakable sound of a gun cocking.

Chapter 3

"**WARTE!**" <WAIT!> FELIS SHOUTED, THROWING HIS hands up further. The rest of us did the same, but we took a cautious step out of the store.

The woman spoke rapidly in German, too fast for me to understand.

"What did she say?" I asked.

"She says it's her store," Felis murmured.

"Tell her we mean no harm. We'll leave." I was too frazzled to repeat what I said in German. I couldn't even remember the word for sorry.

Felis relayed my message while slowly backing up toward us. From the light bouncing off the shelves, I could see the fear in the woman's eyes. She shouted at him and raised the gun higher.

"All right, we're leaving," Felis stated for us rather than her. Hefting our backpacks over our shoulders, she watched our retreat and slammed the door shut, covering her outraged face.

Once we were certain we wouldn't receive a bullet in the back of our heads, the tension in our shoulders relaxed, if only a little. Climbing back over the car onto the main area of Old Town, we followed a smaller crowd than the one we had left behind. The crowd thinned as people broke off to loot or hide in nearby shops. Some shops still had working lights, and others were dark, with only flashlights telling us people were inside.

Passing by banks, sweet shops, clothing stores, candlemakers, and even a cozy tea shop left a bitter taste in my mouth. It reminded me of the good times when Theresa and I would walk these roads on the weekend, eager to explore our new home. Unlike me, she was born in Germany to German parents and chose to live in Salzburg for how laid-back, yet modern, the city was. I simply chose Salzburg because my parents grew up here. I lived off the stories they told me as a child of a city that embraced the old and the new. A city lined by the Alps, with a trickling blue river that snaked its way through it, surrounded by grass far greener than I could possibly imagine.

The brick stone path widened ahead, leading us toward an archway overlooking a bridge stretching over the silvery expanse of the Salzach River. Not a soul was in sight. I swallowed the lump that had formed in my throat.

There were more abandoned cars along this stretch of the road. I didn't want to consider the implications of why they had been abandoned. There were no chokeholds here, no other traffic. It was as if the occupants had decided to take their chances on foot.

Flags on either side of the bridge snapped in the breeze. It was the only sound besides the gentle gurgling of the river below and the heartbeat in my ears. Our shoes skidded across the wet pavement, and I flinched at every squeak. Something wasn't right here. It was *too* quiet. Meteors continued to rain across the heavens in still fewer numbers than before. Where the hundreds careened across the sky had turned to dozens, they now came maybe one or two at a time. I tried to quell my rising anxiety. The meteorite in the parking lot held a single monster. Even if all the meteorites held only one, that was still thousands. How many other countries were affected? Was it just Austria? Europe? The eastern hemisphere? Or would the entire world fall under the scourge of these monsters from beyond the stars?

I needed to find a television or a radio. Someone had to have answers or at least answers I could believe.

Something flew out of the darkness on the other side of the bridge, thudding against the pavement at Felis' feet. He paused, staring down at it.

"What's that?" I called out, slowing to a stop. Osman and Theresa paused at my side, equally wary. Oliver ran to his boyfriend's side, whispering to him.

"A rock." Felis gestured for Oliver to stand behind him. The warning came not a minute too soon as another rock hurtled its way through the air, landing where Oliver had stood.

"I don't like this," Theresa murmured from my side.

Four boys appeared from the darkness on the other side of the bridge, closest to Felis. They couldn't have been much older than sixteen and were dressed in dark clothing, hoods shielding their faces.

"Who's there?" Felis growled out his words.

Part of me rejoiced it wasn't an alien, but honestly, sometimes humans could be far worse than any monster. That was confirmed a second later as they raised their hands outward, revealing long, sharp objects.

"Are they going to attack us?" Theresa's eyes darted between the gang and me.

Are you serious right now? Rage ignited in me. We were under attack from *aliens*, and these pubescent boys wanted to *fight*?

One of the boys stepped closer, calling out in a language I couldn't understand.

Felis raised his hands. "I-I don't understand you."

Shit.

Osman blanched. "I do."

The lead boy, although lanky, towered over Felis and growled out something unintelligible, pointing at Felis with what I immediately knew was a machete. Osman replied, his tone almost pleading. I knew he was trying to bargain, but when the other teenagers came forward, it was clear Osman was losing. They weren't here for a friendly chat. They were here to rob us.

Osman bent over, scooped up something at his feet, and, cocking his arm back, threw with all his strength. Whatever it was hit the lead boy in the head, and his gargled scream incited rage in his companions. They darted forward, machetes and bats raised.

"Run!" Osman yelled at us.

We scrambled across the bridge, my hand grasping Theresa's to encourage her to keep up the pace. I didn't know how close they were, but part of me knew I could not outrun them. The last time I had run was when high school classes forced me to. I generally avoided exercise at all costs unless it included lazy, meandering strolls through a park or shopping mall. And now I was paying for it.

Theresa was struggling too. She had the grace and body for Pilates, yoga, and ballet. She was not a runner.

Felis streaked by us with Oliver hot on his heels. Osman eventually caught up, his nervous glances doing nothing to aid the panic of waiting for a sword in my back. Theresa began to slow, but my grip stayed firm.

"A little farther," I shouted. The end of the bridge was so close.

"A cramp! My leg!" she cried out before tripping. I went down with her, eating a face full of pavement.

The teenagers were gaining ground, and from there, I could almost see their shit-eating grins.

I turned to her. "Run!"

Her eyes widened, a hand gripping her calf. "B-but, Emilia—"

"Run!" I growled out, pulling myself to my feet.

She tentatively hopped to her feet, wincing from the cramp in her leg. I waited for her to take a few steps before I turned to stare the boys down. If my inevitable death gave her a chance to escape, then it would have been worth it. I heard someone call my name, a frantic, panic-filled voice, but I ignored whoever it was and dug the nails of my hand into the flesh of my palm.

I pounded my chest, taunting the boys. "Come and get me, assholes!"

The boys slowed their mad dash, bewildered expressions on their faces. The night around us turned bright and hot, and for a minute, I wondered if the lights had come back on.

"Emi, run!" Theresa cried out before a meteorite hurtled overhead, crashing into the other end of the bridge. A blinding light engulfed me, and an intense pounding headache dulled my senses before an insufferable ringing sounded in my ears.

The pavement before my feet seemed to shatter, and I watched the Salzach rise to swallow me whole. Water rushed into my mouth and lungs. I fought desperately not to inhale and to keep my mouth shut, but panic took hold of me. An odd feeling, like ripples, ran the length of my skin, thrumming within me. Then I remembered where I was and how I got there.

The meteorite!

Tilting my head up, or at least, what I thought was up, I kicked my feet as hard as I could. I burst through the surface almost immediately and scrambled to cough up the water that had entered my mouth while trying to fill my lungs with air. The world around me, as dark as it had been before, now smelled of fire and ash. Twisting around in the water, I saw the shore within arm's reach.

Crawling onto shore, my shoulders heaved involuntarily. and water splattered onto the grass. I took several deep, grateful breaths of air before returning my attention to the river.

"Theresa? Theresa!" I screeched like a banshee, not caring if the monster in the river somewhere below me heard. I could only hope it would head straight for me and leave Theresa alone if it had.

A head popped out of the waves further down, and someone crawled out of the water, coughing and spluttering. I hobbled to her side, my chest heaving as my arms wrapped around her, pulling her close. I drew her face upward, inspecting her for injuries.

"I'm fine." She breathed. Her voice was shaky, and I could feel her shivering in my grasp.

"Are you okay?"

"I said I'm fine." She looked around. "Where's Osman?"

Shit. I'd forgotten about Osman, Felis, and Oliver.

"I'm here." I heard a cry from where I had come. I turned my head to see him limping toward us, his black hair pressed against his head like strangled seaweed.

"We need to leave before that thing emerges." But, even then, my eyes wouldn't leave the river. *Could they survive underwater?* It was a question I knew I didn't want the answer to.

"Guys! You're alive!" A cry sounded from above.

Felis and Oliver stood at the far end of the bridge near Old Town on the other side of the river.

I waved to them, beyond relieved they escaped unscathed. But there was only one problem, the entire northern half of the bridge was missing. I knew it had disappeared into the river from the darkened mounds that peppered the waters.

How did we survive that?

It didn't matter, though. What mattered was finding a way to unite with each other. I followed the river west, where I could make out the long, dark shape of a smaller bridge. I pointed to it. "There's another bridge. Meet us there."

Felis shouted in agreement before he and Oliver disappeared into the shadows.

On this side of the river, it seemed more buildings still had power. Some streetlights flickered on and off, and I could make out furniture, televisions, chairs, and tables in some houses and stores. But no people.

Theresa's teeth chattered, as did mine and Osman's. I had half a mind to hand her my coat, but it was as soaked as everything else. We'd have to find somewhere to lay low until daybreak, preferably a place with electricity and a heater.

My mind kept wandering back to the bridge and the meteorite that simmered beneath it.

"We should hurry," I said quietly.

No one asked why.

Felis and Oliver greeted us at the other bridge, looking everyone over to make sure we had survived in one piece.

"Jesus, I can't believe that happened." Felis ran a hand through his curly locks, his eyes wide.

However, I could barely hear him over the chattering of Theresa's teeth.

"We should find somewhere to lay low for the night." My gaze drifted to the padlocks secured to the metal grates of the bridge.

Somewhere in the middle of the bridge, a bright pink, heart-shaped padlock sat with '*Theresa Wagner and Emilia Bauer, best friends for life,*' scribbled on it in black Sharpie. Theresa had insisted I dotted my Is with tiny hearts. I had half a mind to check, to make sure it was still there, but I didn't want to stay out here soaking wet in the cold any longer than we had to.

"Come." Oliver threw a thumb over his shoulder. "My cousin owns a café near here. I know where he hides the key."

The buildings on this side of the river weren't much different from the south, with the same façade and baroque architecture prevalent and gilded, wrought iron signs and hanging baskets of flowers. We dodged down an alleyway between two apartment buildings with prime riverside views. Unfortunately, whatever beauty there was had been callously destroyed. The graffiti splashed across the stone with no rhyme or reason reminded me of the paintings you could buy from the zoo when a zookeeper gave an elephant a paintbrush. Several cans of spray paint lay nearby, joining half a dozen beer cans and several cigarette butts. If I enjoyed gambling, I would bet a lot of money those teenagers had something to do with this.

We rounded the corner, and the pep in our step faltered. Oliver ran forward, arms outstretched, coming to a halt before a pile of broken stone. The entire half of the building that had stood here was a smoking crater.

It had been a café once. The metal signs were the only recognizable thing in the pile of debris.

"I guess that's not an option." Felis sighed.

In the very middle of the pile of rubble sat a pool of tar. Fear gripped me, and my stomach threatened to empty, although there was nothing inside.

"I don't like this. Can we go?" I asked.

Felis paused, staring at the pile of goo. "Is this what the meteorite looked like?"

I shook my head. "This is what the meteorite became."

"I agree with Emilia. We should leave before whatever crawled out of there comes back." Osman's vigil hadn't paused. He stared into every room, through every window. "I haven't seen a single person, and this is right here? It's not a coincidence."

Felis nodded, but I could see the hesitance in his eyes. As a scientist, he wished to study whatever the monster had left behind. But if Osman was right, we were all in danger.

"Where do we go?" Theresa murmured, her voice but a whisper. Her palpable fear broke something inside me.

We needed to go somewhere—*anywhere*.

I turned on my heel and started walking, pausing at every door to test it. One, two, three, four, five. All locked.

"One of these will be open. Help me check."

Felis and Osman covered the right side of the road, and Theresa and I checked the left. Oliver walked through the middle, keeping an eye out, ready to sound the alarm the moment he saw something bad. At this stage, though, I wouldn't trust the people any more than the aliens.

When we met up at the end, our faces bore equal expressions of exhaustion. None of the doors were unlocked. To our right, a long promenade edged by a low stone wall and heralded by stone statues called to us. I pointed at them, silently asking our companions if we should enter the Mirabellgarten.

"It's very open." Felis had his doubts written across his face.

He wasn't wrong. The gardens were wide and the lawn closely mowed. It would not be an easy place to hide from a bloodthirsty monster—human or alien.

"Yes…but perhaps one of the halls is open?" Theresa's brows furrowed.

Felis arched an eyebrow. "How do you figure?"

"She studies ballet," I explained, nodding at Theresa.

He frowned, waiting for an explanation.

Theresa shrugged. "Sometimes the performers stay late to practice."

Osman rolled his eyes, charging through us. "What does it matter? I'm freezing! We stand here, argue, and get sick, or we move and keep warm. I know what I'd do."

Theresa followed him, and I shrugged at Felis' questioning gaze.

Mirabellgarten, an emerald paradise of manicured lawns and blooming flowers, sat between a host of historic buildings. A palace, several performance halls, theaters, and even a museum edged the gardens. A fountain sat at its center, and we paused there after trying every door we had come across. So far, luck had not been on our side.

"This was a terrible decision," Felis muttered, unable to disguise the annoyance in his tone.

We were cold, tired, and hungry. If we didn't find somewhere to spend the rest of the night to recuperate, I was afraid the odds of survival wouldn't be in our favor. Already I could see the life draining from our pallid skin, and the goose bumps pebbling our flesh were becoming an almost permanent feature.

We moved to the stairs of a nearby building, hope in our step as Osman yanked on the door to no avail. Like all the doors before it, it remained stubbornly closed. A chilly breeze ran over us, ruffling our hair and the faux fur on the hoods of our coats still wet from the dip in the river. My gaze drifted upward, where the lights in a room flickered briefly.

Scaffolding from restoration still clung to the building's façade, and plastic sheets waved in the light breeze. I shuddered when I smelled the smoke in the air. I knew it did not belong to a fireplace. There were no people in Salzburg's most populated area, which somehow made me more uneasy.

Where was everyone?

"I don't like this," Osman echoed my thoughts.

Nearby, a branch snapped, and we whipped our heads around. I heard Theresa's panic in her breathing.

"Think it's one of them?" Felis murmured, circling us, his eyes on the trees.

I took a tentative step back. "We should run."

We had no hope of fighting one of those things. None of us were armed with more than a backpack filled with soaked camping gear. I don't know what the others put in their bags, but a knife or gun wasn't on my list.

"I agree with her," Oliver said in his deep German accent.

Taking the steps two at a time, we ran out into the open, pausing by the fountain to make sure we weren't being followed. What we weren't prepared for was for the entire world to go white. I pressed my hands against my eyes, wincing at the bright light that seemed to have burned my eyes. Squinting into the garden, my hands shading my eyes from the blaring light, I made out many shadows walking toward us.

"We're surrounded," I voiced to my friends. They pressed up against me, trying to cover every direction.

"Who's there?" I knew Felis' voice had asked, but he sounded so far away, so unsure.

Several voices in German shouted out at once, authoritative and deep. They had either rehearsed this or done it dozens of times before.

"What are they saying?" I'd like to consider myself fluent in German, but it was difficult for me to keep up when someone spoke as fast as them.

"To put our hands up," Felis grumbled beside me.

"I guess we don't have a choice." Osman fidgeted beside me, and like him, I raised my hands above my head, trying to squint around the bright light blinded almost my entire view. All I could see was the stone we stood on, the lip of the fountain, and the water within.

Then, the light lowered, and after a minute, my eyes adjusted to the environment once more. A pit sat low and heavy in my stomach, and my breath hitched as I watched dozens of men in dark clothing surround us, guns pointed at our heads.

Chapter 4

"*Die Sprache?*" <Language?> One of the men—I didn't know who—called out.

"English," Felis and I said together.

We could all speak German, but I thought it would go much smoother if we didn't require them to speak slowly or repeat themselves.

"Follow us," one of the men said. The guns were never lowered as they led us northward toward the palace.

Thankfully, the imprint of the bright lights no longer clouded my vision, and I could see clearly again. Looking around, I saw the men had hideouts throughout the gardens. Most of them were near the walls, where I could make out camouflaged nets strung out like cobwebs, hiding heavily armed guards beneath. This wasn't a militia or a group of hunters trying their best to survive but a full-on military operation with guns, vehicles, and turrets. They came prepared for war.

"Where are we going?" Felis asked after several uncomfortably terse and silent minutes of walking.

The man leading us didn't bother to turn his head as he said, "All civilian personnel are being escorted to the palace for evacuation."

I couldn't fathom how the military had assembled nearby and arranged for the safety of the local residents in such a short time. I guessed that explained why those houses and buildings were empty, but the lights were on. They probably weren't given much notice before being spirited away.

"Evacuation?" Osman repeated.

The guy shushed us. "All questions will be answered inside. For now, keep your head down and your mouth shut."

We did as we were told, except our heads certainly did not stay down. Even Theresa let her gaze wander over the operations. At the very end of the gardens sat an ancient crumbling stone wall blanketed with emerald vines. But through the archway we could tell the garden on the other side was scuffed. Deep gouges were cut into the earth, and flowers were strewn over the dirt. Even the Christmas tree-shaped topiaries hadn't survived the touch of the military. Tents had been assembled on either side of the fountain in the center, where a winged horse, stained mossy green, reared toward the sky.

Mercifully, I had noticed the meteor shower was over. Now all that occupied the heavens were clouds and stars, just as it should be.

Tall, skinny wooden doors leading into the marble palace were held open by bricks. Military personnel filed in and out, carrying paperwork and crates filled to the brim. Some crates held food, water, or toilet paper, and others contained boxes of bullets. I swallowed the bile at the back of my throat, imagining what carnage could be wrought with those.

"Through here." The soldier leading us grunted, standing back to let us file into the palace.

Inside was dark and musty. The kind of must that comes from thousands of people roaming these halls over their lives. From stone that hadn't moved in centuries and memories of bygone eras.

It was difficult to navigate the halls as the only light source was from nearby soldiers' flashlights. The palace rooms had been converted, some into sleeping areas, others into reconnaissance littered with maps, laptops, and radios. It seemed the power did not work here, even though the buildings on the other sides of the garden were alive with light.

I felt, rather than saw, the end of the hallway engulf us, leading into a vast room of echoing marble and glass windows. Scattered throughout the hall were cots arranged in careful rows. Some held people snoring, crying, or despondently staring out the windows.

The soldier led us to the very end of the rows, where five cots sat against the windows. I thought it odd such a prime viewing spot wouldn't be taken, but then I remembered Oliver's cousin's café. Some people here might have seen what crawled out of the meteorite and feared waking up in the dark to see one of those devilish things staring back at them.

The soldier turned to us. "These are your beds for the night. You will find food and water and extra blankets under your beds."

"Wait!" He raised his eyebrows at me, and I cleared my throat, trying again. "Sorry. What happens next?"

"Try and get some rest. The next bus should be here soon. Then you'll be evacuated to a safe house on the city's outskirts." He left before we could ask any more questions.

Gingerly sitting down, I didn't realize how much I had longed to sit. My calves ached, my thighs throbbed, and I was positive the blisters on the back of my heels were rubbed raw. Tossing my backpack off my shoulder, I peered inside, and my heart swelled as my fingers touched dried clothes and food. Everything had remained untouched.

The backpacks were waterproof. I guess that explained the odd texture of the fabric.

Against the far wall, plastic screens had been erected as flimsy room dividers, with coats and jackets thrown across them. Not saying a word to my companions, I grabbed the spare clothes and made a beeline for the screens.

The immense pleasure I felt peeling off my soaked clothes and letting them fall to the floor with an audible plop could not be explained. There were no towels to dry off the excess water that clung to my skin, so I flicked off what I could before reaching for the fresh clothes.

Except, something blocked where the clothing draped across the screen. A head cocked sideways stared at me. I nearly screamed, covering myself with my hands. "Dammit, Theresa. Don't do that. I was going to slap you."

She laughed, the sound easing the ache I had in my heart. I didn't know if she was strong enough to recover from what had happened, but it warmed me to know she was stronger than I thought. I needed to give her more credit. She may be a tiny ballerina on the outside, but she was a resilient swan on the inside.

"Mind if I join you? I don't want to change on my own…" Her voice trailed off.

I nodded to her, waiting for her clothes to join mine on the floor before pulling my jeans over my wet underwear and a shirt over my damp bra. Sadly, there wasn't underwear in the bag, but I could handle those being wet.

Theresa didn't waste time, quickly changing into jeans and a long-sleeved turtleneck that looked oddly familiar.

I looked down at my own ensemble. "You know, I almost forgot."

"I couldn't help it!" She gripped my arm, beaming at me.

I playfully rolled my eyes. "Of course you couldn't."

Leaving our wet clothes on the floor, we walked side by side into the hall.

"What do you think will happen to us?" She stood at the window, watching the soldiers patrol the garden.

"We'll be okay." I don't know if I believed what I said, but Theresa seemed to.

I joined her at the window. As if on cue, we craned our necks to observe the magnificence of the intricately gilded ceiling above. I don't know what the inspiration for the ballroom in *Beauty and the Beast* was, but if I had to hazard a guess, this would be it.

Ten-year-old me would have screamed in delight and twirled in her sundresses with pigtails flying around her face.

"Did you know *The Sound of Music* was filmed here?" Theresa twirled slowly, taking in the grandeur of the hall.

From the corner of my eye, I watched Felis and Oliver whispering to each another. Oliver's face was twisted in anger, his brows furrowed, and the lines on his face formed a scowl. Felis reached out a hand to touch his, but Oliver slapped him away, stood, and stomped from the room into one of the hallways.

I walked over to Felis, offering him an apologetic smile when he looked up at me.

"Everything all right?"

He snorted. "Not really."

"Anything I can do to help?"

Felis patted my arm. "Thanks, but not really."

Theresa bounded over, taking a seat on his cot. "What should we do now?"

I shrugged. "Probably try and get some rest before the next bus comes."

Although I knew Felis agreed, I could see he was reluctant to do any sleeping without Oliver. I couldn't blame him. My eyes drifted back to our cots, where Osman was already sound asleep on his. Watching his chest slowly rise and fall, I wished I could fall asleep that easily.

Theresa yawned, the energy she had a moment ago suddenly gone. Settling into her squeaky cot, she threw the blanket over her and turned toward the windows. I did the same, except I lay on my back, staring up at the ceiling until Oliver crept back into the hall, sitting on an empty cot opposite Felis.

I slept or, more accurately, laid on the uncomfortable cot under a scratchy blanket with my eyes closed for maybe half an hour before soldiers burst into the room, calling for everyone to wake up and grab their things. Felis dashed to his boyfriend's side without a backward glance. Osman handed Theresa her backpack, and they walked together with the strangers who were already in the hall when we got there, with me trailing behind.

The entryway, featuring a marble stairwell guarded by statues of children and archways at every entry, was a perfect example of the baroque style common to this region of Europe. Under other circumstances, I would sit here for hours appreciating the beauty of it all. But my heart was heavy, and a pit sat low in my stomach. I had little hope leaving the palace would be better than staying. Something told me things would get a lot worse before they got better.

Soldiers were stationed every couple of feet throughout the marble hallways, watching us carefully. Outside the front doors, a single bus waited. I saw Felis and Oliver situating themselves near the back, and I motioned for Osman and Theresa to follow them.

The driver greeted us with an icy stare, and shadows haunted his face. I'm sure he'd seen his fair share of chaos in the last couple of hours—enough for a lifetime. I know I had. But it didn't seem to end there.

I sat by a window, and Theresa sat in front of me, sprawling across her seat. Osman did the same in a seat opposite us. They no doubt wanted to catch up on sleep, but I knew I couldn't. Anxiety welled within me, building and building like a kettle on the stovetop. It was only a matter of time before I burst. Desperate to find release, I turned my attention out the window, where dark, clouded skies and the eerie silence of a pre-dawn morning did little to help me.

My gaze strayed across the landscape as we moved, and the greenery slowly eased the nervousness welling up within me until I noticed the church opposite the palace. Built of the same white marble as the palace and possibly just as old, one of its two steeples had been shredded. Chunks of stone littered the path before it, and a shattered bell lay in the heap.

For a moment, I thought perhaps it had succumbed to a meteorite. However, as the bus pulled away from the palace, I realized the damage was not caused by a visitor from space but one from home.

Mortar shells inflicted those wounds.

Our slow escape through the eastern half of Salzburg was a sobering sight, making me regret not trying to sleep. Even closing my eyes so I didn't see the carnage would have been enough, but now I had seen the shattered windows, crumbled stones, and ripped flags, I couldn't stop looking.

Although our apparent destination was nearby, the bus constantly stopped to collect civilians who clambered from the ashes of fallen buildings or darkened apartments. No questions were asked, and barely any words were exchanged. The dozen or so hitchhikers sat and stared listlessly out the windows.

The bus came to a rolling stop in the middle of a bridge over a multi-track train line. Soldiers sat on the bridge, and their tarp-covered vehicles blocked our way. The bus driver opened the door and mumbled something to a soldier before he waved us onward. A truck blocking the bridge roared to life and moved out of our way to let us through. The interaction took less than two minutes, yet my anxiety rose with every second that passed. Out over the emptiness of the train tracks, I could see smoke rising from the city. Below us, the trains sat lifelessly, like long silver snakes on the tracks, and people—more soldiers, I realized—moved alongside them.

Settling back in my seat, I tried to tear my gaze away from the window, but I didn't have the strength. The further away from the heart of the city we drove, the fewer buildings seemed to have power. But it didn't make it any easier not to see the destruction on some of them. Stone and cement façades were riddled with tiny pinpricks or black-rimmed holes—bullets and mortars. The military had fought something here. But the sight of the buildings injured by the military faded in comparison to a massive pile of rubble and rebar foundations we drove past. The only intact part of the site was its sign set in stone, which announced it had once been a hospital. I swallowed, praying no one had been inside when it was leveled.

Eventually, the high-rises, apartments, and general hallmarks of city life faded away, replaced by wide lawns, multi-story single homes, and lush trees. For a moment, I could pretend everything was fine. That everything was normal.

Until the bus lights lit up a white sign announcing our arrival into Guggenthal-Kuhberg. We were in the foothills outside eastern Salzburg. On the right side of the bus, a wide field of gently flowing grass led us to a sideroad with a blockade. But unlike the one on the bridge, no trucks blocked our path, and the driver did not stop. Soldiers waved us through, using flashlights to beckon us toward a yellow building with white-bordered windows.

Pulling up to the entrance, my eyes roamed over the building. Dozens of paper flowers plastered the windows, and the archway to the front doors held the word *Volksschule*.

"The evacuation center is a primary school," I whispered, filled with dread.

Theresa sat up, peering over her seat. "What?"

"We're here," I murmured as the lights inside the bus came on and the driver called for us to get off.

Soldiers gestured for us to follow them inside and wait in the entryway, where a middle-aged woman stood with a clipboard. We lined up like the children who would have come before us, waiting for instructions.

As our group drew closer to the front, I realized she was recording our information—names, addresses, nationalities, and next of kin.

Next of kin. I hadn't even taken a moment to think about my mother and father. *Was Australia spared from the onslaught?*

Once we had given the lady our information, she pawned us onto another woman who led us to a nearby room. There were no cots here, only mattresses on the classroom floor. And yet, they were more comfortable than the cots at Mirabell Palace.

After we had claimed our spots, the woman had two soldiers hand out survival bags—frumpy plastic bags filled with food packets and water bottles. There were even chocolate bars.

"When you're ready, shower stalls have been set up down the hall, and there are boxes of donated clothing."

"Donated clothing?" I inquired. Who would willingly donate anything in such a crisis? The other cities in Austria? Other countries?

Were we the only ones affected then?

The woman glanced at me. "The clothing was acquired from a thrift store nearby."

Someone knocked on the door, our heads swiveling to a young woman with frizzy hair and wide eyes.

"Sie haben den Fernseher zum Laufen gebracht," <They got the television working,> she said in German.

Everyone jumped to their feet, ignoring the protests of the lady who had led us there. We followed the frizzy-haired woman, who wasn't much older than us, into another classroom. It was crowded in the classroom, and the television was tuned into a local news station mid-report. The five of us managed to squeeze into a space at the back, leaning against a table covered in bottles of glitter and glue.

All our attention was on the woman behind the desk as her shaky voice filled the small room.

"Today, I am sad to say, we have experienced a crisis unlike any other," she spoke in German, slowly articulating every word. "I know I've said this repeatedly, but I can't find the words to say anything else. We have been invaded. It is as simple as that. What started as a night of stargazing with friends and family has become a national, perhaps global, tragedy."

The anchor's eyes were rimmed red, and glistening tears rolled down her cheeks. "I have been unable to contact my fellow reporters in Budapest, Bratislava, or Prague. My last contact within Austria was an hour ago in Vienna. There is a massive military presence in the region, but…" she took a moment to take a deep breath, "…I've been told there have been mass casualties."

The room was filled with sniffling, and someone bolted into the hallway, a wail following them.

The anchor continued, "Communications with Munich are still open. They are welcoming evacuees from Salzburg and Innsbruck through southern Germany."

There was a pause, and the woman cleared her throat. "However, I have even worse news for those seeking a way out. A storm is approaching from the north, and we are anticipating a freak snow event in Southern Germany. So, I'll be upfront because that is what I would want from the news right now. If you're going to leave Austria, do so now. Avoid the main roads if possible and pack supplies for several days. If it is not safe to leave, prepare for the worst."

She stared the camera down, her shoulders heaving with choked sobs, as she managed to squeeze out, "Godspeed."

Chapter 5

THE STATION WENT DARK, AND A SECOND LATER, STATIC filled the screen.

"*Von wo bericht Sie?*" <Where is she reporting from?> someone up front asked in German.

Another lady answered, "*Das ist Leda. Sie ist von hier.*" <That's Leda. She's local.>

The group went silent save for the occasional sniffle or dejected sigh. Theresa's hand covered her mouth, and her eyes glistened with tears.

"Let's go back to our room," I said, ushering our group away from those too stunned to move.

Once we returned to our room, Felis and Oliver sat on a mattress together and lost themselves in each other's arms. Osman fiddled with his flip phone, desperately calling every number on his list.

Theresa and I watched him, our hope fading with every call that ended with a dreaded busy beep. He muttered something in Turkish and threw his phone on the mattress before curling up into a ball.

As he clearly did not want to be disturbed, I grabbed Theresa's hand and nodded toward the door. She let me lead her silently down the hallway to where a row of white plastic sheets had been stretched between plastic poles. A woman stood at the entrance, counting clothing in the boxes. She stopped counting when we approached and greeted us with a solemn smile that did not meet her eyes.

"The showers are through there. Each stall has a bar of soap and some shampoo. It's not much." She shrugged. "You're welcome to grab clothes from the boxes before heading in. I have them sorted by size. These are children's clothes, but we have women's over there."

"Thanks," I said, noting I hadn't seen a single child among the evacuees.

Theresa immediately grabbed a pair of leggings and a sweatshirt. I picked something similar but chose muted pastels in contrast to her bright colors. As we entered the makeshift showers, I noticed only one of the suspended white sheets would hide our nakedness from prying eyes. Ragged pipes and odd grates were set into the floor, and I took these as signs the military had hastily built the showers. But I wouldn't complain. I would finally rid myself of the stench of river water and sweat.

Theresa hung her clothes over the plastic door of a stall, and I took the one next to her. A second later, her shower started, and I didn't allow myself to think of anything else. I let the hot steam of the water roll over me, washing away the memories of the last few hours. But no amount of scrubbing and washing could make me forget what had happened and what was *still* happening. We were under attack, plain and simple.

"I don't understand," Theresa commented. Her voice was hollow, with little substance, as if she had witnessed an unspeakable horror.

But she had, hadn't she? We all had.

I wiped the water from my face and watched her shadow move on the other side of the sheet. "Understand what?"

"Why this is happening."

Neither do I.

"We'll be okay." I don't know if I believed that, but I was willing to say it repeatedly until I did.

"The news reporter didn't even tell us anything about the creatures." If I didn't know her better, I'd say it almost sounded like she was pouting.

"I mean…we got there late in the middle of her report. Maybe that's what she said at first…or maybe she doesn't know anything," I reasoned.

A moment of silence settled between us before she murmured, "I guess."

I stared listlessly at my bra and underwear hanging over the side of the door. Without a second thought, I grabbed them, scrubbed soap into the fabric, and washed and wrung them dry. I would more than likely be stuck with the same undergarments for a while.

Wicking the water from my skin, I was grateful the towel hung up in the stall was insanely soft. I pulled on the leggings and sweatshirt and met Theresa. We walked slowly back to the classroom, pausing at the door.

Peeking inside told me everyone was asleep or at least trying to be.

"We should try to sleep." Maybe I'd have better luck this time.

We went to our mattresses and unfolded the quilted blankets that sat on them. Before I could make myself comfortable, Theresa scooted across the floor, staring at me. I held my blanket out, and she crawled in to lay next to me. Wrapping my arm around her, I couldn't help but feel lucky we had both survived.

Sleep was quick to come to me this time, as a combination of being clean and safe and being with my best friend lulled me into a deep slumber.

A beam of light hitting me in the face awoke me. The blinds of the classroom had been pulled wide open. A woman with braided hair manned the cords. She muttered an apology when our eyes met, but I waved it away. It was probably time we got out of bed.

Theresa stretched, groaning.

"Morning, sleepyhead," I murmured to her, glancing around the room.

Felis and Oliver were nowhere to be seen, but Osman was chowing down on a sleeve of biscuits, smashing the buttons on his phone.

I looked at Theresa. "Want to get some fresh air?"

She nodded sleepily at me, wiping her eyes. Throwing back the blanket, I stretched my legs and arms, staring out at the cloudy sky.

"Hey, Osman, want to join us?" I knew what his answer would be from the perpetual frown on his face, but I asked anyway.

He glanced up from his phone. "I'm okay." He clearly wasn't, but Theresa and I left him to his own devices.

The hallways and classrooms were more alive now, and people scurried to and fro. Some helped sort food and clothing, others dismantled chairs and tables, and others still lounged around.

"Sucht ihr Mädels etwas zum Frühstücken?" <You girls looking for breakfast?> A voice in German pulled me from my nosiness. A soldier with eyes as brown as his hair stood in front of us.

"Breakfast?" I reiterated in English. *What was this, a hotel?*

He flashed us a smile, answering me in English, "One of the evacuees owns a store nearby. She offered us all of her supplies and made breakfast."

I looked at Theresa and could practically hear her salivate.

"We'd be delighted."

The soldier waved us after him, leading us through a hallway and a set of double doors into a yard between the buildings. High walls sheltered us from the roadside, and the chilled breeze ruffled the trees overhead. Tables and chairs were set up in the grassy yard, and almost all seats were occupied by soldiers or civilians.

A long table against the far wall heaved with pots and pans. Hotplates muddied by attempts at making waffles and pancakes were lined in a row beside bottles of syrup and tubs of butter. Some people stood at the other end of the table, cooking bacon and idly watching the toaster for their bread.

The soldier led us to the front of the table, passing me a plate. I immediately pressed it into Theresa's hands, and the soldier handed me another, leading us down the table.

"Sprechen Sie Englisch? <Do you speak English?>" he asked in German, eyeing me curiously.

Theresa skipped ahead of us, pouring herself a glass of orange juice.

"Yes, much better than my German, I'm afraid."

His eyes widened. "You have an interesting accent. Where is that from?"

"Australia. I was born there."

He passed me a pair of tongs, pointing to a bowl of fresh berries. "That's cool, actually. Never met an Australian before."

I smiled, loading some berries onto my plate.

"I'm sorry for the lack of diversity available, but this is all we could muster on such short notice," he said.

"Oh, this is definitely more than I expected." To be honest, I thought the packets of food in the plastic bags we were given had to suffice.

Theresa joined us again, handing me a cup of apple juice.

"You remembered." I took a swig, grateful for the sugary goodness that quenched the parched feeling I hadn't noticed in my throat.

She winked at me before turning her attention to working the waffle iron. I moved down the row behind the soldier pouring coffee into a mug.

"Your English is pretty good," I said. I could tell he wanted to make small talk.

The dark circles around his eyes made me believe he had been in the thick of this from the beginning. I was more than happy to be a scapegoat for some normalcy.

Such a small comment seemed to lighten up his world. "I spent my high school years at a boarding house in Tonbridge."

I gave him a blank stare. "England," he offered.

"Oh." I was amazed by the diversity Austria had to offer. Still, I had no idea how to respond to him, so I pretended to be busy setting up some bread in the toaster.

"I'm Lukas, by the way," he said after a moment of awkward silence.

"Emilia," I offered before pointing to my brown-haired friend, pouring batter into the waffle iron. "And she's my best friend, Theresa."

He waved to her, and she awkwardly waved back, her hands juggling her plate and a jug of waffle mixture.

Lukas insisted we share a table when we finished making our food and loading our plates. Theresa dug into her food immediately, not caring who watched the tiny ballerina devour an entire plate of food like she was a pro wrestler.

"So, are those guys you came in with…are they your boyfriends?" Lukas leaned forward, his eyes never leaving mine.

I groaned internally, ready to say yes, just to avoid the conversations that would stem from answering truthfully.

"No," Theresa said, between chewing bits of waffle.

I let my hair fall over my shoulder, shielding my expression from him and gave her a steely glare, raising my eyebrows. Theresa swallowed nervously with understanding. That was not the right answer.

He beamed. "Oh?"

Mercifully, a commotion at the table next to us grabbed our attention. Some soldiers were bent over a radio, listening to a man with a gravelly voice barking orders. I could barely make out a word and instead busied myself with fulfilling my angry stomach's wish for satiation.

"Seems we're going to be moving out soon," Lukas remarked with a sour expression.

"What makes you say that?" I asked between mouthfuls of buttered toast.

He nodded toward the soldiers, some of whom were hastily downing their coffees and shoving food into their faces.

"The captain says we're to relocate the civilians at Guggenthal."

I glanced at the other plain-clothed people nearby—men and women of different ages and nationalities, all keeping to themselves.

"To where?" *How could Guggenthal not be safe?* We seemed to have an abundance of supplies, beds, and even showers.

"There's a city in the mountains on the border of Germany south of Salzburg. Berchtesgaden, I believe?"

That's what the anchor had said on the television earlier. That if any survivors were left to escape into Germany. I guess the military was taking her advice seriously.

"I thought there was a storm headed in that direction."

Lukas nodded. "That's why he told us to leave before nightfall."

My eyes strayed to the dark gray clouds that hung on the horizon. Time was against us.

"If you and your friends want to take a shower or anything, I'd do it now." He finished his meal, then got up to leave.

Theresa agreed, and we finished our meal quickly before returning to the classroom. Felis and Oliver were back, but now Osman was missing. We quickly told them what we had heard.

"There are showers?" Felis' eyes nearly bulged out of his skull.

Oliver tugged at his arm. "Let's go."

They were out of the room before we could say anything else.

"Should we shower again?" Theresa seemed antsy at the idea of going however much longer without another shower.

"I'm not going to. But I do think we should grab some warmer clothing." If we were headed for the mountains during a potential blizzard, our current clothing would do little to stave off the bite.

Theresa and I shoved the extra water bottles and food from our rations into our backpacks before rummaging through the thrift store boxes again. We kitted ourselves with woolly socks, hats, and gloves. She managed to find a waterproof coat in her size, and I slipped a vest over my sweatshirt. Mercifully, the military had shared some of their thick, waterproof boots, and the women's selection was far greater than the men's. It wouldn't help us survive hiking in the Alps, but it'd certainly keep us warm until we reached the next leg of our journey.

"Emi?" Theresa's voice sounded so hollow, as if she stood at the edge of a cliff and debated whether to jump.

I turned to her, concern written across my face. "Are you okay?"

She tossed her head back, and tears glistened in her eyes. "Can we go for some fresh air?"

"Of course." I steered her back down the hallway to the yard, but she stopped in her tracks.

"I meant…where no one is." Her voice wavered.

I grabbed her hand, and we turned on our heels, heading for the front doors. Soldiers piled past us, ferrying crates, barrels, and briefcases back and forth. No one stopped us as we walked past the doors and out onto the small road where the bus still sat.

Theresa took charge here and led us up an embankment along the side of the road, sheltered by a row of trees and bushes. But as we crested the top, a smile lit my face. An open field of soft grass and tiny flowers rose to greet us. She charged forward, and at some point, she decided she was content. Folding her legs beneath her, she collapsed into the soft grass, bringing me down with her.

We lay there with the wind in our hair and the soft grass waving around us for what felt like an eternity until I broke the silence because I had to know what was on her mind. "Want to talk about it?" The wind snatched my words, and for a moment, I thought she had not heard me.

Theresa groaned. "I just…I can't get a hold of my parents. No texts, no missed calls…I have to know if they're okay."

The smile on my face was genuine. "You heard the newsreader. Germany is safe. Aren't your parents in Munich?"

She nodded slowly.

"Then you have nothing to worry about," I reassured her.

What I didn't voice was my concern for *my* parents. The news said nothing about the outside world. Other than they couldn't contact Turkey, Slovakia, or Czechia. Somewhere like Australia was more than likely not even registering in her mind.

"Thanks, Emilia." She rolled over, hugging me fiercely.

I patted her on the back before she fell into the grass, staring up at the clouds.

"Think we'll outrace that storm?"

My eyes followed hers. The clouds above us didn't look darker than what warranted a mild drizzle. But the ones on the horizon, settling over the mountains, were heavy shadows blocking all light.

"We might get lucky." I didn't pretend to know anything about meteorology.

We sat in silence, enjoying the sound of the wind whistling through the trees and the cry of a hawk somewhere nearby.

"Do you remember in July when we went to Mondsee for a weekend getaway, and the boy who worked at the restaurant would not stop asking you questions?"

I eyed her warily. "Yes…"

She giggled. "And then when you went to pay for your meal, he said it was on the house if you went on a date with him?"

Oh no, I think I know where she is going with this.

"I think you're about to have a repeat of that scenario." Her eyes glittered with mischief.

I groaned aloud, about to remind her it was her fault for telling Lukas I was single, until a shadow in my peripheral begged for my attention. I stopped with my mouth open, staring at the strange shadow within the tree line at the edge of the field. I didn't know what was in that direction beyond the forest, but something told me it wasn't a tree.

"Emilia…what's wrong?" I could hear the concern in her voice and feel her shift beside me anxiously. I knew her smile had faded, but I couldn't tear my eyes away from the shadow as it came closer and closer to confirm it.

The clouds parted long enough for a stream of sunlight to illuminate the field. The shadow sharpened into a dark shape, with two arms, two legs…and four spikes coming out of its back. My heart skipped a beat, and a lump formed in my throat. My mouth gaped open and closed like a fish, and an odd noise passed my lips before I could squeeze out a single word.

"Run."

Chapter 6

"EMILIA...NOW'S NOT THE TIME TO JOKE—" THERESA started to protest.

"*Run!*" I screamed, cutting her off as I pulled her to her feet and pushed her back toward the school. I hoped a soldier, or even a civilian, had heard my scream and reinforcements arrived before I—or heaven forbid—Theresa, ended up like that man in the parking lot outside our apartment.

We ran and ran, dirt flying behind us, the wind streaking through our hair. But it felt like the school was so far away. Too far. My heart pounded in my chest, and my mind screamed at me to *run, run, run.*

Theresa and I locked eyes, and I knew what would happen if that creature got hold of us.

The yellowed school roared at us from between the tree line, taunting, as if saying, "*You're almost there.*"

And we were until I saw Theresa's ankle roll and her leg buckled beneath her. She crashed to the ground. I slid to a halt and doubled back for her, but I knew it was too late. The monster was already there.

It bared deathly white teeth, and a growl emanated from within its chest and poured out of that mouth as a warning. It appeared similar to the one that had crawled from the crater in the parking lot, but it had hair as black as tar, eyes as white as its teeth, and skin with a purplish tint. I wanted to ponder the reasons for the differences, but the only thing on my mind was ensuring Theresa's safety and survival. But the monster had a different idea. It closed the distance between us. The nasty spikes in its back, winglike structures without feathers or skin, were poised to strike.

I moved closer to Theresa, aiming to stand between her and the creature. But it moved so fast. I watched in horror as the monster raised a hand and swiped at Theresa, who threw up her hand in defense. I saw the blood, the mangled flesh. But I was a statue. Unfeeling, unyielding, unable to comprehend what had happened. Unable to *accept* what had happened.

Theresa gave a death-rattling scream, breaking me from the panic that had me frozen like a deer in headlights. I screamed, too, the sound distracting that monstrous thing long enough to take its eyes off Theresa.

"Down!" Someone shouted behind me, and I dropped to the ground, angling myself over Theresa.

I heard the gunshots, then the bullets entering the monster's body. Over and over and over.

I didn't move.

I didn't look up.

I hardly breathed.

Theresa writhed beneath me, a groan escaping her lips.

"You're going to be okay," I said again and again, trying to convince myself more than her.

Fuck.

Footsteps approached me, even as the guns continued to ring. I heard the curdling death cries of the thing that had tried to kill my best friend, heard its body slump to the ground. But even as someone gripped my shoulder, I couldn't believe it was dead. I stayed over Theresa, believing foolishly if I lived, so would she.

"Emilia," said a familiar voice at my side.

I peeled back my head, my hair flying wildly around my face. Lukas stared back at me, a hand extended.

"Theresa," I murmured.

He hooked his hands under her shoulders, and I grappled for her legs. Together we carried her from the field as soldiers surged past us, weapons raised, eyes straight ahead. I didn't glance behind me as Lukas cried out for a medic. Several soldiers burst out of the school with kits in their hands, running to our side. A smaller group emerged with rectangular black boxes, setting them on the side of the road beside the bus.

"The truck." One of them nodded at us.

I let Lukas lead me to a nearby truck that seemed equipped specifically with medical gear. Two women jumped inside, and Lukas passed Theresa to them. She opened her eyes, tears streaming across her cheeks.

I gripped her knee. "T-Theresa?" I stammered through a shuddering breath.

"I-I'm okay," she said shakily, cradling her ruined arm to her chest.

An alarm, shrill and whooping, sounded from the school.

Soldiers and civilians burst through the doors, angling for the trucks and the bus sitting on the road. Felis, Oliver, and Osman appeared as a group in the doorway. The moment their eyes met mine, I burst into tears.

They ran to my side and hugged me tightly.

Osman was the first to speak. "What happened? Where's Theresa?"

I nodded my head toward the vehicle, where two nurses were using wipes to clean Theresa's arm. The door to the back of the truck was open, and soldiers handed in kits, extra blankets, and pillows.

Felis frowned, looking at me. "How?"

"We were attacked." The words left my mouth, but I still couldn't believe it.

A soldier appeared behind us, barking orders in German.

"They want us on the bus. We're leaving now." Felis' gaze darted between the bus and the truck Theresa was being treated in.

"I'm not getting on that bus," I ground out, stomping toward the truck. They had to let me in. They just had to.

A nurse glanced up as I approached, saying something in German. Her words didn't register because I paid her no heed, my eyes on Theresa. Blood soaked her arm, flecks of it dotting her face. Her eyes were closed, her chest rising and falling slowly.

"She's sedated," the nurse said in English.

I tore my eyes away from my friend's mangled arm, staring the nurse down. "Please...I have to ride with her."

The nurse exchanged a glance with the others, but I could see there was no room in the truck. Black boxes in an assortment of shapes and sizes were crammed into the back, leaving little room for the nurses and doctor, let alone for Theresa.

"I'm sorry." The nurse breathed, her face pained. It was clear she took no joy in telling me I couldn't be by Theresa's side.

I placed my hand on my best friend's booted foot, trying to hold back the tears.

Someone patted me on the back. "Come, we'll take the truck behind this one."

Lukas stood behind me, offering a solemn smile.

"Take care of her, please," I whispered.

The nurse nodded. "Of course."

On the other side of the truck stood Osman and another soldier. They had finished heaving a box into the back when they turned to see me approaching.

"Is it all right if I ride with you?" Osman's eyes were strained, and it took me a moment to remember I wasn't the only person who cared about Theresa's well-being.

I gave him a tight nod before jumping into the front seat. Lukas took the driver's seat, then Osman and the other soldier jumped into the back. The cabin was open to the back of the truck, where boxes and crates were stacked high, secured by cords. Two trucks peeled out first, taking the road south. The bus went next, followed by Theresa's truck. The back had been secured, and I could no longer see my friend.

It wasn't until a bend in the road I noticed there seemed to be too few vehicles for how many people had been at the school.

"Where is everyone else?"

Lukas kept his eyes on the road ahead. "We're the evacuation crew."

His bare minimum explanation set a lump in the back of my throat.

The journey south, under any other circumstances, would have soothed me. Emerald fields of waving grasses flanked the road, and tall tree branches hung like curtains overhead. Here and there, houses popped out of the forest like little mushrooms before being swallowed again. I wondered if anyone still lived in these houses or if they had left the moment they had a chance to. They probably thought they were safe out here, away from the hustle and bustle of Salzburg, where many of the meteorites fell.

My stomach twisted as a pair of monstrous white eyes filled my mind. I shook that creature's deathly glare from my mind, knowing if I focused on it too long, I'd start hyperventilating.

I cast my gaze out the window, hoping for a distraction, as we approached another bend in the road. This time, the trees fell away, revealing a luscious valley of shiny buildings sitting on the banks of a winding river.

Salzburg.

Everything appeared normal in the fractured light that streamed through the dark clouds. I could almost pretend nothing had ever happened, everything was fine, and it had all been a fever dream. Then I saw the black smoke curling into the sky and the shattered hulls of buildings destroyed by meteorites or the military's attempt at vanquishing our invaders.

Invaders. My heart ached painfully, and I reached up to stroke my chest through my long-sleeved shirt. I nearly laughed at myself for thinking such a gesture could ease the pain of knowing what had happened. Most European countries had a policy requiring mandatory military service after high school for a good reason. Borders were quite often redrawn, countries renamed, and nationalities stricken or added. So, it wasn't unusual to think one day, your country might be invaded by your neighbor. And that was what had happened. We'd been invaded, not by our neighbors, but by the stars.

"Did Felis and Oliver take the bus?" Osman murmured after what seemed to be an eternity of silence. Or rather, I suppose it felt like silence to them. To me, I was lost in my own mind and memories.

I shrugged. "I guess so."

Part of me thought they might have joined Osman and me, but I tried not to let my disappointment show. We were strangers, even though we had been through a lot in a short time. I had to keep reminding myself of that.

Osman leaned back against a crate, staring aimlessly out the windshield. "What happened out there?"

I swallowed, finding the courage to speak. The event had replayed in my mind repeatedly since we left the school, yet it still didn't seem real. Things could change so quickly in the mere blink of an eye.

"She was nervous about her family and wanted some fresh air." I took a deep, steadying breath. "We didn't go far. I could still see the school through the trees…we were right there," I choked back a sob, my eyes watering.

Lukas reached out, gripping my hand. I couldn't deny the warmth and slight squeeze of his hand soothed the angry part of me. I simmered and looked up at him.

"It's okay. Natalie will take care of her." He glanced at me briefly before returning his attention to the road.

"Natalie?" My eyes strayed to the truck in front of us.

"The nurse you talked to. She is my cousin."

That did make me feel better. But not seeing Theresa's face or being there when she woke sat at the back of my mind as we continued ascending the mountains.

More than once, our parade of military vehicles, sandwiching a giant blue public bus, faltered in their stride. Someone would call over the radio, instructing us to turn left or right. The instruction would almost immediately be followed by a warning our new route had added time to our journey.

Normally this wouldn't have bothered me. I enjoyed long, winding drives through the hills and countryside and marveling at the beauty of nature. Theresa did too. And that was why I couldn't enjoy myself now. Even though my eyes strayed to the beautiful, lush fields and wilds of the Austrian countryside, my mind never wandered far from the girl in the back of the truck ahead of us.

The landscape had changed since we struck south of Salzburg, the mountains inching ever closer. The hills were rockier, the ravines craggier, and the rivers flowed fervently as if they had somewhere to be. The trees grew darker and closer together, and something fell from within the darkened clouds. Small and white, it sat on the windshield, taunting us.

"Snow," I whispered.

Another snowflake fell, then another, until a steady stream of glittery whiteness cascaded around us.

"What route are we taking?" Through the dusting of snow falling silently from the sky, I couldn't tell left from right. The radio chatter was the only distraction from the nervousness that ate away at me.

"I'm not sure why they're sending us this way, but I don't ask questions. I do as I'm told," Lukas murmured.

"Should it have taken this long to reach the town?" I thought it was a half-hour drive, but we had been traversing the hellish mountainside for nearly an hour.

The rocky ground and bright grass outside our windows had been swallowed long ago by a smothering blanket of snow.

"No." Lukas was nervous, and only then did I notice the shifting of his eyes and the sweat beading on his brow.

He knew something.

One of the other soldiers pulled out his map, reviewing it carefully. He murmured something in German I didn't quite hear, causing Lukas to hiss at him to be quiet. Not even a second later, an urgent warning sounded over the radio, a muttering that made no sense to me.

We careened to a halt. The seat belt dug into the skin of my neck. Calming my beating heart, I surveyed the road where the other trucks had been. But there was no road, only a glaring mound of deathly white snow.

An avalanche had swallowed the road.

Chapter 7

Lukas pinched the bridge of his nose before grabbing the radio and contacting the vehicles on the other side. He spoke hurriedly in German, and his companion pulled out a map to try and figure out a way around our predicament.

It took me a moment to realize what this meant. Theresa was stuck on the other side of the avalanche.

Tossing open my door, I made to jump down from the truck, but a hand gripped the back of my vest.

"I have to help her!" I panicked, trying to disentangle myself from his grasp.

Gripping my upper arms, Lukas shook me back and forth. "Listen, Emilia. Your friend is safe. Hear that on the radio?"

Calming myself, I listened to a woman shouting over the radio.

Lukas looked me dead in the eyes. "That's my friend. She was driving the truck your friends are in. They're safe."

I felt the anxiety that had been rising slowly dissipate. I remembered that voice and Lukas telling me before the nurse who sat with Theresa was his cousin. Lukas released me, but his eyes never left me. Leaning my head against the headrest, I shut my eyes against the headache starting to form.

"What now?" I managed to whisper.

Lukas murmured something to his companion, and a chill breeze entered the cabin as the two soldiers exited.

Osman leaned forward. "Come."

Jumping from the truck, I waited for Osman to follow before we approached Lukas and the other soldier. They stood at the edge of the snow mound, their faces showing equal amounts of annoyance and disdain.

"*Wir könnten da hoch klettern,*" <We could climb it> his friend said in German.

Lukas eyed him. "*Und das Auto hierlassen?*" <And abandon the vehicle?>

The man's mouth twisted, and he returned to the truck, hoisting the radio near his mouth, speaking fast to someone on the other end. They were but a murmuring of voices, whispers on the wind from where we stood.

"I think I've had enough exercise for a lifetime," Osman grumbled.

I couldn't stifle the giggle that escaped my lips. Lukas eyed me curiously before joining the other soldier.

Osman raised an eyebrow. "That was an odd reaction."

Leaning forward, I pressed my gloved hand into the snow, my mood souring as my hand pressed a hole straight through it. The walls of snow left behind crumpled immediately, burying my hand.

"I don't know if we can climb this."

Osman glanced behind us at the road slowly filling with a thin dusting of snow.

"Well, we can't go back the way we came," he remarked.

True. It'd add an hour or more to our travel. I could hardly handle being in the truck behind Theresa, let alone dozens, if not hundreds of miles away. There had to be another way. My gaze swept over the darkened shadows between the trees. On our right was a cliff plunging toward an icy river, but to the left…

"We could walk around it." The trunks were deceptively short where they met the snowline, but it couldn't be any worse, or more dangerous, than trying to walk right through the mound in the road.

Osman followed my gaze. "You know what, that's not a bad idea. I'll go pitch it to the boys."

He returned to the truck, leaving me in the middle of the road. Snow flurried around me, and a breeze ruffled my loose hair across my shoulders. I shivered and noticed how cold my exposed face already felt.

I wish we'd hurry this up.

Looking at the woods around us, I thought I could make out a viable path through it, where rocks seemed to have held back most of the snow. It left a sliver of bare ground, almost imperceivable amongst the sea of white snow and brown bark. A clump of snow fell from a nearby branch, drawing my attention. A shadow shifted behind one of the trees, and my heart lurched in my chest.

It's just snow.

There it was again, at least twenty feet up the embankment. The shadow was too big, the movement too familiar, to be *just* snow.

An animal, perhaps?

Taking a tentative step toward the nearest tree, I placed my hand against its trunk, my eyes narrowing at the spot I last saw the shadow.

There!

It definitely was something. Part of me hoped it was a deer or even a bear. Anything would be better than what my mind wandered to. Because deep down, I knew it was not the familiar shape of a bear or a deer but something fast becoming too familiar.

"Guys…" My voice wavered slightly, and I stepped back, my eyes never leaving the tree.

I could hear them behind me in the truck, their murmuring a drone in the back of my head. Spinning on my heel, I bolted toward the truck, sliding to a stop before the open passenger door. They glanced down at me.

"Everything okay?" Lukas raised his eyebrows at me.

It took me a moment to find my voice. "There's something in the woods!"

The men exchanged a look before their gazes drifted to the trees.

"I don't see anything," the unnamed soldier said in English.

Oh, God, they're probably going to think I'm insane.

"I swear I saw something."

But even as the words left my lips, I could see the doubt settling on their faces.

"Could be an animal?" Osman offered.

The men jumped out of the vehicle, but their glances toward the forest were dismissive.

"There is a lot of wildlife in these mountains," Lukas agreed.

Shaking the premonition that set goose bumps creeping along my arms, I reluctantly nodded.

Osman placed a hand on my shoulder. "Well, if there is something there, we'll find out."

"What?" I looked at him with wide eyes.

Osman cocked his head sideways. "They think your idea to climb through the forest is our best shot."

Lukas glanced at the truck. "We'll need to grab some supplies, though."

Osman, Lukas, and the other soldier emerged from the back of the truck a moment later, carrying a long, black box between them. It was like the black boxes littering the side of the road outside the school and sitting in the back of the truck that held Theresa.

Grabbing my backpack from the truck, I pointed out the sliver of a navigable path through the snow.

"Well, lead the way." Lukas flourished his hand toward the woods.

Swallowing the nervousness that had settled into a leaded weight in my belly, I pressed my boot into the snow, waiting for it to stabilize under my weight. My eyes never left the tree where I had seen the shadow.

As we progressed further up the embankment, the trees crowded around us, the canopy protecting us from the flurry of snow sprinkling down from the graying sky. But it was quieter here under the shadow of the trees. Every time snow fell from a branch or a limb snapped under the weight, I'd flinch, jumping in the direction of the sound.

Calm down, Emilia. The woods make weird sounds all the time.

And yet none of that would account for the shadow I had seen.

Animals. My mind tried to reason with me.

"Can you see them yet?" Lukas called to me.

Peering into the underbrush, all I could see was snow and trees.

"Not yet."

The other soldier fiddled with his radio, calling out to the trucks on the other side. There was a moment of static before a woman responded in German.

"They can see us." Lukas hefted the box higher, and the boys increased their pace.

Up ahead, I could see the embankment taking a sharp decline. And at the very edge, swallowed by snow, was the shiny reflective surface of something metal. I instantly recognized it.

The guardrails.

"We're close," I said with encouragement.

The snow, although still soft and fresh, stopped giving as we approached the road. There, the snow was older, hardened by a day or more in the sun. We moved faster, and before I had time to question where the road was, the trees disappeared, and I found myself standing on the asphalt.

"*Da sind sie,*" <There they are,> someone called out in German.

Several men emerged from the trucks, and I was pleased to see the bus sitting idly in the road, the civilians eyeing us. Felis and Oliver's faces were lit by identical smiles as they waved at me. I raised my hand to do the same.

The men emerged after me, placing the box on the ground. Several men came out of the trucks to snatch the box before I could even process what had happened. They inserted it in the back of another truck, and I was moving toward Theresa's truck when Lukas' voice called out from behind me.

"Anyone seen Julian?"

The half a dozen soldiers froze, confusion on their faces. The man who had sat in the truck with us from Guggenthal was missing.

"Julian?" Lukas shouted his name into the breeze.

"H-he was right there…" Osman murmured, taking a step back from the woods.

That's when we heard the screams. Our heads swiveled to the forest we had emerged from, and almost immediately, another scream broke through the silence. The soldiers scrambled for the trucks, pulling out weapons. Kneeling at the guardrail, weapons trained into the woods, they waited with bated breath.

Lukas grabbed my wrist and pulled me toward the nearest vehicle. Osman followed, muttering something in Turkish.

"Aren't they going to help him?" Even as Lukas tried to put distance between the soldiers and us, I couldn't help but be concerned about the man I'd spent the last few hours with, even if it was only now I knew his name.

Lukas' gaze hardened as he pressed us against the side of the nearest truck.

"No reason to send six other people to their deaths." His tone contained thinly concealed anger, but the words he chose had me doubting his concern.

Now he believed what I saw wasn't an animal. His hand reached for mine, but I slapped him away.

His face crumpled with hurt. "What's wrong?"

I turned on him. "If you had listened to me and taken me seriously, this might not have happened."

He took a deep breath, pinching his eyes closed before he looked at me again. "Maybe. Maybe not. But then it would have just been someone else out there."

I glowered but didn't say a word. Osman stood wordlessly beside us, trying not to be seen. He clearly wanted no part in this. I wanted to be mad at him for dismissing me too. But at least he wanted to believe something was there.

"Da bewegt sich was!" <Something is moving!> someone shouted in German.

"We've got movement!" another soldier said in English.

They started shouting over each other in German, dropping to their knees, weapons cocked and raised. I didn't know whether to be relieved or terrified no other noises had come from the woods. There were only those two bloodcurdling screams, then silence.

"We should leave," Osman whispered beside me, his hand resting on the door of the truck.

I found myself agreeing with him. Why fight when we could flee? Especially since the snow didn't look like letting up any time soon. In an hour, the asphalt would probably be invisible under a layer of white.

"Hold fire!" The command echoed through the soldiers.

One of the drivers in the trucks ahead of us radioed in with someone, but his words didn't make sense to me.

"Movement at eleven!"

The soldiers swiveled left, where I could make out a shadow behind a tree.

"Julian?" One of the soldiers called his name, lowering his weapon to lean over the guardrail.

He took another tentative step, calling the guard's name

again. The other soldiers monitored his every move, poised to strike like vipers.

"*Julian,*" the soldier said, louder this time.

The shadow shifted, and something slumped forward, rolling toward the soldier. My stomach lurched as I recognized a trail of shiny crimson following it. Lukas froze beside me, but I didn't tear my eyes away to see his reaction.

"It's Julian!" The soldier confirmed, bounding toward the body. Leaning down, his eyes darting between the woods and the unmoving corpse, he placed his fingers on his neck. But I didn't need to wait for him to check for a pulse to know Julian was dead.

Standing, the soldier turned to the others, his face a mixture of horror and confusion. He opened his mouth to say something, and his body shuddered. A choked sob wracked his body, and for a second, I thought he would cry.

Before he could, his head lolled to the side, and his body slumped forward into the snow.

I heard the screams on the bus before I could process what had happened. Behind the soldier's unmoving body, clad in tight, dark clothing like leather armor, stood one of the creatures. Blood-red eyes stared at the line of soldiers, pink lips parted to reveal sharp canines, and black hair waved in the breeze.

"Fire!" The command was drowned out by gunfire and the sharp whir of bullets.

They shredded the trunks of the nearest trees, sending a spray of fractured wood flying. My hands flew to my ears, desperate to protect them from the sound of gunfire.

"*Get the civilians into the truck,*" a soldier shouted at Lukas above the racket.

Lukas made to move, but strangled screams caught our attention. The monster had emerged from the woods, avoiding the spray of bullets and standing to the far left of the soldiers. The nearest soldier didn't even have time to cry out before one of the rigid spikes struck out, slicing open his throat. The other soldiers raised their weapons to fire, but the creature surged forward with dizzying speed. It lashed out with its hands and the spikes on its back, and, one by one, the soldiers fell into the snow like dominoes, staining the ground red.

"Go, go, go!" someone cried out over the radio in the truck I was standing next to.

The first truck in the convoy began to move, causing Lukas to snap out of whatever spell had him frozen to the spot. Running to the driver's door, Lukas started the engine, calling us to get in. Osman climbed across the passenger seat into the back, waving his hand at me to hurry.

The trucks and bus in front of us began to roll forward, but my eyes fell on the last truck. The driver was pounding the dashboard, desperately trying to get the engine to start.

Theresa.

I abandoned Osman and Lukas, ignoring their cries. The snow was slick beneath my boots, and even though they were made for tough terrain, I had to fight to keep myself upright. I watched the horrified faces of the soldiers in the truck staring me down. The passenger door creaked open, a soldier ran out, raised her weapon, and began firing.

"Run!" the soldier cried to me.

The driver was frantically turning the key in the ignition, the engine spluttering as it fought for life.

"No!" I heard the screech, the moment of panic, before a garbled murmur and then silence.

Shit.

A shadow slunk past me, and I turned my head. Everything moved in slow motion, my heart pounding painfully in my chest. The creature was headed for the truck Theresa was in. As he neared the hood, the driver jumped out, pulled a small handgun from her pocket, and aimed at him. She hesitated for a split second, and it cost her. The monster lashed out, leaving jagged gashes across her throat and chest. She slumped to the ground, clutching her wounds.

The creature showed no care for the human who lay dying at its feet. Instead, its attention was on the truck.

Theresa.

I didn't know what overcame me, but I had a single thought as I barreled my way to the monstrous creature stalking toward where my best friend lay injured.

Save her.

Ten feet, five feet, and suddenly I was upon it. The monster turned slightly, and its crimson eyes narrowed. But I didn't care, didn't pause. I plowed into the monster who threatened my friend with all my might, and we fell off the cliff together.

Chapter 8

THERESA.

She was the only thing on my mind as the snow flurried around me, and the monster I clung to finally realized what had happened. We weren't airborne for long before we collided with the branches of a tree, slowing our descent before we plunged face-first into the river.

The chill of the depths raced into my eyes, ears, and mouth and settled in my lungs. I was too cold to shiver, too cold to realize what had happened, until a rock grazed my back, sending a bolt of pain through my shoulder. I cried out, but no air entered, only more water. I felt my grip on the monster loosening, and I only hoped if I died there, at least it meant Theresa was safe.

The faces of my friends flashed before my mind. Theresa, with her pronounced dimples and annoyingly perfect bedhead every morning. Osman, with his infectious smile and enveloping bear hug he'd give me when we met in the hall on our way to class. Then there were my parents. I pictured my mother, with her short, curly hair and big baby-blue eyes, knitting me another scarf for Christmas. I made it a habit to wear one on every holiday card I sent her. My father would always get jealous, wondering why I never took photos with the care box loaded with my favorite Australian snacks he'd spend an embarrassingly long time collecting to send me on my birthday. And even though I barely knew Felis and Oliver, they, too, took up real estate in my mind.

But my attention was dragged away when my head burst above the surface of the water, and I was assaulted by fresh air. I tried desperately to breathe, to flush the water from my lungs, but the coughing and spluttering only caused me to inhale more water. The current had softened, and up ahead, I noticed a bend in the river. A log jutted out from the riverbank and over the water, offering me salvation. When I got within reach, I kicked off from the rocky bottom of the river and stretched out my hands. I clung to the log and wrapped myself around it like a cat to a fish-shaped toy.

Out of immediate danger of drowning, I hauled myself further out of the water, coughing up what liquid was still inside me. My lungs burned, my head ached, and my entire body came alive with the assorted injuries that lurked beneath the surface of my clothes.

Once I had composed myself, I took in my surroundings. The river gurgled past me over graying rocks along a pebbled shore coated in snow. The trees, crowded close, obscured the sky, smothering me in shadow. But none mattered as much as knowing the alien was gone. I only prayed it meant the horrid thing had died, its corpse carried downstream.

Breathing a sigh of relief, I crawled along the surface of the log, ignoring the splinters that cut into my gloves. It only took me a moment to haul my entire body out of the water and find my way up the rocky shore. Laying on my back in the snow, I stared up at the sky. Or, at least, what I could see through the trees and the dizzying sprinkle of near-constant snow.

If I never saw another river again, I'd be eternally grateful.

I thought I'd surely hear my friends looking for me or, at the very least, calling my name. I couldn't have traveled too far from where the convoy had been, could I? Sitting up, I yelped as pain exploded through my leg and ribs. I doubled over in the snow and clutched at my calf, wincing as lightning bolts of anguish swept through my body. Shuddering, I had the horrible realization I might have broken something. I could feel bruising, especially around my ribs, but my leg felt far worse. I'd never broken a bone before, so I had nothing to compare the pain to. If ever I would dredge up a comparison, I'd think this pain had to be pretty damn close.

Resigned to the thought I might have broken a bone, I flipped onto my side and scanned the cliff edge. Following the rocky terrain upward, I could barely make out the shiny glint of metal guardrails around a bend. I didn't remember seeing a bend in the road.

Maybe the river had brought me farther than I thought.

Shaking the thought of being lost alone in the mountainous wilderness along the border of Germany and Austria, I gave myself a moment to breathe. Given how bad my situation seemed, there was no hope of me relaxing, but it allowed me to gather my thoughts and plan my next move.

But the moment I took to breathe and collect myself would cost me dearly.

That monster had gone over the cliff with me, had hit the river with me. At the very least, my friends should be safe. The convoy was headed to Berchtesgaden, a town nestled in a valley between white-capped Alps in southern Germany. Unfortunately, I wasn't paying nearly enough attention to my surroundings as we drove, my mind clouded by Theresa's plight. We'd changed our course so many times, doubled back, and turned left instead of right. I wasn't even sure if Berchtesgaden was still the destination.

Even if the river had dragged me some ways, as long as I didn't lose sight of the road, I should be able to make my way back to civilization. According to the last sign I had seen, a town somewhere nearby sat along the river's shoreline. My best bet was to inch along the shore, expecting I'd eventually come across it. Or, at least, I hoped I would.

Sighing, I pushed myself against the nearest tree, holding my breath against the flood of pain. There was no guarantee I'd have a better chance following the road than staying where I was. But nighttime would fall soon, and out here, exposed, during a blizzard, I stood no chance.

Once I was certain I could handle another wave of pain and had no choice but to, I used the tree for leverage and propped myself up onto my feet.

Pain immediately reverberated from my calf, through my knee, and up my thigh into my back. I cried out, slinking into the snow once more.

"Fuck," I muttered through clenched teeth.

You've really done it this time, Emilia.

Grinding my teeth in frustration, I ignored my inner self-doubt. Casting my gaze around me, I saw a long, sturdy stick lying under a dusting of snow, just within reach. I grasped one end of it, giving it a few exploratory squeezes and jabs at the rocks. It was firm and unyielding, and I knew what I had to do next.

A broken leg or not, I had to get out of there. Surprisingly, when I sat still doing nothing, the pain was nearly nonexistent. It gave me hope that perhaps it was a simple fracture or even a muscle injury. But I was no doctor, and the most intense medical training I had received was when I took a first-aid course to placate my mother about moving halfway around the world. Sadly, it didn't prepare me for being lost in a forest during a snowstorm after plunging off the side of a cliff into a river.

"All right. Into the unknown," I murmured to myself for encouragement.

Propping myself against the tree again, I jammed the stick into the ground and leaned against it heavily to pull myself to my feet. I wavered slightly, my heart beating painfully against my chest. But so far, the pain was more akin to a bruise than anything worse.

Maybe I haven't broken anything.

With steely determination, I set my sights on a grouping of boulders twenty feet ahead along the shoreline. With agonizing slowness, I shifted my weight from one foot to the next, trying to put all my strength into holding myself upright with the stick. I was wobbly and in considerable pain, but it was doable. I ignored the shivering and the horror at knowing I couldn't feel the tips of my toes.

A problem for later. I swallowed nervously. *If there is a later.*

I shuffled across the rocky shore, leaving a line like a snail through the snow in my wake, the boulders drawing closer and closer. Streaming out of my mouth like steam, my breath curled before me for a split second before the breeze snatched it away. I could feel myself tiring, the stick digging into my palm. With every deep breath I took, an ache vibrated from my ribs. I had to control my breathing, taking shorter, shallower breaths. But every step I took required more exertion, and my vision became starry as my head began to spin.

Approaching the first boulder, I shifted the stick to my other hand, using the boulders to push myself further along. The snow between the rocks was deceptively deep, and I stumbled more than once when I expected to feel solid ground. Luckily, I managed to keep myself upright.

Moving among the boulders, they seemed to get larger and flatter, forming small outcroppings and hollows free of snow. Temptation pulled at me, begging me to make my bed for the night by lying beneath one. But common sense told me if I lay down now, I might never get back up, especially in such an exposed area.

I looked at the sky, which had grown darker since I'd last checked. The snow had thickened considerably, and what was once a simple dusting now rose above my ankles. Time was running out. The ground leveled out ahead, and the rocks—boulders, really—widened considerably before blending into a wall of pure stone that stretched upward to where I suspected the road should be. It was in there, at a bend in the river, I spotted a dark opening in the cliffside. I knew before I reached it that it was a cave.

Standing at the mouth of a cave, I squinted into

the darkness within. The temptation to rest here was overwhelming compared to what I felt at the outcroppings, but a gaze out across the wilderness told me I still had a lot of ground to cover. Did I risk spending the night in the cave to rest? Or did I continue on my path, hoping to reach this town whose general direction could literally be anywhere? It was a choice between potentially freezing in a cave or alongside the river.

While I stood there, debating which death would be more welcome, an odd sound reached my ears. It was a whistling, like air rushing through a gap in rocks. I was still straining to hear the sound when the ground beneath my feet began to shake.

"What the—" I glanced upward, my heart skipped a beat, and my stomach lurched. A rush of snow had dislodged from the mountain.

Another avalanche and it was headed straight for me.

Panic welled up in me, and I desperately looked for an exit. It wasn't a simple slipping of snow hurtling toward me. It was easily the accrual of all the snow that had fallen and built up where the road would have been. I stared at the oncoming wall of snow, an icy drift of ivory threatened to smother me whole.

I could run. Best scenario, I would squeeze out of its path. But the worse would have me pushed back into the river and possibly drowned. The only other option I had stared right at me—the cave. Be smothered and eventually die due to lack of oxygen, be pushed into the river and drown, or be buried alive in a cave? My options were not appealing, and I was running out of time. The avalanche moved surprisingly fast, and clumps of snow had already rolled ahead of the main body. Some hit me, light flecks that would be mere tickles if not for the larger clumps that followed.

I decided to take my chance at running and had started moving when a clump of snow broke free from the avalanche and struck the stick I was using as a cane. The trusty piece of wood went flying, and I collapsed into the snow.

No…

Panic took control, and I grappled for purchase on rocks that cut into my flesh, fresh pain erupting from my calf and ribs. The fall knocked the wind out of me, yet surprisingly, my breath was the first thing to come back. But it didn't matter, because I was about to die.

Watching the raging snow roll closer and closer, part of me tried to reassure myself it wouldn't be too bad. Not the fastest death but perhaps one of the least painful. Being buried alive by an avalanche would be like falling asleep. That's what I'd read, anyway. I'd find out the truth of it soon. Snow fell around me in clumps, forming small mounds like anthills.

As the avalanche neared, all I could think about was Theresa. I could die peacefully in the knowledge my sacrifice had given her the time to escape. Her and Osman, Felis and Oliver, and Lukas.

Survive.

I closed my eyes, waiting for the inevitable end. Fractures from the avalanche and tiny snowballs thudded against my chest, shoulder, and leg. I ignored the searing pain of my fractured and nonfractured wounds. They wouldn't matter soon enough.

Please let death be quick.

In my acceptance, with shoulders relaxed and eyes closed, I heard the commotion of the world around me more clearly—the gurgling of the river as the slower water at its bank began to freeze over, the whistling of the breeze through the trees, the ruffling of the leaves. But even though I could hear the rushing of the snow and the dislodgement of the rocks as the avalanche hurtled toward me, there was a single sound that made no sense. A crunching, as if something was walking briskly. But I didn't dare open my eyes. Whatever it was would perish with me in this waterfall of snow.

The sound drew closer and closer. The roar of the avalanche was slowly drowned out by the roar of my heart. Still, I could hear the crunching of snow, leaves, and rocks underfoot, something advancing upon me. I could no longer attribute the shivering in my core to the dampness of my clothes and the frigid air. As the end drew near, I was no longer afraid of dying. I feared those few short moments, where I would be alive but drowning, starved of oxygen, buried beneath the snow. I could only hope it would be quick.

The crunching sounded directly behind me, and my eyes fluttered open. A shadow loomed over me, the shape somewhat familiar. Before I could turn to face down the shadow that had come for me, arms wrapped around my waist, gripped me tightly, and carried me into the cave. We collided with the hard rock, and pain shot through every part of my body, and my head swam with stars as my temple grazed a rock. The avalanche hit less than a few seconds later, sealing the mouth of the cave. The light trickled away with each pound of snow that fell, leaving us in total darkness. My—our—fate had been sealed. But all I knew was pain, and my consciousness ebbed in and out.

Maybe I would still die here today.

Maybe I would still be spared from knowing what happened to my family and friends.

But as I lay there in the darkness, all I knew was pain.

Chapter 9

It was deathly cold, and the sounds of the world were muddled and distilled like I sat at the bottom of a bucket and listened to noises echoing off cold, dead walls. Everything ached, and I fought to stay awake and even to open my eyes. Then the events that led to this moment came rushing back like an out-of-control freight train. Darkness gathered at the edge of darkness, begging me to let it take me somewhere else. I had already made peace with my inevitable end, so I gave in and shut my eyes against the cold.

However, my mind wouldn't let me forget I wasn't alone as the darkness shifted, and the distinct sound of someone pacing beside me echoed around me.

It's a figment of your imagination, my mind pleaded with me. *Born of desperation. Sleep, and this will all disappear.*

It was hard to argue with your consciousness when it made sense. Why would I care what lived in the cave with me, what had shoved me in here, clear of the avalanche, so callously?

I froze, coming straight to wakefulness. Something—someone—had purposefully shoved me out of the way. Whoever paced endlessly on the stones beside me was my savior. Waiting, I listened to the steps of what sounded like boots scuffing the stone and kicking small pebbles from their path. Eventually, the pacing got further and further from me until I heard shuffling at the other end of the cave before it returned to my side. Almost instantly, the distinct noise of rock scraping rock echoed, and a sudden warmth chased away the cold at my cheek.

It became warmer and warmer, light dancing behind my closed eyelids. But there was a shadow beyond the light, and I knew my mystery savior sat on the other side of the fire watching me.

I should open my eyes.

A part of me feared what I would see. Surely, if it were Osman, Felis, Oliver, or Lukas, they would have said something by now. There would be voices outside the cave, the sound of people digging. Maybe even Theresa calling out to me. But there was no sound but the crackling of flames and spitting of wet fuel on the fire.

The world was silent, cold, and deadly.

The warmth of the fire as it hungrily devoured whatever debris my companion had found grew and grew. Suddenly, I found I wasn't shivering as much. My clothing was still damp, and surprisingly, I realized it didn't bother me so much.

There was a shifting behind the fire. The shadow moved behind my eyelids until it blocked the light of the flames entirely. Then, trying desperately not to show my savior I was awake, I set myself as still as I could. I wore a mask and hoped to God it didn't reveal the turmoil roiling through my mind. And although my mind was active, playing memories and yelling at me, I found it difficult to grasp a single one. The memories were jumbles of pictures with blurred faces. No names, no sounds, no colors.

Then I realized what was happening.

I was becoming hypothermic.

A rough hand brushed against my forehead, moving the stringy strands of my slightly wet hair. I discerned after a few strokes the odd sensation came from a glove. But I still couldn't open my eyes, even as I felt this stranger stroke my hair, heard them remove their glove to check my pulse, and felt a hand on my forehead. I felt the warmth of the fire, yet there was an odd wetness around my scalp.

Am I sweating?

The stranger's fingertips brushed my temple where I had hit my head, and I couldn't hold the flinch that followed in check. An annoyed tut sounded under their breath, followed by the distinct sound of a zipper being pulled. I was desperate for a peek, but when I tried to flutter my eyelids, the blinding light of the fire forced them to shut again.

The stranger moved about the cave, shuffling fabrics, kicking rocks, and zipping or unzipping something. *Maybe a backpack?*

A few moments passed by before I felt their presence at my side. I could not deny the sense of relief that washed over me at their nearness. Somehow, I felt safer. Which made no sense, considering I had no idea who it was.

The stranger's shadow enveloped me, blocking out the heat and light. Their hands fiddled at my hood, pulling it back. They tossed my hair over my back, then the hands moved toward my chest, gripping the zipper of my vest and pulling it down.

"Stop!" I cried out, my hand weakly gripping the hand that held the zipper.

Even under my gloves, I could feel the strength in the hand, especially as it made to pull the zipper down again.

My eyes shot open, "I said—"

No words could describe the pain that erupted in my chest and how my heart lurched when seeing who—*what*—kneeled at my side. Its shiny, black hair was as dark as a starless night and rolled across muscular shoulders with pale gray skin splashed with dancing golden runes.

"Nooo…" I whispered in horror, recoiling from his closeness.

How…how could he have survived?

There wasn't a single mark on him, no evidence he had fallen from a cliff, let alone into a river.

Oh, God, I called it him.

Crimson eyes narrowing, it towered above me. Cocking its head sideways, his deadly eyes roved over me from head to toe. Taking a step forward, it reached out a gloved hand. I couldn't back away fast enough, far enough, and the moment my back hit the side of a rock, I cried out in pain. My ribs were still tender, and the ache in my calf still throbbed. But I felt more alive at that moment than I had in the last… however long it had been.

But what does it matter how I feel when the reason I'm here is staring at me like a science experiment?

It took a few steps forward to stand above me, its eyes locked on where my hand gripped my injured leg. My ribs were inconsequential. I was almost certain they were bruised, nothing more. But damn, did they hurt. The creature cocked its head sideways, and strands of silky black hair fell across its face. Memories came flooding back. I replayed them over and over, yet I couldn't accept what was plainly laid before me. I could not deny what it had done. It had saved me. There was no way around it.

My savior was a monster.

Why did it save me?

"What do you want from me?" I seethed, my voice shaking with rage and fear.

I'd be lying if I didn't admit I looked around for some way to rid myself of it. But there were only rocks, snow, and sticks. Of these, the latter was currently the only fuel source for the fire that staved off the cold. It didn't stop me from considering taking a burning twig and shoving it through the monster's eye socket.

It should be dead.

I could say it a thousand times, but it meant nothing if I wasn't prepared to do something about it. Angling myself into a seated position, with my back resting against the rock wall, I stared him down. I couldn't deny the pain that throbbed in my side with every breath I took or the dull ache in my calf.

If I wanted to do anything, I'd have to surprise it. There was no way I could brute force my way out of this situation. Considering my condition, I wasn't sure what I could do. I'd never experienced this level of pain before, but I was positive what I felt now paled in comparison to what this creature would do to me.

The creature kneeled less than a foot from me, staring intently like I was the thing to be studied. It reached a gloved hand toward me again, but I flinched out of its grasp, resting my cheek against the stone surface.

What does it think it's doing?

My back was as close to the wall as possible, but I still tried to put more distance between the creature and me. My gloved fingers clipped a rock, and I immediately grasped it in my palm. Undeterred by my obvious dismissal of its closeness, the creature moved a bit closer, raising its gloved hand again. Its hand came closer and closer until it hooked a finger under the strands of hair clinging to my face. I shuddered at the feeling of the rough fabric on the exposed skin of my cheek.

What is it doing? I asked myself again. My head was heavy with fog, and my mind still raced. Although there were no more memories, faceless faces, or reels without sound and color filling my thoughts. All I saw was the creature, and my mind was consumed with discerning its intentions.

It didn't seem concerned by my wide eyes, labored breathing, or how I shook as its fingers brushed my hair behind my ears. Heat flushed my cheeks, the sensation odd since the rest of my body felt deathly cold. Unperturbed by my obvious disdain at our close quarters, the creature's fingers trailed down my throat to rest against the zipper of my vest.

Not this again.

Rage built inside me, and I knew it was now or never. Gripping the stone tightly, I raised my hand and struck out. The rock hit it just above the eye, and the creature recoiled. Its hand shot out like a viper, wrapping around my neck.

The force knocked the breath from me, and I growled in response, but the only noise that left my throat was a pained whimper. The rock tumbled from my grasp and clattered to the cave floor.

It immediately released me, its eyes searching mine.

Coughing, I rubbed my neck, positive I could still feel its hand there.

"Just kill me already." I breathed in exasperation.

Those crimson eyes widened, and an odd expression lined his features. If I weren't convinced I was suffering from hypothermia-induced confusion, I'd say it looked *concerned*.

"What are you?" it whispered.

Wait! I froze as the realization dawned on me, my heart skipping a beat. He spoke and in *English*.

"W-what…" I was completely dumbfounded, unable to process what had happened.

It can speak. Does anyone else know this? The military? NASA? My mind couldn't grasp the concept.

"What are you?" it repeated in a silky, rich voice that melted my mind.

I shook my head, but no matter how hard I tried, I couldn't escape that voice. He sounded so innocent, so *human*. But of all the things he could have said, he wanted to know what I was.

"W-what am I? What are *you*?" I stammered.

The curiosity on his face had me baffled, but I knew it wasn't just natural curiosity. Something else sat beneath the surface, and I wasn't quite sure what it was.

Let's try a different approach.

I cleared my throat, trying to stem the shivering. I didn't know if it was induced by the cold or anxiety, but my trembling made it hard to be indignant. "You invaded my planet, and you have the gall to ask what I am?"

"You shouldn't be here." His eyes narrowed.

I couldn't stop the laugh that came out. "I shouldn't be here? This is my planet!"

He raised a hand again, and I batted it away. The motion caused pain to flare along my ribs, and I winced.

"You're injured."

I stared at him with a dumbfounded expression. *No shit, Sherlock.* Did he not remember me ramming him off the cliff?

"You're not." My words were icy, and I did not regret their venom. How could he survive the fall without injury?

If I wasn't mistaken, the expression, although fleeting, was more akin to guilt than anything else. I leaned forward, trying to discern what shadows were real and what were cast by the flames behind him. But suddenly, my vision blurred, and I was overcome by the overwhelming urge to lie down and close my eyes. My hands shot out to catch myself. The coldness of the air seemed to seep into every nook and cranny inside this cave.

"I-I don't know what's happening." Darkness clawed at the corners of my mind. The world spiraled around me, and the walls of the cave closed in.

The creature removed his glove and pressed his warm hand against my forehead.

"You have a fever," he murmured with a faint tone of annoyance.

"D-does my illness displease you?" I managed to say, although my head was spinning. *Now what, monster?* "If I die, you will be stuck in a cave with a corpse. Afraid I'd ruin the natural aroma of dank stone for you?"

He ignored my comment and moved forward, trying to unzip my vest again. "Your clothing is wet. It must be removed."

"Don't touch me." I tried to bat his hands away but had little strength to put into my attempts. I was certain I couldn't even fight off a fly.

Those flaming eyes narrowed. "If you don't let me help you, you'll die."

I laughed at him, a hollow pathetic noise that used far more energy than I should have been comfortable with. "Wouldn't that solve your problem?"

"Problem?"

Although the darkness gathered at the edges of my vision, I fought to stay awake. Anger was a great motivator. "Y-you had no issue killing everyone else. What is one more human life to something like you?"

He flinched, and the skin around his eyes crinkled.

Maybe it was disorientation from hypothermia, but I swear I saw pain in his eyes from my statement. *But that doesn't make sense. And neither does him wanting to help me.* Part of me considered his words, however. For now, I was alive, and he seemed to know how to help me.

With the shadows from the fire smothering him, all I could make out were the crimson irises of his eyes.

"You think I'm a monster."

I frowned, jerking my head back. The motion caused my head to swim. "I have no evidence to the contrary."

The creature gathered his hands before him, where the light barely touched them.

"I'm not the monster here," he said in a tone I couldn't quite decipher.

I scoffed. "It's not my job to prove otherwise. It's yours."

For all that I'd seen so far, the murder spree of his kind was greater than my own.

My shivering was overwhelming now. Goose bumps prickled every inch of my skin, but oddly enough, I couldn't tell if I was cold or hot. Everything felt the same.

"Time is running out," he said solemnly, but he made no move to close the gap between us.

Maybe he finally understood consent.

A moment passed before I replied. "I've accepted my fate." I was weary now, my voice shaking with the effort.

"You might have, but have your friends?"

That brought me back from the edge of the darkness enough for Theresa's face to appear in my head.

"W-what about them?" *Was he using my friends against me?* The friends he had tried to kill?

"I know where they are taking them."

I gave an odd laugh that sounded more like a shaky breath.

"What *do* you know?" My tone was of disbelief, but deep down, curiosity begged me to discover what he knew.

He moved closer to me and angled his body to the right so the light and warmth of the fire hit me in the face. I instinctively leaned toward the heat, hungry for the life it offered me. Maybe I wasn't yet ready to die.

"Where they are taking your friends." His voice was icy.

I rolled my eyes. "Even I know where they're headed."

He leaned over me, and the twitchy appendages coming out of his back hovered over me. "But do you know *why?*" There was no ignoring the venom in his tone. He knew something I didn't. Instinct forced me to shy away from his closeness.

"An evacuation. All the civilians—"

He laughed, a mesmerizing noise that, although it sounded fully sarcastic, sent a tingling sensation through me.

"Is that what they told you?" His appendages twitched.

I swallowed, nodding slowly. Part of me knew fear and the promise of seeing my friends again were the only things that stopped me from succumbing to the darkness that had hooked its claws into my soul.

"That pretty mountainous town with the odd name?" He waited, prompting me to say it.

"Berchtesgaden." Was it even safe for me to reveal that? I only questioned it once the name slipped past my lips.

"Yes, odd name indeed." He mused, his eyes peering into mine. "They may have told you they were securing your friends for evacuation in the mountains, but that pretty town is not their destination."

I drew my arm under me in an attempt to prop myself up. It was hard to stay focused because the room began to blur. "How do you know that?"

"I know a lot of things." Those crimson eyes glowed.

So cryptic.

I glowered. "Then where are they taking my friends?"

Anger rippled across his features. "A facility born of malice and greed, where they experiment on the living and the dead."

And dramatic, apparently.

But I knew what he was not saying. That facility was evidently operating on his kind. "I hardly see how that's any of my concern."

"You are mistaken if you believe your friends are safe there." He waited a moment for the realization to sink in, for my eyes to widen at the implications. Theresa, Osman, Felis, and Oliver weren't safe, after all. And Lukas, *did he know?*

And he claims he can help me find them…

I shook my head. "What's the catch?"

Cocking his head sideways, a frown of confusion marred his features. "Catch?"

So, the creature understood English, but our expressions were a bit beyond his language skills. An odd thought surfaced. Talking to him wasn't unlike talking to someone whose first language wasn't English. Colloquialisms and expressions were foreign and misunderstood.

"What must I do?"

I didn't care what happened to me in the end. But my friends, Theresa, Osman, and even Felis and Oliver, didn't deserve what might happen to them, assuming the alien wasn't lying.

"Let me save you," he stated firmly.

Those four words rang in my head over and over. He *wanted* to save me. Even if I hadn't been teetering at the edge of passing out, I still wouldn't have comprehended why.

"Surely, my life isn't worth this? You could easily abandon me here and save your own."

Pain mottled his features. I knew the look well, but when our eyes met, the pain vanished, leaving that stoic-looking expression behind. "You and I will travel to the facility together. Those are my terms." It was very clear from his tone he was done answering questions, and all he wanted now was an answer.

The darkness around my vision blurred further, melding the inkiness of his hair and the crimson of his eyes until he, the night, and fire were one. Time truly was running out.

But I'd been given a second, no, *third* chance, at redemption, at saving my friends. They deserved to know what was about to happen to them.

"Yes," I murmured before letting the darkness take me.

Chapter 10

Warmth awoke me, and I felt a firmness beneath me that was somehow yielding.

The crisp scent of wet snow was in the background of burning wood and the aroma of cooking meat. My eyes opened slowly, and my disorientation caused me to flinch away from the brightness of the firelight. But the rumbling in my stomach wouldn't let me ignore the juiciness of what wafted in the breeze.

A set of connected metal rods was propped over the flames, reminding me oddly of the guardrails edging the mountain roads. Hanging from the topmost rod was the seared corpse of what used to be a rabbit. The fur was long gone, but the long ears and unmistakable feet were still attached. I hated myself for salivating at the sight of it and the rumble my stomach gave in response. I was not a fool, ignorant of the origins of what I shoveled into my mouth day in and day out. I knew veal came from baby cows, venison from deer, and the cute cow at the petting zoo would one day be the patty in my burger. But somehow, seeing the carcass strewn over the pole like a flag, being licked by the flames, made me uneasy.

"Hungry?" came a voice from above me.

Twisting beneath the blanket that enveloped me, I turned to see I was entangled in the creature's arms. I froze, anxiety rising to the point where I thought I might scream. It wasn't that he held me like a child, keeping me warm and safe. What caused my panic was when my eyes followed his gaze downward, and I realized I wore only my bra and underwear.

"Oh, my God!" I groaned, tearing the blanket from his grasp and wrapping it around me before scooting across the stone and out of his arms.

A crisp breeze tickled my bare skin, and I shivered. "Why am I naked?" I sounded nearly hysterical.

He didn't seem bothered by my reaction in the slightest, sitting upright, eyeing me curiously.

"Your clothing was wet."

I stared at him, dumbfounded. "What?"

He pointed behind me, and my eyes followed to where another set of metal poles sat on the other side of the fire. My vest, long-sleeved shirt, jeans, and socks were spread over them. My backpack sat against it, and most of the contents were laid out in a neat row.

"When I asked for help, I wasn't giving you permission to *strip* me!" With the blanket wrapped around me, I scooted around the fire to my backpack, keeping the flames between us. Testing the clothing on the poles, I found them soft and dry, ready to go.

"How long was I out for?"

They were soaked before...

He seemed undisturbed by my rush to put distance between us. "A day."

"A *day*?"

He frowned. "Is that not the word?"

I held up a hand, dismissing his concerns. "Yeah, that's the word." At least, I hoped so. "I find it hard to believe I was out for so long."

How much did I sleep through?

"You were on the verge of death. Do you realize that?"

I fidgeted under the intensity of his gaze. Not wanting to tempt any more awkwardness, I focused on balancing the blanket on my back as I pulled on my mercifully dry clothing. After grabbing the scarf and hat that sat on the cold ground of the cave, I sat back on my feet and watched the smoke curling above the rabbit.

"Are you hungry?"

My eyes snapped to him. I guess he took my nonverbal response as a positive answer. He crossed the space, kneeling beside the fire as he maneuvered the metal rod with the rabbit off the flames.

As he began to tear pieces of the flesh from the carcass, I did a double take.

"W-where did you get that?"

He eyed me curiously. "I killed it."

Well, yes, obviously. "I can see that…but where did you get it from?"

Pausing in his dutiful stripping of the meat, he pointed toward the mouth of the cave. I followed his finger to where, at the very top, where the snow met the cave ceiling, was an unmistakable hole.

What the…

"There was an opening this entire time?" I knew my reaction was irrational, but by God, I wanted to hit him.

He studied me curiously. "What good would it have done for you to know? Your injuries would not have allowed you to leave."

He was right, I suppose. I guess it also explained why we didn't die from smoke inhalation. I hadn't even considered where the smoke was going this entire time. My eyes drifted to the cave roof, where puffs of gray smoke hugged the ceiling before slithering along the stone to the hole. The light out there was blinding, begging me to come out and see it.

He seemed oblivious to my inner dialogue. Skirting around the fire, he placed several strips of rabbit meat on a metal plate. It seemed familiar, yet I wasn't entirely sure of its origins.

"Where did you go?" I lifted the plate to eye level, inspecting it.

Fiddling with the slices on another metal plate, he took his seat on the other side of the flames, eyeing me. "Your friends left a vehicle behind."

I swallowed nervously. *The vehicle Theresa was in. Does that mean…*

He noticed the concern etched on my face, and I quickly chastised myself for being so obvious. I hated I was so easy to read. It made it extremely hard to lie. Not that I ever had a need to before.

"Your friends were nowhere to be found," he said quickly.

Breathing a sigh of relief, my shoulders sagged. For a moment, I thought maybe he had escaped to finish the job. But if he could leave whenever he wanted, why didn't he?

"Why did you come back?" I asked, curious.

He cocked his head. "What do you mean?"

I swept my hand over the food, the blanket, and the dry clothes. "Why?"

"We made a deal, human." A deal. He said it like it was obvious.

"So?"

His eyes narrowed. "I know deals are easily broken by your kind, but mine do not take them lightly."

I shivered at the venom in his tone.

Ignoring the chill that crept along my spine, I took a tentative whiff of the rabbit strips. There was no denying it smelled oddly like chicken, perhaps with an earthier tone. Part of my consciousness begged me to consider maybe he poisoned it, but why waste the energy of saving me to poison me? I took a deep breath, closed my eyes against the pointed ears on his plate, and bit into a strip. Immediately, I was assaulted by a flavor palette I had no words for. The meat was dry and gamey, yet I scarfed down every strip on my plate. I couldn't deny my guilt, but the gnawing feeling in my stomach subsided. Now all I needed to do was cure the aches in my rib and calf and solve the headache slowly blooming around my forehead.

A gloved hand appeared before me, and I looked up to see the creature handing me my canteen.

"Why are you..." I fought for the best word to describe what I was struggling to understand, "...being nice?"

He placed the canteen in my outstretched hand. "I've already told you."

I scoffed. "We have a 'deal.' Yes, yes, I know that. But that doesn't explain what you're doing."

"Maybe the way we treat our enemies is different." He shrugged.

I took a swig of my canteen, the icy water soothing my parched throat. "So, I am your enemy," I stated simply.

Something danced behind those crimson eyes. "For now."

I tried to ignore the implications of his words. *For now.* Admittedly, it was hard to accept I was talking with one of his kind. He could easily pass for a human if it weren't for the weird bone wings sprouting from his back, his odd skin color, and blood-red eyes. It certainly didn't hurt he wasn't bad-looking, either.

I squashed the thought as fast as I could, stomping it into oblivion. *Don't you dare.* My inner voice immediately raised my arms, and who could blame her? He was a monster, just like the others. I couldn't forget no matter what sort of kindness he showed me, his kind invaded Earth and was slaughtering humans, and no amount of goodwill could change that. It certainly wouldn't bring back the guy in the parking lot or the soldiers whose corpses were buried under a foot or more of snow on the cliff above us.

We finished our meager meal in silence. When the strips were gone, my stomach protested at the little nourishment, and I fished around in my backpack, noticing the food bars. As desperate as I was to fill the pit in my stomach, I knew this could easily be the only food I would have for a while. With hunger rumbling in my belly, I packed up, zipped my backpack closed, and tossed it over my shoulder.

He watched me with a bemused expression, but I did my best to ignore him. Half-limping across the cave, I eyed the hole through the snowbank at the entrance. It was decently sized. I certainly wouldn't struggle to get through it, but getting up to it was another problem. Although the pain from my ribs and calf was nothing compared to yesterday, they still ached. I was almost certain my left leg would buckle if I put too much weight on it.

Steeling myself, I placed my hand against the stone wall. There were divots, sections of stone weathered from rain and wind over countless years. They seemed sturdy enough for me to hold myself steady as I climbed, but the moment I set my foot on the hard, packed snow, I knew this wouldn't be easy.

Who knew snow could be slick?

Ignoring my mind's stupid comments, I kicked at the snow until a small nook formed, allowing me to slip my foot into it. Without giving myself time to second-guess my actions, I gripped the divot and pulled myself upward. Almost immediately, my boot began to slide, and I fell backward in slow motion. I didn't have time to cry out as I slid back onto the cave floor.

"Do you need assistance?" The smugness in his voice was nothing compared to that on his face.

I barely contained the urge to swear, instead opting to ignore him. I'm sure for someone like him, it was a breeze. He was all muscle and judging from how quickly I'd seen his kind move, it would probably take him no more than a few seconds to get through. I waited for him to zoom past me like a weasel, but he remained beside me.

"After you." He flourished his hand toward the hole in the snow.

I eyed it warily. I knew this wouldn't be easy, but after I made myself look like a fool, it should be smooth sailing.

Or at least, that's the lie I told myself.

Taking a deep, steadying breath, I tried again. With my hand in a different, deeper divot and my foot angled into a sturdier, flatter part of the snow, I pulled myself upward and didn't slip. Renewed at the fact that, for now, I was stable, I moved forward. From one indent to the next, I kicked my foot into the snow. Halfway up, the aching in my ribs and burning in my leg became apparent. My face contorted with every step, especially when my weight shifted to my left leg.

I was much farther up than before and knew I could easily make the last few feet. With the sun shining so bright on the other side, the hole taunted me. I could do this. I shifted my hand to the next divot, leaning forward. Almost immediately, the snow beneath my feet shifted, and I felt myself falling backward. I sensed him surge forward, and strong arms enveloped me as my back collided with his chest.

"I didn't ask for help," I grumbled, sagging in his arms like a petulant child.

I could almost feel the eye roll, but his grip did not loosen. Standing behind me like a barrier, he let me use him as a point to push off. The arms around my waist relaxed, and I crawled toward the hole, the snow constantly shifting beneath me.

Ahead, the hole yawned wide, calling to me. I gripped the edges of the snowbank and hauled myself to the surface, poking my head out into the world. My face was assaulted by a deathly chill, and my eyes were blinded by the sun. Once my sight adjusted from the musty darkness of the cave, I could appreciate the transformation of the landscape around us. The world was bathed in a pristine blanket of ivory. Even the river was a silver ribbon struggling beneath a thin layer of cracking ice.

Hauling my entire body through the hole, I perched atop the snowbank, angling myself to slide down it to the ground. The snow barely gave beneath my weight, and the rocks that lined the river beneath me were not even visible. *He* joined me a moment later, with far less noise and far more dignity than me.

"This way." He stepped out in what I hoped was a westerly direction.

I followed behind, leaving a healthy distance between us. Mainly, it was in the hope he wouldn't notice my limp and how I struggled to keep up. Every step was worse than the one before, and yet, I couldn't bring myself to ask for rest, let alone for his help. Something told me he would be more than willing to make this easier on me, but I couldn't trust him.

I didn't want to trust him.

After several minutes of silence, disturbed only by the crunching of the snow beneath our boots, I spoke, "How did you know about this facility?"

He gazed over his shoulder at me but didn't say a word.

All right, let's try something else.

"Do you have a name?"

"I do," he replied.

That's it?

"Okay…what is it?" *Like, clearly, I'm asking because I want to know.*

I bet his kind had weird names, like the names given to characters in fantasy novels and television shows. Maybe there was an Imlerith. Or a Caranthir, Nithral, or Geralt. Or maybe they had more of a science-fiction vibe with names like Ronon, Teyla, or Teal'c. But after a while, it was clear he wouldn't reveal his name.

"All right, if you don't want to share it…what do your people call themselves?"

A moment of silence passed before he spoke. "You talk an awful lot."

I glowered, relegating us to silence once more.

But I could only listen to the gurgling river and crunching snow beneath our boots for so long before I started going insane. I was in a unique situation. For whatever reason, this creature had not only spared me but also promised to help me find my friends. The least I could do was try and understand who he and his people were.

"Where do you come from?"

His eyes darted from one tree to the next. "Far from here."

Finally, a response! But not the one I was hoping for. Then again, would it mean anything to me even if he had told me where his people came from? I knew the Andromeda Galaxy existed, but maybe it's called something else to them.

"Do you miss it?"

He mumbled something under his breath, then his head whipped around to stare behind us.

I stepped into his view, staring him down. "Hello?"

"Quiet, human," he warned, sinking low to the ground like a hunter waiting diligently for prey.

"Why? What's—"

His hand clamped over my mouth, dragging me against his chest. I railed against him, but he placed a single finger against his mouth. I was quiet long enough to make out an odd sound coming from somewhere ahead—crunching steps, murmuring, the rustle of clothing.

There were people!

We stood sheltered by a thicket heaving with snow beside

a group of what I suspected were young oak trees. I knew they wouldn't see us unless we moved through the dense brush. My suspicion was confirmed a moment later when a group of four men appeared, hauling themselves over a nearby snowbank.

They were dressed in camouflage gear with rifles slung over their shoulders. One of them hauled a sled weighed down by the corpses of three deer and an icebox I suspected was filled with beer.

I wanted to run to them and beg for help, but something told me these people were more dangerous than the creature I stood beside.

My eyes strayed to the creature at my side. *What was the saying? 'The enemy of my enemy is my friend.'*

The four men joked to one another in what I knew was German. Yet the words were hard to understand, except for one that did more to chill the blood in my veins than the frosty weather. I immediately chased the word from my mind as my heart beat painfully against my ribs.

The creature beside me stirred, removing his hand from my mouth to pull me closer to him. I didn't know if he understood German, but if he did, I was instantly thankful for the gesture.

Once the coast was clear, he dropped his hand and led me into the woods once more. After a while, the terrain slowly rose upward, and a small hill covered in trees blocked our view. The struggle of climbing had me limping every step of the way, just like back in the cave. He seemed to notice my predicament when I was halfway to meeting him at the top. Maneuvering through the snow with all the grace of a damn god, he held out his hand. Pride demanded I ignore the offer, but the pains in my ribs and leg demanded otherwise.

Placing my hand in his, I let him support me to the top of the hill. We stood at the zenith, staring out over a landscape of snowy cliffs, silvery ribboned rivers, and trees dotting the landscape like little toothpicks.

The light streamed through the dense gray cloud cover, and from the corner of my eye, I noticed it reflecting off something below. My heart skipped a beat as my eyes roamed over the sleek, black body of a truck not more than sixty feet from us, and I spied a barely visible road curving around a bend. With a start, I realized I knew that truck. It was one of the ones the military had used in Guggenthal. My heart raced, and I could hear and see nothing else as I skirted around the tree line to get closer. If that truck was here, my friends couldn't be far away. I had to check.

I had to make sure.

I barreled through the snow with only one thing on my mind. The truck got closer and closer and, ignoring the burning in my leg, I took one final step. My foot met nothing.

I'd stepped right off the cliff.

Chapter 11

WITHIN THE SPAN OF A SINGLE BREATH, I FELT HIS HAND grip the back of my vest and yank me backward. I collided with his chest and slipped on the soft snow beneath my feet. My leg buckled, and I brought him down with me.

Sprawled into the snow beneath the evergreens, the creature stared down at me. In the gentle light, I could appreciate his high cheekbones, strong jaw, and dark, thick lashes over what I now realized were not entirely crimson eyes. Flecks of gold streaked through his irises like glitter in a marble countertop. My eyes trailed from the silky, black hair that rolled across his broad shoulders and barely brushed my own. The sunlight streamed through the leaves, casting a heavenly aura around him. Right now, he looked like an angel, not a demon—an otherworldly creature I had the privilege to be in the vicinity of.

That was until those bony, featherless wings spread out from his back. They resembled long spider legs in the speckled sunlight and reminded me no matter how handsome or nice he was, he was still a monster. And he had still killed people.

I couldn't help the shiver that ran through me. I broke eye contact, untangling myself from him. Wiping the snow from my jeans and vest, I stood and surveyed the small glade at the top of the hill. He joined me a moment later, his black leathers unmarred by our romp in the snow.

"Are you okay?" His eyes paled with concern, and I couldn't help the fluttering in my chest. When I didn't reply, he turned toward me and said, "Human?"

"Emilia." I breathed.

He paused. "What?"

"My name."

I saw him watching me from the corner of my eye with an odd expression I couldn't quite discern.

"Emilia." He purred in a dangerously honeyed tone.

I blanched, turning away from him. My cheeks heated, and my stomach started somersaulting.

What the fuck! Why would he say it like that? But an even worse thought occurred to me. *Was it wrong that I liked it?*

"A storm approaches," he murmured, oblivious to the effect he had on me.

I was too flustered to speak, instead opting to follow his gaze to the horizon. Dark, near-black clouds kissed the peaks of the mountains, and even from where we stood, I could see the flecks of snow falling like confetti. I couldn't catch a break.

"Are you coming?" he called out.

I hadn't noticed he was no longer beside me and turned around to see him descending the cliff face. Part of me panicked, thinking about how close I'd come to falling off the edge. Swallowing my nervousness, I hugged the side of the cliff, ensuring I copied each of his footsteps. The pain was easier to ignore when I was focused on not plummeting to my death, but as we neared the very end and he stood on the road waiting for me to join him, my leg threatened to buckle. Grasping a long taproot that jutted out along the cliff, I eased myself closer and closer to the road, focusing solely on the path in front of me. But the pain worsened as the trail steepened, and I suddenly lurched forward and crumpled.

Gloved hands immediately reached out for me, gripping my upper arms and steadying me. The creature's crimson eyes watched me carefully as he supported my weight onto the road.

"Must I carry you?" he murmured, cocking an eyebrow.

I glowered at him. "Surely, it'd be easier to simply leave me here."

"I told you—"

"A deal's a deal. I *know*." I rolled my eyes.

Ahead of us sat the black truck we'd seen abandoned. Behind it, a large sign listing the names of nearby towns and cities was peppered with snowflakes. But I only cared about one town.

"Berchtesgaden," I whispered, nodding at the sign.

We stared at it in silence.

Berchtesgaden – 15 kms

He glanced toward the truck no more than twenty feet from us. "I'm afraid we'll need to shelter here for the night."

I hated he was right. It couldn't have been too much after midday, but it was easily a four-hour walk to Berchtesgaden. *If I wasn't injured.* Part of me considered his offer to carry me

125

the entire way, but I didn't want to be more indebted to this creature than I already was.

Shrugging off the hands still holding me upright, I limped toward the vehicle. A thick layer of snow surrounded it, so it had been abandoned for a while. But my heart still hammered in my chest as I got closer. *What if someone was still there? What if it was someone I knew?*

Horror hastened my steps, but my heart calmed as I rounded the truck and pulled the first door open with a light squeak. It was empty. Of people, at least. The inside still contained some bags, and I made quick work of going through them.

The creature appeared at my side, peering over my shoulder, but I paid him no heed as I noted what could be useful. My stomach had other ideas, grumbling loudly enough I heard him snort in response.

"I'm sure you're hungry too." The military bags had no food or water. So, I had to make do with what I already had. Slinging my backpack into the seat, I pulled out two trail bars, turning to press one into his gloved hand.

He raised it to his nose, sniffing tentatively.

I rolled my eyes. "It's food, not poison."

Sliding into the seat beside my backpack, I ripped the corner of my bar and popped it into my mouth. I was thankful for the sweetness of the honey and the nutty aftertaste. But the joy was gone after I had devoured the entire bar a second later. I looked at my new companion, who had pulled open the wrapper to stare at the contents. Delicately, he took a bite off the corner, those bleach-white canines sending a shiver down my spine. Chewing, he swallowed quickly.

He noticed my staring and passed the bar back to me.

"This is disgusting."

Excuse me?

"What's wrong with it?" I don't know why I felt so indignant at his response. It wasn't like I had made it.

He raised his eyebrows. "It's hard and unbearably sweet. You humans enjoy this?"

I shrugged, almost offended. "I mean, some of us do."

"You need real food," he said matter-of-factly, his eyes scanning the horizon before he climbed over the guardrail and slid out of sight.

"W-wait!" I hollered, limping after him.

Did he just jump off the cliff?

Peering over the guardrails, I watched him blaze a trail through the snow toward the nearly frozen banks of the river. I hadn't realized the river was so close, but I didn't know what difference it made. Crawling over the guardrail, I slid down the embankment and limped to his side, careful not to give him a reason to carry me.

Standing awkwardly by his side, I watched his eyes, trained intently on the free-flowing water. Here, only the banks had a thin layer of ice atop them, and it took me a moment to realize why that garnered his interest. I could almost make out the glittery, lithe forms of fish darting beneath the surface.

Navigating the icy bank, he stood on a rock out of the water's reach, staring at the fish streaming past.

"W-what are you doing?"

I blinked, and, in a single heartbeat, a wriggling fish appeared in his gloved hand.

"Finding us real food."

I glowered. "Trail bars are *real* food!"

He gave me a look and, without a word, stalked away from the riverbank.

Pausing after walking past me, he tossed a look over his shoulder. "Coming?"

Repeating his approach, I crossed the icy bank, standing on the rock out of reach of the water. "I'll get my own, thank you."

But unlike him, I kneeled at the edge. I didn't have the grace, power, or speed to pull a fish from the river like he had. But if I were smart enough, I was sure I could tempt one to come close enough to snatch it. I hated to admit he had the right idea. The protein from the fish would help me go a lot farther than the sugary crash I'd get from the honeyed nut bar.

Sitting at the very edge, my hands hovered above the water, and I swear I could feel the chill without even touching it. Fish darted beneath my fingertips, too fast for me to catch. But I waited. I knew if I was patient for once, I could do it. Moments passed, and still, the fish darted back and forth. I became a statue, unmoving, barely breathing, hoping the fish would forget about me and calm their manic frenzying. I'd seen it before in a nature documentary.

Photographers would wait, even after the animals had caught sight of them. Eventually, the creatures would forget the photographer was there. There was no reason to believe a hunter lying in wait for the hunted was any different.

And soon enough, I was rewarded for my patience when a small fish slithered into view, swimming in place right below my hands. I didn't think. I plunged my hands into the icy river, and my fingers gripped the slimy fish. I plucked it from the shallows, water splashing across my jeans.

I did it!

"Hah!" I said triumphantly, adjusting myself to show my catch to the creature who no doubt thought I was inept. Steadying myself on the rock, I turned, and the fish slipped right through my fingers, splashing back into the river.

His derisive snort drew a glance over my shoulder. Standing on the bank, a flurry of snowflakes twinkled around him. My eyes roamed from his crimson eyes to his harsh black leathers, which starkly contrasted with the ivory landscape around him. In every sense of the word, he was handsome. Deadly but handsome.

Letting out an audible sigh, I shook the sight of him from my mind, turning back toward the river to try again. But the snow falling around us had thickened, and the chill in the wind was baneful. My hands were freezing from the few seconds they spent in the river, and my first attempt had scared off the remaining fish.

A shadow appeared at my side, followed by his deep voice. "Come."

Fine. *Trail bars it is.*

Reluctantly, I dragged myself away from the river. He got back to the truck much faster than me, and by the time I caught up with him, he had made something on the road beside the truck. A tarp was stretched from the truck's passenger door and tied to two trees on the side of the road at a slight angle. Below it, protected from the harsh wind on one side, a fire was beginning to gain life. He motioned for me to sit in the passenger seat, and I watched him descale the fish before folding it over a tire iron to roast above the crackling fire.

Snow flurried around us, and the black clouds above

darkened the world. We sat in silence listening to the crackle of the fire and watching the smoke be carried away by the breeze. There was no denying the scent of the fish cooking made my stomach rumble and my mouth salivate. A reaction that simple trail bars had never accomplished.

When the outside of the fish was nicely toasted, the skin verifiably crunchy, he removed it from the iron. Picking it apart, he placed several large pieces on a metal plate he had found in the truck, holding it in front of my face.

"What?" I asked in confusion.

He pressed the plate into my hands. "Eat."

"Why are you doing this?" I couldn't handle this, couldn't understand it.

The hands that plucked a fish from the river, cooked it, and helped carry me to safety were the same hands that had slaughtered innocent soldiers just doing their job. So saying I was greatly confused and conflicted was an understatement.

"Doing what?" His brows furrowed, eyes squinting in obvious confusion.

I didn't know how to voice my concern. "Being…nice."

He sighed and placed his plate on the snow that had gathered beside him. Emotions roiled over his perfect face like a wave. They came so fast I couldn't hold on to one. But there was one I couldn't deny when those crimson eyes slid to mine, and from his peripherals, I knew he was looking me over.

"I don't know," he finally said.

God, I hated myself for what I was about to say. "I think you do."

An awkward silence settled over us. Several minutes passed before he turned his attention to the fish. We ate in silence until my plate was empty and my stomach full. I was grateful the warmth of the fish had transferred to my body because I was *freezing*. I wanted to shut the door, huddle down with the banket, and shiver myself to sleep. But the pull of the fire and my mysterious companion won out.

The orange hue of the flames reflected against his pale purplish-tinted skin, showing the hollow in his eyes. He looked tired and haunted, and part of me felt for him because I understood those feelings. But common sense demanded I not forget this was my world, my people, that his had invaded and killed.

"You remind me of the Beast."

His eyes didn't stray from the embers as they spat at his feet. "The Beast?"

I chuckled at how stupid it sounded. "It's a fairy tale. A story my people tell children. It's about a man who appeared to be a monster, but deep beneath the exterior was a good man." I didn't add he learned to overcome his nature with the help of a woman. That was far too real for me. "Sometimes I wonder if you and he aren't the same." Even as I said that my stomach twisted, and the images of those people dying flashed before my mind.

When he didn't respond, I blurted out the one question that had been on my mind since the moment I saw him. "Why did you kill them?"

His eyes never left the flames. "They were dangerous."

I couldn't help the anger that boiled to the surface. "You don't know that. They were defending themselves, doing their duty. You struck them down without a second thought."

"You defend your kind, and I applaud your loyalty." Those crimson eyes turned on me. "But I can see now you are an innocent bystander who knows nothing about what your kind has done."

My eyes zeroed in on his. "Then tell me."

"Do you know what you carried in those vehicles?" His tone changed immediately. It became dark and careful.

I frowned. "Civilians? Supplies?"

He let out a huff of air, the cloud of cold curling away and dissipating. "Those *humans*…" he stressed the word with disgust, "…carried the mutilated remnants of my breed like they were nothing more than dirt."

I froze. "The black boxes."

He nodded.

Horror filled me, the realization of what he said chilling me more than the frigid air ever could.

Did we really butcher his people?

"Why?"

He tore his gaze from me, returning to watch the fire slowly turn into nothing more than a sparkling pile of embers.

"I don't wish to speak more of this right now."

I understood that, but I was also desperate to know. Even if we did have a reason for doing it, did that justify it? There was something I wasn't being told, something either the military or this creature wasn't sharing. He wanted revenge to save his people, just as I did. Were we so different?

Could I sit here and call him a monster, creature, or thing when he was as complex as me?

Time passed, an hour spent staring at the dying embers as they were enveloped by the downfall of snow. I crawled onto the truck's back seat, sprawled beneath a blanket, and used my backpack as a pillow. I turned to him. I could see his outline in the darkness of the passenger seat.

"If you won't tell me your name, then I shall assign you one."

He shifted in the seat, and I knew his gaze was on me only because his eyes held the slightest shimmer like a cat in the shadows.

Could he see in the dark?

"Leviathan." I smiled, knowing the word meant nothing to him. "But I'll just call you Levi for short."

There was silence before I saw the glow disappear as he shifted again.

"Levi, it is," he murmured.

Chapter 12

"That was probably the worst sleep I've had in my entire life." I stared listlessly out the windows, obscured by a thick layer of frost.

Levi sat in the passenger seat in the front of the truck, allowing me to sprawl across the back. But even with the space and the blanket he insisted I use for myself, I had shivered and remained awake through most of the night. The moment light streamed through the tiny gaps of frost in the windshield, I begrudgingly sat up, prepared for the day of travel ahead.

In the silence of the abandoned world, I couldn't help but think about what Levi had told me the night before. Part of me wanted to believe he was wrong, he didn't know what he was talking about. I never knew what happened to the creature at Mirabellgarten or the one at Guggenthal. But I distinctly remembered the black boxes piled in the back of the military vehicles.

We only paused long enough for me to shovel a trail bar into my mouth before Levi struck out down the road. Once again, the ivory blanket of nature swallowed the landscape, the crunch of the snow beneath our boots the only chorus on the silent walk to Berchtesgaden. Several houses loomed up between the evergreens, but they had been abandoned long ago, evidenced by the untouched snow piled up by the doors.

Levi didn't pause to check them, and neither did I. The last thing I needed was to misstep and break an ankle. So far, my leg and ribs were tolerable, simple aches I could dismiss if I focused on literally anything else. And that's exactly what I did. I focused on making it to the next tree, the next mailbox, or the next bend in the road.

Eventually, we made it. More and more houses had crowded out the trees, all as abandoned as the ones before them. A sign rose from the snowbank alongside the road like a stick in the snow, welcoming us to Berchtesgaden. The eerie silence set my teeth on edge, and I couldn't help the shiver that ran up my spine.

Where was everyone?

Levi seemed equally unnerved. We'd both expected the military and civilians to be here. But there wasn't so much as evidence of a military presence. No tarps or rudimentary tents. No vehicles, mortars, or bullet shells. Not even a banner. Guggenthal had all those hallmarks and then some. So far, on the outskirts of Berchtesgaden, it didn't look like the military had even come through.

Where were my friends then?

Suddenly, Levi's words were starting to make sense. Maybe they were in danger. We'd taken such an exaggerated path into Germany that it had made no sense.

A gloved hand shot out, holding me back. Levi's eyes were trained ahead, where a gathering of abandoned cars sat on the side of the road.

"What is it?" Nothing seemed out of the ordinary. There were cars and buildings, garbage cans and everything you'd expect to see in an urban town center. Everything except people.

"That car." He nodded at an old gray sedan sitting outside a hair salon. The paint on the bumper had peeled from years left in the sun, uncared for.

"What about it?" When I finished my sentence, I knew why it had caught his attention. In the driver's seat, a shadow flickered. My heart skipped a beat. Someone was inside.

Levi slunk along the side of the buildings, sneaking up on the gray sedan. I followed in his footsteps, careful to make as little noise as possible. Whereas my companion moved with the grace and litheness of a stalking leopard, I would liken myself to a baboon. There was nothing graceful about my limp or how my heavy footfalls found every twig, leaf, and rock beneath the layer of snow on the sidewalk.

However, Levi wasn't deterred from revealing our location to whoever sat in the car. Instead, he stalked on, stopping at the edge of the sun-damaged bumper.

As soon as I slid to his side, I could hear a voice emanating from within, irritation evident in the many swear words being uttered in German. What startled me more was the voice didn't belong to military personnel or some teenager trying to steal a car. It belonged to an elderly woman.

I pulled on Levi's arm, prompting him to step back. A part of me hoped the expression in my eyes would be enough to convince him to stay back. The last thing I needed was to give somebody's Oma a heart attack.

"Why won't you start?" she seethed in German, punching the steering wheel.

Circling the car, I stood at the passenger door behind the driver's, waiting for her to notice me. But she continued fiddling with the key in the ignition, and I grew more and more concerned.

Maybe she had dementia.

My stomach knotted uncomfortably. Was she too much of a burden to evacuate? Did someone leave her hoping one of the creatures—Levi's people—would solve the issue for them?

Ignoring the anger building up in me, I loudly cleared my throat. The woman jumped, clearly startled. A hand flew to her chest as she turned around in the seat and stared at me.

"I'm sorry if I scared you." With my hands raised, I gave her an apologetic smile.

She let out a deep breath. "No, no. Not scared, only startled."

I nodded at the key. "Do you need help?"

Glancing between the key and me, she waved me over. I had to admit, I knew nothing about cars. My knowledge ran as far as it did with computers. If it wasn't working, I turned it on and off again. But from the sounds of the struggling engine when I approached the vehicle, it seemed she had already tried.

Skirting around to the open window, I reached in and pulled the lever, releasing the hood. I waited to hear the click before rounding the front of the car, my face scrunching at the sound of the metal screeching as I propped it up.

"Are you a mechanic?" I heard her call from inside the car.

I laughed nervously. "No, far from it."

My enthusiasm waned as I looked over the metal innards of the sedan. There were wires and tubes and all sorts of things. As far as I knew, everything seemed to go where they were meant to go. Nothing looked loose or otherwise degraded. Unlike the paint job on the outside of the car, the engine appeared to be in good shape.

"I-I'm going to be honest. I'm not sure why it's not starting." Honesty was better than keeping up this charade, giving her false hope.

I closed the hood, returning to her side.

I gave her an apologetic smile, "Look, it might be easier to find another car."

Levi moved closer, eyeing the vehicle curiously. But the woman had yet to see him.

She threw the keys at the dashboard, shoved her handbag under her arm, and strode from the car like she was mad at it.

"Ma'am?" I called out to her.

Her eyes roamed over the other cars nearby. All seemed viable candidates, but I knew even less about jumpstarting a vehicle than trying to start one.

"That one." She pointed to an SUV ahead of us, and I swallowed the bile that rose at the back of my throat. A 'Baby on Board' sticker and a small stick figure family were pasted on the rear windshield.

"Ma'am, I don't know how to hotwire a car." Where would we even go? I glanced at Levi before returning my attention to the old woman. She fiddled with the car doors, but as I predicted, they were locked.

"*Scheisse,* <Shit,>" she swore, moving onto the next vehicle.

I stood by her side, awkwardly waiting. Levi snuck closer and closer, and I waved at him with my hand, hoping he'd get the hint and back up.

You're too close. I mouthed at him, my eyes widening. All she had to do was turn her head.

"Where is it?" the lady mumbled in German, wandering through the street.

Something fell, perhaps snow off a roof, or the breeze knocked something over. But it didn't matter what fell because it immediately drew the attention of the frail old lady. She turned so comically slowly, her eyes growing wider and wider as recognition flickered behind them. She had seen Levi.

A bloodcurdling scream echoed around the empty street, and my heart skipped a beat.

Fuck.

She immediately turned and ran.

"Wait!" I tried calling out to her, but she was surprisingly fast for a woman who was easily pushing eighty.

Levi was the last thing on my mind as I darted after her. She turned down an alleyway, skirting around the piles of snow pushed up against the wooden fences. Snow, leaves, and trash were smooshed beneath her feet as she took a right at the end of the alley, darting into the yard of a nearby home.

The house was small and modern, and I watched her fiddle with the doorknob. Like the SUV, it was locked. She spotted me walking up the footpath with my hands held out.

"Hey." My voice was strangely calm.

She kept trying to look around me as if convinced one of those things or Levi would pop out of a nearby bush.

"Did he follow you? Did he see you? How did you escape?" She spoke incredibly fast, and it took me a moment to translate her words.

"It's just me. It's okay," I whispered, getting closer and closer.

Skirting around the porch, she made to dart past me.

"Wait—"

She spun around to face me. "For what? For that thing to find us? I've seen what they can do, and I'm good, thank you very much. I may be old, but I still have quite a few years ahead of me."

Well, here goes nothing.

"He's not like them," I blurted out.

Her eyes widened. "You're…you're with him?"

I was not sure what she was implying, but it set an uncomfortable feeling in my chest. "He saved my life."

I didn't know why I tried to disprove her opinion of his kind. Just because Levi was like this didn't mean the others were.

She scoffed. "Are you delusional, girl?" The frown on my face was instant, her face twisting in response. "Is he threatening you? Is it Stockholm syndrome? Maybe you're the one who needs the help, not me."

Shuffling away from me before I could respond, she forced me to dart after her down the road. She was slower than before. No doubt, the cold and age were catching up with her.

"Ma'am, please. Listen to me."

Waving me off dismissively, she took the next left, dashing across the street to a considerably dirtier side road.

Behind me, I could hear the crunching of the snow, and I knew Levi was close behind.

Could she see him? Is that what spurred her onward?

I was too nervous to glance behind me, knowing the moment I did, I might lose sight of her.

Part of me wondered why I cared. After all, she was a stranger. But she was an elderly woman alone in a large city under attack by aliens. I couldn't in good conscience allow her to roam around here, to fall and hurt herself, and die alone in a gutter. If she were my grandmother, my sweet Oma, I'd want someone to do the same.

"Let me help you…" The words died on my tongue as we skirted around a hedge decorated with fairy lights.

On the other side, the landscape was chaos. Not even the fresh dusting of snow covered the crimson splashes of blood on the sidewalk, the mortar blasts in the sides of the buildings, and the giant crater that reared up in the center of a park. Tents, no doubt leftover from the military, surrounded the crater. Boxes and crates and all manner of equipment lay around the park. Whatever had happened here, the military had left in a hurry.

The old lady dashed toward the park, past the razor wire fence and sandbags, to a tent whose sails were pockmarked with holes I was certain were caused by bullets. Skirting around a puddle of dried blood, I paused by the entrance, watching her dig inside one of the boxes.

"All I want to do is help you," I said quietly.

Nervousness prickled beneath my skin, and a part of me screamed I was being watched. But I squashed it down. Of course, I was being watched. Levi was somewhere behind me.

Pulling something small and dark from the box, she turned to me. Tears glittered in her eyes, and my stomach knotted.

She jabbed her finger at me. "I don't know what he did to you or what you think he wants to do. But that *thing* you follow around will turn on you, and when it does, you'll wish you listened to me."

I shook my head. "He has had so many chances to kill me, yet he has done nothing but help me. He told me the truth, about the military, about what they're doing…"

Her instant laugh disturbed me. "And you believed him?"

Doubt clouded my mind for a split second. *What if she was right?*

"Humans aren't the only ones capable of lying."

The snow crunched behind me, and I turned to see Levi emerge. He looked at me.

Immediately, her demeanor changed—eyes wide, hands shaking. She fiddled with something behind her back and raised her right hand at me. It took me a few heartbeats to realize the small, black object in her hands was a gun.

"Wait!" My hands shot up automatically.

She wouldn't shoot me, would she?

Levi moved closer, the sound of the snow crunching beneath his boots causing my heart to skip a beat. And I realized it wasn't me she was going to shoot. It was Levi.

"You want to save me? Well, I'm going to save you," the old lady said, cocking the gun and taking aim.

I threw my hand out as if somehow that would stop the bullet.

"Emilia!" Levi's voice rang out in the cold, dead silence, echoing off the empty buildings. My name on his tongue stirred something within me, and by God, I could not decide if I liked it or hated it.

I watched helplessly as her finger wrapped around the

trigger and made to pull. But then, nothing happened. She shuddered, a puff of steam exited her mouth, her shoulders shook, and a soft gasp escaped her thinning lips. The gun clattered to the ground at her feet, and a moment later, her body followed it, falling into a heap beside it.

It took me a moment to see what stood in her stead—a long whitish spike covered in blood. Emerging from behind the bullet-ridden flap of the tent was a pair of fierce golden eyes set against a backdrop of pale blue skin shrouded behind a curtain of long hair as white as the snow that crowded the banks of the city.

"No…" The horror in my tone belied the fear in my bones. I took several steps backward, my heart thudding painfully in my chest. It was another creature, one of Levi's.

The creature took a few steps out of the tent and glanced around before its golden eyes trained on me. It smiled a vicious smile, gleaming white canines sparkling. Levi appeared by my side, eyeing him down.

The creature smiled and uttered a single word, and it took me a moment to realize he had spoken in English.

"Brother."

Chapter 13

Levi held his head high and stared down at the creature. "Brother."

The woman's blood still dripped from those nasty bony wings, the crimson droplets hitting the snow at his feet in a steady stream. Bile rose in my throat, and my legs weakened. He had killed her—a confused, scared old woman. I couldn't get the image of her final breath out of my mind, and with it came the last breaths of the others. The man in the parking lot, the two soldiers on the road in the mountains, and the countless others I had not seen. Those crimson splotches surrounding the park, were they because of him?

He spoke, but not in English. I was pretty sure it wasn't in any earthly tongue. The words were smooth, honeyed, strung together like fairy lights on a hedge. They were whispers in the wind.

Levi did not reply. His eyes clouded, and a shadow crossed his face. It was such a human reaction, one I recognized well.

Anger.

This creature, Levi's brother, was taller and bulkier than he was. But his voice was just as deep, just as honeyed. His golden eyes locked onto me, sending goose bumps across my skin. It was an odd contrast, and yet, his yellow eyes unnerved me more than Levi's red ones.

The newcomer came closer, peering around Levi to stare at me.

"Raak," Levi warned.

The creature—Raak—circled me, those deadly golden eyes roving over me. It reminded me of the way my neighbor's cat would watch the birds from her living room window. I knew he did not see me the way Levi did. I was not a help but a hindrance.

He stopped in front of me, eyes narrowing. I did not miss how Levi angled himself, so half of me was hidden behind his shoulder.

"Who are you?" That dark voice, rich and powerful, unsettled me as much as it made me swoon.

Was this an ability they had?

Their voices sent a thrill through me, like an animal that used a song to attract its prey. That was the only explanation for why I could even possibly consider having such feelings.

They're monsters, Emilia. Get a hold of yourself.

Levi spoke for me. "None of your concern."

Those golden eyes turned to his own, crinkling in amusement. "A pet then, perhaps. Weak and inferior, it serves you as nothing more than amusement."

Levi hissed, saying something in their language. Even though I could hear the anger, the rage in those words meant nothing to me, they still sounded hauntingly beautiful.

Raak raised an eyebrow but continued, seemingly changing the topic. "Where are Tress and the others?" His voice was darker like he was expecting bad news.

Why is he speaking in English if they have their own language? Which quite frankly sounded so much better than my language if I was honest with myself. And then Levi turned to me, and I understood. Raak spoke in English for me so I could understand everything.

"*They* took them," Levi ground out.

Raak cocked his head sideways, eyes roaming over the boxes and tents the military had left behind. "Do you know where they have gone?"

"North." Levi's curt and straight-to-the-point answers were starting to grind on me. But I had no right to be upset. After all, I agreed to go with him based on what he had told me.

I tried to dismiss the background noise of that old lady's final words.

"Humans aren't the only ones capable of lying."

Raak pondered that single word before replying with one of his own. "How?"

"The beacon."

I wasn't sure how much longer I could handle the short, vague responses. "I'll rendezvous with the other sites, see who I can find. I'll meet you..." he glanced at me before returning his golden eyes to Levi, "...at the facility."

Levi muttered something in their angelic language, causing Raak's eyebrows to rise. Sighing, he skirted around his so-called brother to stand directly before me. He raised his gloved hand to cup my chin, looking me straight in the eyes. Fear, anxiety, and the tiniest bit of desire gripped me, but I wouldn't admit that to him. I wouldn't let myself be read like a book. Setting my jaw, I stared him down, daring him to see through me.

His eyes widened in amusement, lips parting. But then, something odd happened. His eyes darted to Raak for a split second, and a shadow of recognition passed over his perfect marble features.

Raak uttered a phrase, and in his tone sat alarm. "The Link."

Levi glowered, but I could see horror written across his face too. Whatever *The Link* was, neither saw it as a positive thing.

Should I fear it too?

Raak cackled, a sound that was as enticing as his voice. He released me, taking a step back, and I noticed now he was clothed in the same ensemble as Levi. The outfit matched that worn by the creatures from the parking lot, Mirabell, and the field in Guggenthal. They all wore obsidian leather like it was armor. Maybe it was.

Levi moved forward, gripping my arm, tearing me away from the presence of his brother. He uttered something to him in their language, and Raak responded with a smile. I couldn't help the backward glance I gave him or the furrowing of my brows. His face darkened, but eventually, he turned, walking south back to Austria.

We walked together in silence, and slowly the distance between us grew. Saying I felt uncomfortable was an understatement. I began to doubt everything. There was something Levi wasn't telling me, something to do with this thing called *The Link*. Part of me wondered if I was a sacrificial lamb and he was preparing me for slaughter. But what difference would my death make tomorrow compared to today? I was human, and he was…whatever he was.

We crested a small hill as we followed the road northward, and the city's high-rises, apartments, and offices faded away. The yards grew wider and the houses taller, then those, too, faded away. From urban to suburbia to the very edge of the rural landscape, we spoke not a single word.

I was growing tired. The occasional pain in my ribs was nothing compared to the pain in my leg. I was slowing, limping, and stumbling. It was painfully obvious to me, and I was positive he could see it too.

Up ahead, a small grocery store sat on the side of the road, with welcoming signs in English, German, and French. It boasted about its café and orchards, promising a once-in-a-lifetime experience.

Not saying a word to Levi, I left the road and stumbled to the barn-red oak door. But, like all the other places we had tried, the door was locked. Limping across the stones, I pushed every window and turned every knob without success. Following the white stone walls to the back of the establishment, I found a small back door whose screen was hanging off its hinges, gently blowing in the breeze. It squeaked when I opened it, drowning out the birds' tweeting and the flags snapping in the breeze.

Levi made to follow me, but I turned to him.

"Stay." It was the only word I could manage, but luckily, he seemed to understand my need to be alone and disappeared down the length of the building.

It took me a few good pushes to force the rickety door to unstick itself, but once I managed to get it open, I was immediately assaulted by the scent of sweets and spices.

The door led into a kitchen, where the tables were still with pastries and sweets in various stages of cooking. It was eerie, knowing the people had woken at the crack of dawn to begin work and had no idea what had happened. They had gone about their business like all was well.

I swallowed my nervousness, heading to the nearest refrigerator and grabbing a bottle of sparkling water. It surprised me to see the electricity still flowed freely. It made me feel like I was somewhere I shouldn't be. As if I would turn a corner and be admonished by a chef returning from his break at any moment. Technically, I was trespassing and stealing, but I didn't linger on it for too long. I grabbed a sandwich from the lower shelf, tucked it under my arm, and crossed into the front half of the café where tables and chairs sat ready for customers who had never arrived. Sliding into a booth by the windows, I put the bottle of sparkling water and sandwich on the table and dug in.

The edges of the bread were tough, and the inside was stale and soggy. But the sparkling water tasted exactly as expected—like a static television with a hint of lemon zest.

My mind wandered to Theresa and Osman, my parents, the other people who stood on the roof with us, the people in the parking lot, and those we had passed on the street. If Levi was right about what the military was doing to his kind and my friends, it felt wrong to sit here and enjoy a meal in silence. Because if I were honest with myself, out of everything I'd experienced, this silence had been the best part so far. I loved my fellow humans, but under the blanket of their absence, I felt peace.

Shaking the guilt from my mind, I slid out of the booth and wandered through the dining hall. An archway led from the café to the gift shop, and I allowed myself to spend a few minutes walking through it. It had all the hallmarks of a country gift shop, from rows of shirts with Germany or Berchtesgaden splashed across them to plush toys shaped like goats and elk. It held a scent that all gift shops did, an odd musty musk like dust and mothballs.

"What am I doing?" I let out a deep sigh, not even bothering to hide my frustration.

My best friend was gone, my neighbor was gone, and I had no idea if my parents were safe, let alone alive. And here I was, traipsing across the mountains with a creature from outer space that had murdered innocent people without blinking, based on mere hearsay my friends might be in trouble.

Returning to the kitchen, I shoveled as many wrapped pastries into my backpack as possible and refilled my canteen. A small archway at the back of the kitchens led to a narrow room filled with floor-to-ceiling lockers and two smaller rooms marked as toilets. I don't know what compelled me to try the lockers, but the entire row on the left was locked. The right had a mixture of open and locked ones, but all were empty. All except the very last locker, which contained an assortment of wrappers and a pair of pants that smelled like dirty water. But it wasn't the garbage or clothing that caught my attention. On a shelf at the top of the locker, barely covered by a magazine containing tasteful photos of lingerie models, was the shiny black handle of a handgun.

What are the odds?

Curious, I grabbed it, marveling at how solid and heavy it felt. I couldn't say I knew anything about guns or even cared about them, for that matter. But I had watched enough television to know how to check the chamber. I swallowed when the click of the chamber opening echoed in the small hallway, and anxiety gripped me when I saw several bullets sitting within. I knew Austrian law regarding gun ownership was perhaps the laxest of the European Union countries, but technically we were in Germany. Why would someone leave a loaded gun sitting nonchalantly in their work locker? My blood chilled at the implications, but it didn't stop me from checking the safety was on and slipping it into my backpack.

Leaving through the door I had entered, I followed the length of the building back to the front, where a small garden sat heavy with snow-covered tables and chairs. Out there, the air was crisp and fresh. I drank in the scent of nature. The only thing that pulled me from my moment of quiet peace was a dog barking. It was muffled as if far away or perhaps inside a building.

No. Humans were one thing, but I couldn't stand to know an animal was in danger.

Speedwalking through the snow, I followed the barking. It grew louder and louder, and yet, it was still muffled. The dog's frantic cries led me through the parking lot to a row of hedges. On the other side was a small community of townhouses, and a sedan sat in one of the driveways. Inside the car, a dog darted back and forth between the driver's seat and the back seat. I would have moved forward, but Levi stood beside the car, watching the dog with crimson eyes.

He eyed the dog with a mixture of curiosity and confusion. The dog didn't seem aggressive or even disturbed by Levi's presence. If anything, it seemed as curious as the alien. Levi placed his hand against the window, and the dog leaned forward, pressing its snout against the glass where Levi's palm lay.

Cocking his head sideways, the dog barked, ears set forward. Levi muttered something, his lips moving, but I was too far away to hear. Whatever he said, the dog reacted, moving away from the window to sit patiently in the passenger seat. Levi raised his hand, balling it into a fist. In the blink of an eye, his fist plowed into the window, shattering the glass. It clattered to the asphalt, and the dog barked in terror. Reaching in, Levi opened the door and stood away. The dog bounded out and held its ears tight against its fluffy head as it darted past Levi into the wilderness. When I could no longer see it, my attention returned to Levi.

"You may come out now, Emilia," Levi called.

God. I absolutely *despised* how much I loved the way he said my name.

Sheepishly, I walked to his side, acutely aware of the nearly indistinguishable weight of the gun in my backpack.

"How did you know I was there?"

A smile spread across his lips, but he didn't say a word.

"Fine then, keep your secrets," I muttered.

His eyes rose to the sky, where the sun had begun to descend.

"We should move." I followed his gaze.

The mountains hugged the horizon, a faded blue silhouette against a sky of fluffy white clouds. The sky was streaked with marigold and magenta, and birds flitted through it to their resting places for the night.

The temperature continued to drop, and the breeze picked up. It cut to my bones, and my breath streamed out before me in a cloudy haze. Levi led me from the café up the road, continuing forever northward. From there, the houses were farther apart on acreages. Horses, cattle, sheep, pigs, anything and everything lay out in the pastures, mindlessly chewing on the emerald seas of grass. It was only September, but here in the valley between the mountains, winter had come early. Farmers would soon send their livestock south of the mountains or lock them in barns to survive the frost.

But what happens when the humans are gone, and the animals must fend for themselves?

I tried not to think too much about it. Out of the corner of my eye, I saw Levi stealing glances at me. I don't know why that made me more nervous. Was it because of whatever *The Link* was or because he saved the dog? I had more important things to deal with, and the pain in my calf reminded me survival involved finding somewhere to lay low for the night. Somewhere warm and safe from the wrath of nature.

Then something warm and firm wrapped around my upper arm, yanking me off the road and down an unbeaten path. I turned to stare up at his crimson eyes, which stared straight ahead.

"What are you doing?" The indignation in my voice was laughable.

He nodded ahead, opting to remain silent.

Between the evergreens at the end of a long unpaved road riddled with overgrown weeds sat a two-story farmhouse. It embodied the unique rural Bavarian architecture, with its sloping roof and shuttered windows. Baskets hung under the sills were still ripe with blossoming flowers. However, their time was numbered, as was mine.

Levi's hand released its grip on my upper arm and rested it against my back as he maneuvered me to the front door. Like many rural houses, the door was unlocked.

"Hello?" I called into the darkness. But this house was as deserted as the ones before it. This one had possibly been abandoned longer, given the layer of dust on the shelves and furniture.

Levi steered me into the living room, where I went to work on starting a fire in the fireplace. The wood, coal, and lighters were all neatly stacked in baskets by the hearth, begging to be used. When the flames roared to life, I grabbed several cushions from the couch and threw them across the floor. Taking a seat on the one nearest the hearth, I was surprised when Levi sat beside me. I let my backpack slide to the floor and removed my vest, grateful for the sudden freedom.

I hadn't considered how much the vest constricted my ribs, and I sighed in relief, holding my ungloved hands before the flames. The heat soothed the aches in my body as much as those in my soul. I had always loved winter, especially the crisp, cold days where you were bundled under layers of clothes, with a cup of tea in your hand and a warm hearth billowing hungry flames before you. But as much as that memory warmed my heart, it also pained me. Theresa enjoyed the atmosphere, too. Because of her, I knew what a *Stroopwafel* was and that I could never enjoy another cup of coffee in the winter without one.

"Emilia?"

A thrill ran through me like a lightning bolt.

Oh, my God, please stop saying my name like that.

I turned to him, my heart skipping a beat at the look in his eyes. I knew that damn haunting look. I'd seen it in Osman when he caught a glance of Theresa in the hallway. I'd seen it in the tortured faces of the men I'd swooned over in television series and movies.

But those were men and Levi?
Levi was a monster.

155

Chapter 14

"Your mind is busy," Levi said, breaking the silence.

I didn't bother disagreeing. "Yes."

Gathering my legs beneath me, I grabbed the flashlight from my backpack, flicked it on, and left the warmth of the living room—and Levi—behind. The hallway beside the living room led past a lonely kitchen before swinging back toward the entryway, where a stairway spiraled upward into darkness. But past that, to the right of the front door, was a room heralded by large dark doors on rails. Pulling them back revealed a room with floor-to-ceiling bookshelves loaded with books of all sizes and colors. Statues and framed photographs joined them, placed artfully on the shelves. The aesthetic called to me. It begged me to run my hand along the spines of the books and to hear soft classical music echoing through the wooden paneled halls.

My eyes strayed to the far corner, where a love seat sat before a coffee table and two leather armchairs. Against the wall behind them was an ancient relic of a bygone era. I knew it all too well if only because my professor had one in his office, a hand-me-down from his father from World War II.

The gramophone had a shiny golden trumpet set on a wooden body, and an unmarked obsidian disc sat on the plate, begging to be played. A handle, curved and ending in a rubber grip, waited for me. Grasping the rubber, I cranked the machine until my arm burned, then lowered the needle onto the disc. The sound was scratchy at first, but it cleared, releasing the familiar melody trapped within the record.

It was a classical song, a tune I'd heard before in music boxes for children or on horror shows involving porcelain dolls. It was hauntingly beautiful. I never thought I'd miss dancing so much, but my body was overcome by the urge to sway to the gentle notes. I gave in without even realizing I had, twirling in the emptiness of the room from one book-covered shelf to another. My feet flew across the carpet, and for a few moments, I even forgot I was wearing boots, or that my leg hurt.

In my mind, I was back in the university hall, hearing my flats slide across the dance floor in rhythm with two dozen others. A metronome ticked loudly in the background, back and forth, back and forth. I heard and felt my heart pounding in my chest, and although I knew it was useless to try, I still aimed each breath for that ticking. I spun, twirled, and raised my arms above my head. In those moments, I never saw or felt anything else. Music dominated my mind, heart, and soul.

Then my eyes opened, and I wasn't at the university with my friends and classmates.

I was in a dark room, with my flashlight gripped in my hand, dancing on the carpeted floor of a study to music played on a gramophone. It wasn't as peaceful as being on the dance floor with my friends, but even alone, I couldn't help but be invigorated by the music that welled in my soul.

For the first time since this began, I felt truly relaxed. Until I saw the flash of crimson eyes watching me that literally stopped me in my tracks. I skidded, throwing out a hand to keep myself from falling over. I winced as a lightning bolt of pain traveled up my calf.

Glaring at him, I waited for him to speak. When he didn't, I ground out, "*What?*"

"Will you speak with me?"

I eyed him with suspicion. Why would he want to talk?

"I want to know about you." His voice was eerily calm and soft like he was afraid to even ask me such a thing.

Pinching my eyes shut, I slowly released a breath, "I don't want to talk about myself."

Silence, broken only by music, stretched between us before he found the courage to speak again. "Then, if you do not wish to speak, perhaps I shall."

My eyes snapped open, and I faced him. *Was he going to share something personal about himself with me?*

To say I was excited was an understatement. Part of the excitement involved soothing the curiosity that wanted to worm its way out of me. The other was the sheer privilege of knowing perhaps I was one of a blessed few, or even the *only* one, to know anything about them.

Levi looked to where I hugged myself. I hadn't realized, but without the warmth from the fire or my dancing, the cold returned with a vengeance.

"Come," he said, disappearing down the hall.

I removed the needle from the record before following him to the living room, where I found him standing beside the hearth. Taking my seat on a cushion, I let my mind wander. I watched a flame crawl across a burning log, the wood splintered beneath its destructive touch, and embers flickered to life as it was devoured.

Levi stood above me, staring down into the crackling flames. "I owe you nothing, yet I want to share everything."

That earned him a glance from me. *Why?* I wanted to ask, but I stilled my tongue.

Encouraged by my reaction, he continued, "I know curiosity grips you. Who am I? What am I? Why am I... *why are we...*here?"

Now my interest was piqued. I turned my full attention to him, the only eagerness I would demonstrate.

Levi continued, the flickering light of the flames splashing shadows and orange hues across his perfect face, "I suppose they told you nothing." I remained silent. "Of course they wouldn't. After all, how could you tell a civilian you offered refuge and then changed your mind?"

I knew he could see the reactions on my face, reading them as easily as a book. I didn't want to speak to ask questions for clarification. I wanted to hear everything he had to say.

The fire snapped and popped, breaking the heavy silence.

"My world, my people, were on the verge of extinction. We had no choice but to flee across the stars. In the darkness and the cold, a beacon sounded, and we responded. It promised safety, a home to start anew."

They were aliens, then. From another world, another

galaxy, some far-flung civilization like in *Star Wars*. But his history sounded more like *Superman*.

If that is the case, my mind couldn't help but whisper, *then what is his kryptonite?*

"But the closer we came, the sooner we realized it was a lie. A fallacy, and for what?" His voice darkened. "In the name of preservation."

What did we do?

"Hundreds were destroyed. Men, women, children. They did not discriminate. All perished in the flames." His tone was laced with venom. If I had spoken, mine would have been too.

The meteor showers. It wasn't the pods but the flaming debris of those they had plucked from the sky. My throat thickened, tears glistening in my eyes. We had lied to them, to him.

"We knew whoever made it to the ground would be murdered on sight, and they were. The first reports were hard to stomach. But if we were designated to be killed on sight, we had no choice but to retaliate."

Outside, a breeze howled around the house, and flurries of snow sprinkled in the firelight that touched the windows.

"I thought you were all irredeemable. Monsters for the slaughter. That was…" he leaned his head against the stone above the hearth, blazing eyes fixed on me, "…until I met you."

I swallowed, waiting for him to continue.

He moved away from the hearth and walked to the window to stare listlessly outside.

"You were only trying to survive. You sacrificed yourself to save your own."

I snorted. Anyone would have done the same.

Levi turned to me, and his gaze softened, "That's the hallmark of a hero and someone worth sparing."

No, that's the hallmark of someone incredibly stupid. And yet, given another chance, I don't think I would have changed what I did. What I did was born of love for my friends and my fellow man. I didn't think the lives of my friends or the people who fought to save us were worth less than my own. The life of a twenty-year-old student from Australia who had spent three years learning to dance in Austria did not weigh more on the scales of life than a soldier willing to sacrifice everything.

"You had as much chance to kill me as I did you. Yet, without knowing anything more than me being just another human, you chose to spare me." I raised my eyebrows at him.

Silence passed between us, and an unusually heavy feeling settled deep in my bones. I wanted to know more about him, about his people, and yet he'd made this conversation about me.

More. *I need to know more.*

But Levi had other ideas. "Will you tell me what you enjoy?"

Please…I can't.

"What you did in that room, that box with its song…is that what you enjoy doing?"

Stop!

"Emilia?" His voice wavered, and he abandoned the window, coming to stand beside me once again. I saw the silhouette of his hand from the corner of my eye, coming closer and closer.

Why is he so obsessed with knowing about me as a person?

He'd seen enough, knew enough. But even though he tried to explain it, I didn't feel any less nervous around him.

Why does he care so much?

I was a nobody, a nothing. My life didn't even register on the vast timeline of humanity. I wasn't even a smudge on the cosmic lens.

But him? He was clearly somebody. He was the last in the line of a civilization on the brink of extinction. Yet, he was fighting for survival, persevering like the others. The names of his people—Raak and Tress—were as sharp in my mind as if they had been carved there. Still, I hadn't come any closer to knowing who he was.

"What's your real name?" I had no idea why that question came out of my mouth when so many others would have been better.

He raised his eyebrows. "Now you speak."

Insufferable creature.

"Does it matter?"

I shrugged. "I guess not."

He smiled. "Besides, I like Levi."

I chuckled, a light, airy noise. "You don't even know what it means."

"You think I don't know what a leviathan is?"

I turned to him, curiosity carved across my face.

What?

Even if he didn't know what a leviathan was in the biblical sense, the word clearly meant something to him.

"Tell me about your world. What was it like?"

He held up a hand, a smile playing on his face. "A question for a question."

Ugh!

"Fine," I muttered.

He sat on the cushion beside me, staring into the flames, which slowly began to die.

"My world is smaller than yours, and yet, not so different—a blue orb floating endlessly in a sea of black. There are mountains and valleys, seas and lakes, and trees grow tall enough to block the pale blue sky. But the differences lie in familiarity. Our trees are violet, amber, and obsidian. Our grass is not green but daffodil, lilac, and crimson."

"It sounds beautiful."

A shadow crossed his eyes. "It was."

I could feel the pain in those two small words. *It was.*

"What happened?"

"Aah. A question for a question, Emilia."

My stomach flipped at the sound of my name again. *Why did it sound so beautiful coming from him?*

"Ask your question then."

His eyes twinkled with amusement, and I could not look away. "What is it you were doing in the room?"

I frowned. "What do you mean?"

"You moved, swaying in time to the melody."

Does he really want me to explain such a mundane thing?

All right, I'll humor him. "You mean dancing?"

"Dancing? A strange word."

I gave him a look. "You're joking, right?"

He cocked his head.

"Your people don't dance?"

Levi shrugged as if the concept of dancing made no sense. I stared at him in disbelief. An entire civilization had no idea what dancing was, surely not. Perhaps they had a different word for it. Maybe he was lost in translation.

"You play music and move your body to the beat of it. Do your people not enjoy such a thing?" *Surely…*

He gave me an apologetic look. "No."

Every civilization on Earth has had dance at the core of their way of life. But I supposed that was the difference here. Those were Earth civilizations, and his was not.

"Well, to answer your question…it's one of the things I enjoy." I let out a stuttering breath. "Or rather, I guess, I used to enjoy."

I gave him a sideways glance.

He ignored the jab. "Will you do it again?"

I frowned. "Do what?"

"Dance."

I…don't see why not? It might be the end of the world, but as I had just proven, I still wanted to dance even with my people threatened and an alien in the other room. But I didn't burst into dance spontaneously. I wasn't an overly jiggy person. I danced when the mood struck me or the music gripped me, and all I could see, feel, and hear was the rhythm coursing through me.

When I didn't reply, he gave me a look. *Does he want me to dance?*

"Where?"

"In that room, with the soft floor and the haunting song."

I scoffed. "Why would I do that?"

He fought for the words he wanted to use. I saw the turmoil in his eyes, those gold-speckled crimson orbs darkened as I rose from the cushion I sat on and stood before him.

"I don't know how." He seemed ashamed, embarrassed even, to admit that, but I expected such an answer. He looked more like a soldier than a dancer.

But an odd thought crossed my mind. *Is he asking me to teach him how to dance?*

I held my hand out to him. "I'll show you."

Hesitation flashed across his marble features before he raised a gloved hand and placed it in mine. I led him through the cold halls to the study with its carpeted floors and wood-paneled walls heaving with wooden shelves. Hovering by the gramophone, I lowered the needle over the record. After a scratchy moment, the haunting melody filled the silence between us.

I turned to him, his hand still in mine.

"What now?"

"Now, we dance," I whispered, staring into those crimson eyes.

Chapter 15

Teaching Levi to dance was much harder than I
thought it would be. It wasn't like I was teaching him the
tango or the salsa but simply how to swing his hips and sway
his upper back. He was stiff and impatient, moving before
I had finished my instructions. His boots thudded against
mine, and his steps stuttered across the carpet.

I stopped. "Here, let's try something different."

Taking his hands, I placed one on my waist and took the
other in mine.

"What are you doing?" I couldn't help the thrill that ran
through me at the alarm in his voice.

I smirked. "Shush. Just do what I do. Now watch my
feet." I moved back and forth. "One, two, three. One, two,
three." I counted to match the tempo of the melody.

He watched me like a helpless child.

"Say it with me," I goaded him on.

I moved a foot forward, and he moved his back. "One."

And then again. "Two."

One last time. "Three."

A smile played on his lips as he followed my instructions flawlessly. It was easy once it was broken down but now came the real test.

"Perfect. Now we do it all at once." In one fluid motion, we swayed back and forth across the carpet. The music continued in the background, but at that moment, I could only focus on him, and it seemed he felt the same.

His crimson eyes stared into mine. He no longer stared at his feet, trying to match my steps. He had memorized the routine and confidently followed my lead. The music quieted down, getting lower and lower. No doubt the gramophone required a crank to bring it back to life. I let it teeter to silence, and we stopped in the middle of the room, staring at one another.

I did it. I taught an alien how to waltz.

But the pride I felt disappeared instantly when I saw the smoldering gaze in his crimson eyes. My heart thumped painfully against my chest, and yet my core writhed at the sight. I hadn't even realized my leg didn't hurt. All I could focus on was him. He cocked his head, and his inky locks fell across his pale gray skin. If it weren't for the jagged bone wings flailing behind him like some macabre Halloween decoration, I'd say he looked like a prince.

Alarmingly, I found myself entranced by his unusual eyes, the way his lips turned up at the corners every time I made eye contact with him, and the strength of his muscles rippling beneath the leather under my hand. I could feel the strength in the way he held me, and I, him. I felt like a doll, fragile and inconsequential, as if he could snap me like a twig in the blink of an eye. But he was gentle and patient now, and I suddenly couldn't remember what I was even thinking about. Until those jagged wings folded forward, and I remembered where I was and what I was doing. I released him, taking a step back.

He watched me. "I think I enjoy dancing."

I snorted. What an odd way to show his appreciation.

"It's fun, isn't it?" I couldn't hold back the smirk.

No wonder he couldn't dance. It couldn't be easy with a pair of those wobbling behind you. But it was more than that. Every muscle that rippled beneath his dark armor was not made for the delicacy and innocence of something like dancing. I could never let myself forget that, first and foremost, he was a warrior sent into hostile territory. He didn't have to confide in me he more than likely spent most of his life training.

"Have you always been a…soldier?" I wanted to still my beating heart, to focus on anything but the handsome creature I had taught to dance.

He smiled at me.

"What?" I frowned

"I believe it's my turn."

I nearly snorted. "You've been keeping count?"

That smile widened. I was almost certain he was wrong, and it was my turn, but right now, I found myself not caring if it was. I simply wanted to hear him speak.

"All right then, ask your question." I rolled my eyes and settled on the loveseat beneath the window.

He crossed the room to stand by the window and stared out into the darkness.

"I want to know more about you," he said like it was a simple request.

"You'll have to be more specific."

Where would I even begin?

I caught him watching me out of the corner of his eye. "Tell me who Emilia is."

"Like my favorite color, and what I would do with a million dollars?"

"Her passions, her desires, the dreams that sit in her head, playing on repeat as she sleeps." That honeyed voice nearly broke me.

It took me a moment to compose myself, to shake the sight of him from my mind. Because I couldn't see Emilia, I honestly couldn't see myself. I could only see him.

"I-I…I'm a nobody, really."

He didn't seem particularly pleased with that response. A frown wrinkled the skin between his brows, and I sighed.

All right, let's get this over with.

"Emilia." Talking about myself to an alien felt easier when I referred to myself in the third person. "Was born far from here and dreamed of growing up to be a dancer. She moved to the other side of the world, away from friends and family, to follow her dream. She's been a background dancer in music videos and live performances, but she dreams of something more, something bigger. But she doesn't know what. So, she just dances."

He had an intent look on his face, his attention no longer on whatever lay beyond the window. He was focused solely on me.

So, I continued, "She likes the cold, the crisp scent of fall in the air when the leaves change colors and the world grows quiet. She claims that pumpkin is her favorite soup, but she's only ever had it at a restaurant. She once thought a dolphin was her favorite animal, and then she discovered the lemur."

I stopped there. How would he know what a pumpkin was? Or the difference between a dolphin and a lemur?

"She made friends with a girl who taught her how to be herself, and now, while she gallivants across the countryside, her friend writhes in pain as a possible prisoner in a place Emilia can't even imagine."

The tears stung my eyes yet clung defiantly to my lashes, refusing to fall. I leaned forward, letting my hair fall as a curtain between us, hiding my face. Somehow referring to myself in the third person made it so much worse.

Levi took a seat beside me. "We'll save your friends, and we will save mine."

I released a breath that shook my shoulders, and my voice broke. "We're not like you. We're fragile and weak. Your people are strong and resilient. Against all odds, you have persevered."

His hand reached out, pulling golden strands of hair away from my face.

"You're just as strong. Just as resilient." His fingers grazed my cheek, lighting a trail of warmth across my jaw and under my chin, which he turned so I would look into his eyes.

"Why are you so nice to me?"

He smirked. "Is that your question?"

I froze. I didn't want to waste a question on that. He'd probably give me some roundabout answer. I needed to ask him something he couldn't skirt around.

Well, in that case. "What is *The Link*?"

He blanched, his eyes widening for a split second before he fought for composure, but it was too late. I'd seen the nervousness with a hint of terror. *The Link.* It sounded ominous, and yet, Raak had almost seemed to taunt him about it as children do to their friends on the playground.

"I…" He paused, and I knew he was giving himself time to formulate a response that served him better than me.

"Tell me the truth, Levi." I swallowed the bile that sat at the back of my throat. "Are you using me?"

He stilled, his eyes wavering.

"No," he whispered. His voice was barely audible and wavered slightly.

Bull*shit.*

"Ugh!" I growled.

I fucking knew it. If it wasn't my own kind doing it, it was aliens. I jumped to my feet, making to leave. I didn't care where I went so long as I was far from there. Part of me tried to rationalize it. After all, what should I have expected? He was an alien wronged by my people. Of course, he was using me.

A hand gripped my upper arm, pulling me back onto the loveseat. My knee buckled, and I fell, sprawled across the sofa like some 1950s pin-up girl. Levi stood above me, silhouetted against the darkness of the study. All I could see within the outline of man and wings was his glowing eyes. Tears fell across my cheeks as I tried to sit up, but he leaned over me, his hands splayed against the cushion on either side of my head.

"Emilia." The thrill of my name on his tongue stirred my core, and a soft gasp escaped between my lips.

I turned my gaze from him, focusing on a statue of a rearing horse on the bookshelf. It was useless, though. As much as I tried to breathe life into that horse in my head, Levi was everywhere.

His hand shifted, cupping my chin and turning my face to his. "I am not using you."

My brows furrowed. "Then why am I still alive?"

He sighed. "Emilia…"

"What is *The Link*?"

Stop playing with my emotions.

His head lowered for a moment, the blanket of obsidian hair falling across his face like a curtain. I could almost feel him grappling with himself, with some inner dilemma. His grip on my chin softened, his face so close I could feel the warmth of his breath on the cold skin of my cheek. He carried an odd scent, a mix of earthy vetiver and citrusy bergamot. I was unable to tear myself away. His scent filled me, entranced me, and I felt like I was trapped under his spell.

"The Link…is a bond. A sensation that tugs us together, a presence that is impossible to ignore."

I froze. *What is he trying to say?*

"And you…" His gaze was smoldering, and I whimpered under his touch and his gaze. His scent in my head, his warmth on my cheek. "Are my link."

His lips were so close to mine. All I had to do was angle my chin slightly, just a little bit. He wanted it as much as I did. But as those crimson eyes grew closer, my heart skipped a beat. What was I doing? I untangled myself from him, jumping to my feet to put space between us.

"I-I…" There were no words.

What do you say when an alien declares you're his soulmate? Fuck.

"I need air." Darting for the front door, I yanked it open and ran out into the frigid darkness of the night.

Chapter 16

THE BITTER BITE OF WINTER SEEMED TO BE IN FULL swing. The wind had increased in its viciousness, and yet, even without a vest, scarf, or gloves, I couldn't bring myself to go back inside. Suppressing the shivers by hugging myself, I skirted along the overgrown path, the snow crunching beneath my boots. Behind the house, a large barn reared out of the snow. Darker than the house itself, the style screamed Americana more than traditional Bavarian.

Skipping past a line of raised garden beds, whose plants had long since died, I pushed at the big red barn doors. They squeaked open, revealing anything but your typical barn experience. This was not made to contain animals. There were no hay-filled stalls, farm equipment, barrels, or baskets filled with fruit or vegetables. Quite the opposite, in fact.

The middle of the barn was a gray tiled strip filled with couches, chairs, and tables. In the very center sat a stone fireplace flanked by a metal tray of cut firewood. On the left and the right, where the stalls would have been, were doors. The walls were decorated with paintings, and the roof was partially separated into glass panels, allowing those inside to see the night sky.

And what a beautiful sky it was.

It had to have been a bed and breakfast back in the day, and I wished I could have stayed here for a day or two on vacation in Bavaria or the Alps. *Theresa would have loved this.*

Swallowing the anxiety that threatened to take hold, I crossed the strip of floor to the other end of the barn. A smaller glass door led out to a raised private patio hedged by a tall wooden fence peppered with lanterns. I noticed with excitement they emitted a soft, yellow glow and knew they must've been solar-powered.

The door opened with an audible squeak that echoed through the silence of the night but didn't deter me from crossing the patio to stare at a circular, covered seat in the middle of it. A large pipe came out of a metal box at the back of it, where a stack of cut wood sat in a metal basket. Wrapping my fingers beneath the lid, I peeled it back to reveal water sitting within but not just any water. The strong scent of chlorine smacked me in the face.

"Oh, my God." I breathed, my breath curling into the air before me.

It was a hot tub.

Excitedly skirting around the back of the tub, I pried open the metal plate leading to the stove's interior. A handy cartoon on the panel door showed how to start the stove and warm the tub. Following the instructions, I shoved several planks of firewood within and turned on the gas. The fire roared to life, igniting the wood, and soon a steady trail of smoke billowed from the metal pipe.

I didn't know how long it'd take to heat up, so I returned to the repurposed barn, scrounging through the rooms for supplies. I wasn't sure exactly what I was searching for, but I was pleasantly surprised to find a towel, a bathrobe, and even a pair of socks.

When I returned to the tub, I found steam rising above the water's surface. Laying the towel, bathrobe, and socks on a nearby chair, I immediately stripped to my underwear and climbed into the tub. The warm water burned my skin in a good way. My muscles relaxed enough to let my mind wander. Then my eyes roamed upward, where a bright sky peppered in fluffy white clouds stretched wide overhead. Twinkling in emeralds and sapphires, golds, and silvers were galaxies, stars, and planets whose names I did not know.

Was one of those distant glittering places Levi's home world? He said it was beautiful, as beautiful as our blue marble. But if his world existed somewhere at the edges of space, how many other worlds lay unknown in the expanse, populated by creatures as complex and intelligent as our own?

I shook the thought from my mind and submerged myself to my neck. It would have been the epitome of tranquility if the creaking of the barn hadn't alerted me to the presence of an intruder. Sighing, I laid my head back against the wooden rim of the tub, staring up at the clouds passing by overhead.

"What?" I grumbled, not bothering to hide my disdain.

His boots thudded across the patio, pausing beside the tub. I could see his shadow in my peripheral vision, and part of me thought he was copping an eyeful. But when I turned to look at him, there was sorrow in those crimson eyes as he looked to the stars.

Stretched far above us, the arm of the Milky Way reached out from the horizon, slowly becoming smaller and smaller as it rose across the sky.

"Can you see it?" I asked, curious.

"See what?" His eyes didn't leave the glittering heavens.

"Your home."

He tore his gaze from the heavens to stare at the bubbling water in the tub. "There's nothing left to see."

My heart ached at the sadness in his voice, the longing would never be fulfilled.

His planet was gone.

His civilization was destroyed, and soon, his people would follow.

"I'm sorry, Levi." There were no words to describe the sorrow I felt for him. There was nothing I could do except help him get back his friends and mine.

"What is this?" He watched the smoke curl from the top of the pipe, disappearing with the breeze.

I covered my breasts with my arms. Even though I still wore my bra, I suddenly felt more exposed than before.

"A furnace to heat the water in the tub."

He gave me a sidelong glance.

"Let me guess. Your kind don't have these either?"

He shrugged. "Not quite like this."

Raising a hand, I patted the water, letting the bubbles slip through my fingers. "What do you have?"

"Well." A memory flashed across his eyes. "There were pools of water, so very hot, that sat at the base of mountains.

They always held an odd smell, not exactly unpleasant, but you knew it when you smelled it."

I snapped my fingers, instantly recognizing what he was referring to. "We have those, too. They're called hot springs. They form naturally near volcanoes."

"So, you have harnessed that power and turned it into a place to relax?"

I smiled. "Something like that."

"Sounds…relaxing."

I couldn't believe what I was about to do, but his dumb response brought a genuine smile to my face.

"Why don't you join me?" I moved away from the stairs at the side of the tub, giving him ample room to climb in. The tub was large enough to easily accommodate six adults, yet I knew it would feel immeasurably small if he joined me.

He hesitated, angling his body as if he fought between saying yes or no.

"Come." I hit the top of the water, letting it splash against the side of the tub.

What am I doing?

He nervously glanced around us as if worried someone was watching, but there was only us and the twinkling expanse of the cosmos. After another moment of deliberation, his demeanor changed, and he seemed to have decided. He turned his back to me, and I watched rather ashamedly as he removed his gloves and jacket. Beneath was a jagged black tank top covered in rips and shreds, like someone had taken a knife and carved out a few strands. It would have been an Earth fashion statement, but I had no idea what it meant to him.

The moment that black top joined his jacket on the floor, my jaw dropped. He *glowed*. The pale gray skin across his back was marked by the same golden runes that shone on his chest. I had almost forgotten about those. Since I'd seen him the first time, he'd kept his jacket closed. Usually, the only skin on display was his face and neck. But, right then, I had the privilege of seeing it all. Undisturbed by my obvious peeping, he unzipped his pants, letting them fall to the ground, revealing underwear as black as the tank top but without rips. Then, before I could even register what had happened, his underwear joined the pants on the floor, and I found myself staring at the well-muscled behind of an alien. I turned away immediately, heat had nothing to do with the hot tub painting my cheeks bright red.

Adverting my eyes, I pretended to be entranced by the fake flickering of the LED lantern on my left. I only realized he had lowered himself into the tub when the water shifted. Once I felt it settle, I returned my gaze to that impeccable creature, and my cheeks heated again.

He was staring right at me. "You are uncomfortable."

Oh, my God, yes.

I cleared my throat, "Uh, my people are—"

"Prudes," he stated, cutting me off.

I stared at him, flabbergasted. "Excuse me?"

He smirked. "I am not unaware of the modesty your kind has placed on such a normal and natural thing as nudity."

Rolling my eyes, I pouted. "You're telling me your kind has no need for privacy or *shame?*"

His lips twitched. "What do I have to be ashamed about?"

Nothing.

I maintained eye contact with a raised brow, avoiding the near-impossible-to-ignore temptation to follow that muscled chest downward. "Awfully cocky, aren't you?"

"You have nothing to be demure about, Emilia." He purred, shamelessly looking me over.

God*damn*. I bit my lower lip, looking anywhere but at the alien sharing the hot tub with me. But the golden runes shimmering on his pale gray skin called to me, and I found my gaze sat solely on him.

"What do those mean?"

He followed my gaze before holding out a hand. "Let me show you."

Show me?

Tentatively, I reached out, placing my hand in his. He coaxed me closer to take the seat beside him. Even in the hot, bubbling water, I felt his warmth beside me, and I had to remind myself not to look down.

Facing me, Levi took my hand in his, his crimson eyes glowing. "Do not be afraid."

Afraid? "Whatever would I be afraid of?"

He placed my fingertips against one of the runes, and my entire body went rigid. Every nerve and vein in my body came to life like electricity, flames, and water poured through me simultaneously. There was a feeling of warmth, and a soft breeze carried warmth through my hair and across my skin. The colors were muddled and smooth, like a watercolor painting at an art gallery. Pastels of lilac, tulip, and peony swirled across a landscape beneath a glistening golden-laced sky pregnant with ivory clouds. I could smell wet grass and feel it beneath my feet. A sweet aroma laced with earthly undertones. My skin prickled at the softness of the earth beneath my feet and the cool, sweet, scented breeze on my skin. And then, as soon as it began, it was over. I was once again myself, sitting in a hot tub with an alien in southern Germany.

"What was that?" My voice was filled with awe, and I didn't bother trying to compose myself. That was amazing. I had no words for it. I could feel, see, and smell as if I were there. But the world didn't feel real. It was fragmented. Incomplete.

"A memory," he whispered.

The golden runes across his chest glittered, begging me to reach out, feel what he had felt, and see what he had seen.

"What was the one you showed me?" My fingers no longer touched the mark, yet I could still feel the whispers of it.

"One of my favorite places back home. I went there when I needed peace and quiet."

My heart ached for him, the sadness in his eyes and the deep breath he exhaled.

"How does this…work?" I waved my hands at the runes covering his body.

He chuckled. "I suppose the easiest comparison is to the devices your kind use to record your own memories."

Like a camera?

"Are you saying you're not entirely…organic?" A cyborg alien. Now, wouldn't that be something?

He mused over the answer. "Organic is relative, is it not?"

"I mean…is it?" Science was not my strong suit. It's not to say such things didn't fascinate me, but I was content with knowing things worked, not how.

I loved my mobile phone and appreciated the quality of the camera. Still, I didn't really care nor need to know how the technology allowed it to capture the essence of what I wanted a picture of.

"Your understanding of the universe is very different from ours. Earth, and thus humanity, has long been sheltered from the rest of the cosmos. Comparatively speaking, this end of this galaxy is barren and lifeless. This blue dot in the middle of nowhere was a gamble. If your planet had been but a few light years closer, you would have seen what life is capable of."

"And those runes are one of those things?"

He nodded. "This is an organism, another creature. It mimics sights and sounds, smells and feelings. It preserves an echo before it dies, and that echo is what we paint on our bodies."

I watched the water wash against his skin. And although it washed the dirt, grime, and sweat from his body, it did nothing to the runes.

"Are they permanent?"

He considered the question for a moment. "It's similar to the markings some of your kind wear on their skin. They are meant to symbolize something important to you. Ours are no different."

No wonder the military wanted his kind for experiments. Imagine the technology we could derive from such a thing. My mind immediately went to intricate tattoo ink, but reality came butting in all too soon. Tattoo ink would be the last thing on the menu of what humans would derive from this organism. His runes encapsulated memories that brought him joy, but imagine what would happen if they were used to inflict pain instead. I shuddered at the thought, letting the silence stretch between us until flecks of glittery whiteness floated down around us.

"It's snowing." I held out my hand, watching the flakes vanish the moment they touched my palm. Steam rose around us, settling above the pool as the flurries fell. "Do you have snow where you are from?"

He watched the flurries alight on my shoulders and hair. "Your hair reminds me of that field."

I swallowed, remembering the marigold that streamed through the other pastel colors. It was vibrant and embodied the background, sitting as a base for the other pastels to frequent, like a wheat field dotted with multi-colored wildflowers.

Reaching out, his hand touched the strands of golden hair that had come loose from behind my ear. I let the blush creep along my cheeks without breaking eye contact.

"Will you show me more?" I sounded hungry, and I was. I needed to see more, feel more, and know more.

His hand fell, gripping mine. The warmth of his palm was reassuring, even as he dragged it to another rune on his chest. This one was smaller, and the colors that splashed through my mind were iridescent. These pastels were sharp and ever-changing, like the surface of a bubble rising into the air on a bright sunny day. The image shifted, and I felt both frigid cold and blistering heat. I heard bubbling and smelled the distinct scent of sulfur and crisp water. I then understood what he was showing me. This landscape had morphed into a colorful pool edged by rocky outcrops was a hot spring. And then, as soon as it had appeared, the world vanished, and I once again found myself in the hot tub, surrounded by drifting snow.

"It's so…beautiful."

His eyes met mine, a smile spreading across his face. "Would you like me to show you more?"

"Yes." There was no hesitation. I could spend hours experiencing his memories with him, which was precisely what I would do.

Chapter 17

WHEN SUNLIGHT STREAMED THROUGH THE BEDROOM window, caressing my face with its warmth, I finally found the energy to tear myself from beneath the soothing weight of the covers. Luckily, the pipes were working, and I didn't pause to see if Levi was anywhere nearby. I slipped into a nearby shower and scrubbed my skin pink, letting the hot water scald my soul as much as my flesh.

Last night was something. I replayed it over and over in my head and couldn't find the words to describe the inner turmoil between my brain and heart. I was a broken record player on an infinite loop of Levi's memories—the scents, feelings, sights, and sounds. I felt like I had spent all last night in another world.

Even as I poured coffee and devoured one of the sweets I'd stolen from the café, my mind would not be distracted from those watercolor memories. I was so lost in them, mindlessly munching on the sweet bread I didn't notice the barn door open or Levi entering.

"Good morning." He purred.

I choked, my hand rushing to collect the crumbs falling from my mouth. Holding a finger up to him to give me a moment, I composed myself with a swift swig of the coffee. The heat and light of the sun caressed my skin, and I turned to see him eyeing me curiously.

Swallowing, I placed the bread and coffee on the side table. "I was daydreaming. Didn't even hear you come in."

"I see."

He had an odd expression on his face, one I couldn't quite digest. But no matter, I decided not to waste time deciphering it.

"Were you here for something?"

He nodded, glancing out the barn door to the fresh snow that sat beyond. "I found a vantage point overlooking the facility."

I raised my eyebrows at him. "Oh?"

"I thought you'd like to join me for reconnaissance."

My chest ached at the thought. *We are that close?* Is that why he chose this place?

"Yeah, let me get dressed."

The only clothing in the barn consisted of comfort wear—bathrobes, fluffy socks, and knitted hats. Nothing that would keep me warm trekking who knew how far through fields of snow to sit on some cliff in the middle of nowhere. But the clothing I came in wasn't good enough, either. First, the bright colors were a horrible idea for a mission meant to be stealthy and unseen. Second, they smelled like sweat and were covered in tiny snags and tears from my previous gallivanting across the wilderness.

Excusing myself from Levi's curious gaze, I returned to

the main house, where I found typical skiwear in a small, unassuming closet upstairs in a hallway. I mouthed a thank you to whoever it belonged to that it was my size. It was a combination of white and black in color and would help me blend in seamlessly with the landscape. Dragging out the jacket and pant one-piece ensemble, I went to the master bedroom, where I also found thermal underwear and a matching long-sleeved top. Standing at the mirror, I grabbed a scrunchie off the vanity table and tied my long hair into a messy bun.

Sitting under the vanity table was a square black box with an unfamiliar logo. Curiosity got the better of me, and I placed it on the wooden table, pulling the flap back to reveal the snazziest pair of binoculars I'd ever seen.

Now these will come in handy. I hadn't even considered how we would view the facility from the top of a mountain.

Wrapping the binoculars around my neck and tucking them into my jacket, I strode downstairs to find Levi waiting patiently by the front door. He was dressed exactly the same. His black hair wasn't oily, his skin wasn't dry or shiny, and his stomach didn't growl like a hungry lion.

"Do you bathe? Or even eat, for that matter?"

Other than spending last night in the hot tub, I hadn't seen him use soap or shampoo. Yet, his scent never changed. He always carried an earthy, citrusy musk around with him. I couldn't help but feel a twinge of jealousy. *Was his species blessed with not knowing what oily roots felt like or what sweat smelled like?*

"I do."

I paused, considering this admission. "When?"

He shrugged like it wasn't a big deal. "When you were sleeping."

What?

"What did you eat?" I don't remember seeing anything missing, and I recalled his disdain for my trail bars.

"I don't quite enjoy the foods you seem fond of." I remembered the odd expression he had given me earlier. *Was it because of the bread and coffee?*

Pushing the idea from my head, I dropped it. Maybe he grabbed another fish, rabbit, or some other animal in a field.

"Okay, ready to go?"

He nodded and led me around the house and past the barn into the snowy pastures. Out there, the world was deathly quiet. The wind was almost still, the fresh scent of crispy snow hung in the air, and the new layer of snow crunched beneath our boots.

My cheeks stung the moment I left the house, and as we walked, I felt them getting colder and colder.

Twenty minutes of walking led us to a fence line with a gate that took more than one jiggle to pry open. The pasture it led to had been reclaimed by the forest. Dead branches, shattered rocks, and long weeds poked out beneath the snow cover. The distance we had covered in twenty minutes on flat grassland now took almost forty. I didn't even notice the asphalt road crossed right through it until my foot hit the firmness instead of crunchy snow. A weight settled in my stomach at the sight of tire tracks along the road. They appeared mighty fresh.

That's when I heard the familiar sound of squealing tires as a truck turned at the bend down the road.

"Levi—" He grabbed my arm, cutting off my alert and yanking me off the road behind several large rocks and a dying bush that hugged the asphalt enough to begin lifting it.

We sat with our backs against the rock, hearts beating wildly in our chests. Or at least, my heart did. My face no doubt reflected the turmoil, but Levi looked calm and collected. He'd obviously done this before.

The engine roared as the truck came closer, and I prayed with our landscape-matching outfits, we hadn't been spotted. A shaky breath escaped my lips, and I stared upward at the cloudy sky. Levi reached out for my hand, our gloves wrapping around one another. I turned to him, mouthing a thank you. Then, in the blink of an eye, the truck had passed us, careening northward into the mountains.

Giving ourselves a buffer of a few moments, we once again struck out toward the mountain.

The mountain at our side drew closer and closer, rearing above us to cast a long, chilling shadow over the world. Levi pointed to a flight of what looked to be hand-carved steps in the rockface, leading me up the side of a cliff to a flat gray stone outcrop. There, the wind buffeted us, explaining why the gray stone was so exposed, with barely any snow clinging to it. It took a moment for my eyes to adjust to the chill wind that sliced away my tears, and I pulled out my binoculars, waiting for Levi.

Flattening ourselves along the stone, he pointed a few miles northeast where the mountain bowed inward for a mile or so. Nestled within the valley sat the facility Levi had mentioned. Even without the binoculars, I saw the black dots of vehicles sitting on a flat tarmac covered in snow.

Bringing the binoculars to my eyes, I watched people dart across the tarmac between the vehicles and a gathering of tents before disappearing behind the arm of the mountain. There were several buildings out in the open as well, but I had dismissed these as mounds of snow until a door opened, and someone walked out.

"Do you see them?" I could barely hear his voice over the wind.

Pulling my binoculars back, I followed his finger, searching the compound. He pointed to the leftmost side of the tarmac, where the arm of the mountain closed in. I spied a concrete building with a metal door. Two guardsmen stood watch there with guns in their hands. A man emerged from the building, clad in a white lab coat with a small handheld device and clipboard in his hands. Two soldiers emerged behind him, following him across the tarmac to the newest vehicle that had rolled up. Curiously, I watched them, wondering what they were doing.

It was clear the man in the lab coat was a scientist. The vehicle's doors swung open, and a ramp appeared at the back. Two more soldiers jumped from the truck and started handing large, rectangular black boxes to the two soldiers escorting the scientist. He held up a hand and flicked his wrist toward one of the boxes. A soldier leaned forward, typing something into a keypad. Then the lid flew open, and the scientist kneeled, staring at the contents.

Levi hissed beside me, but I couldn't take my eyes off them. The scientist touched something within the box before bringing the handheld device down to scan it. A smile crept over his face, and he snapped at the soldiers. They closed the box, securing it, before following the scientist back into the white building that was seemingly built into the mountainside.

Sliding my sight over the tarmac and its many parked vehicles, I watched a truck idling by a gate with a guard house.

The soldier inside leaned forward and, after a moment's deliberation, pressed a button. The boom gate rose, and the truck lurched forward, following the path toward the other vehicles. But I didn't watch the vehicle. Instead, I followed the road it had driven on south, through a forest alongside a deep river. And with a start, I realized the road led toward the very mountain we stood on. Toward us.

It seemed the military was using the road we had crossed to access the facility, and from what I could see, it was the only way in or out unless we wanted to hazard crossing the mountains. My skin prickled with goose bumps, shuddering in response to such a ridiculous idea. Levi could probably manage, but I certainly could not.

Setting the binoculars down, I glanced back the way we had come, hoping to make out the start of the road. But although pastures dotted the landscape, clumps of evergreens blocked my view. There was no hint of the road behind us, although I was certain I'd see a hint of it around the mass of rocks below if I squinted enough.

I turned to my companion, watching his face writhe in obvious outrage. "Levi?"

He had every right to be angry, but the malice I could feel rolling off him like a vapor set a weight in my stomach.

"We should go." He didn't drag his gaze from the facility.

I sucked in a breath. "Go…where?"

"Back to the house." It was clear from his tone he wanted to do anything but.

"Are you sure?"

Before he could answer, my stomach growled loudly and with displeasure. Not even the wind that assaulted us could muffle it. My cheeks heated, and I averted my gaze.

Damn stomach.

The edges of his lips lifted upward, and he dragged his gaze from the facility to stare at me.

"Yes. I'm sure."

Crawling back the way we'd come to the stairs carved into the cliff face, Levi guided me downward. Even without me verbalizing or making it obvious, he was somehow aware my calf was beginning to bother me. I swear I could feel the warmth of his hand through the fabric of my jacket, and I couldn't deny it helped soothe the dread that had begun to settle within my bones.

As we began our journey across the rocky field toward the road, I couldn't help but acknowledge from here on out, things would be different. Whatever plan Levi mustered together would surely end badly. One, or both of us, wouldn't make it out of that compound. And if I were the macabre or betting type, I'd wager it would be him. I also had no clue if my friends were there or whether civilians were in danger.

But Berchtesgaden was empty, and Levi's explanation was the only one that made sense.

The road was empty when we crossed it this time, but the field we entered after wasn't. I saw a blur of chocolate, a flash of red, and suddenly Levi and I found ourselves standing before a herd of horses. Their ears pricked up at our arrival, but after a moment's deliberation, they must have decided we weren't a threat and returned to what they were doing. We stood there, watching the six horses toss their heads and whinny. They raced across the field, kicking up the snow and pausing to rub their faces against one another.

"What are they doing?"

I wonder if he knows what they are.

"They're playing." I didn't pretend to know anything about horses, but I was certain their carefree movements could be attributed to joy.

Levi watched on in wonder, and for the first time, I thought perhaps he was awestruck. I couldn't blame him. They were beautiful with their long manes and tails that trailed out behind them like veils. Their shaggy winter coats almost didn't match the mood, reminding me of 1970s shag rugs.

The horses stopped their play abruptly, heads whipping up, nostrils flared. They smelled or heard something they weren't comfortable with. Stamping their hooves in annoyance, they sped off across the field, the thunder of their departure distracting me from the real issue. Whatever it was they were running from. Levi must have felt the same trepidation as his gaze swept the field with mine. But whatever spooked them wasn't easy to discern. The field was empty, filled with snow and shoots of weeds desperately poking out of the cold.

My stomach growled, loud and annoyingly.

Levi smirked. "We should continue."

I groaned, tossing back my head.

We continued across the field, and soon enough, the top of the barn appeared on the horizon, welcoming us. My stomach growled again in response, eager for more trail bars. Although I was sure more sweet breads were left, I couldn't remember what I hadn't eaten. My mouth salivated at the knowledge sugar and honey would soon be on my tongue.

The fence reared up before us, and somehow, we had found ourselves far from the gate that led onto the farmstead. The snow crunched beneath our boots, and the breeze picked up the closer we got. I was more thankful now I'd found this outfit. I couldn't imagine trekking for hours in the snow up a mountain without it.

There's no way I wouldn't have gotten frostbite.

We came upon the gate, and I froze, my heart racing to keep up with the mental gymnastics in my mind.

Levi paused, turning to me. "What is it?"

"This was open."

He frowned. "Are you sure?"

"Yes, I'm sure." My voice shook, and it had nothing to do with the cold. I had left it wide open.

Levi's hand shot out, grabbing my arm and yanking me behind him. I couldn't even mutter a single word. The crunching of snow somewhere beyond us near the farmhouse carried on the air, and I angled myself to peek around him. There, in the garden beds framing the lawn between the barn and the house, were people. A group of six men and women, anywhere from sixteen to fifty, stood in the snow, staring us down. Their eyes were wide, their lips trembled, and my heart ached as I saw the exact fear I had felt when I saw Levi for the first time.

A silent moment passed between the eight of us—an awkward, unsteady stretch of time that seemed much longer than it was. But it was broken the second the oldest man in the group dropped the crate he was carrying in his arms and yelled, "Run."

I snapped back to reality, watching them drop whatever was in their hands as they fled through the garden toward the side of the house.

Levi's grip released my arm to fall to my side, but that small action made me realize he didn't do it because he was squeezing far too hard. No, he released me because, in the very next heartbeat, he darted across the snow, closing the distance between them and us.

He was going to kill them.

Chapter 18

"No!" I CRIED OUT.

Levi had jumped the fence but skidded to a halt in the garden. His eyes jumped between me and the retreating backs of the strangers. I could feel his eyes begging me to let him go and stop them.

"Levi, please…"

He bared his fangs. "If I don't stop them, they'll bring others."

I gripped the gate latch, tearing it open with some difficulty. "They're just hungry, afraid. They're looking for food and shelter…"

"Emilia—"

"No," I said firmly, my voice darkening. "Not everyone has to die, Levi."

He glared at me, crimson eyes blazing.

"Prove to them your kind are not all bad." The tips of his fangs disappeared, and he straightened his back, staring me down. "Show them peace is an option."

Some invisible cue drew our gaze to the side of the house, where the last stranger's dark green jacket disappeared. I could see the tension in Levi's stance, in his back and shoulder muscles visible through his black leathers. He wasn't pleased I had stopped him, but I could tell he cared about what I said. And maybe, possibly, part of him agreed. I couldn't disagree letting them leave might bring others, but they were clearly unarmed. And judging from the remains of broken drink bottles and smashed food littering the ground in the garden, I suspected food and shelter were all they were after. Even from the momentary glimpse of them, I could tell they were not military. The patchwork repairs on their coats and baggy pants were evidence enough.

"I hope for our sake you are right," Levi muttered when I crossed the distance to stand at his side.

Violence wasn't always the answer, and sometimes peace was not either. But I was certain I—*we*—had made the right decision.

Without a word passing between us, we salvaged whatever food and drinks we could from the crates and bags the group had left behind. I didn't recall apples and packets of noodles being in the barn, so they either brought them with them or raided the farmhouse pantry. Even though we'd been here long enough, I hadn't explored every nook and cranny of the house and knew there were still things to discover, especially when I bent down to grab a bottle of wine that had survived. It was full, and the cork sat nice and snug at the top, begging me to indulge.

Maybe tonight.

"How long are we staying?" I asked, following him into the barn to place the food on the nearest table.

He glanced outside, where the sun was beginning its descent, although it couldn't be later than four or five in the afternoon. September was that odd child of the group, where winter liked to poke her head around the corner, reminding you she was waiting in the shadows, even as the trees and grass still clung to summer.

In Australia, the seasons were reversed. Winter was in the middle of the year and summer at the end. Although where I lived, there wasn't much difference. What told me if it was winter or summer was the rain.

My heart ached as I remembered my childhood with my mother and father and my friends and neighbors. Times were simpler then. Memorable.

I watched Levi stoke the hearth in the center of the barn, blowing gently on the embers to coax the spark into a roaring flame.

Stripping off the snow jacket and pants ensemble, I rested it on the back of a chair beside the fire, relishing how free I felt with it off.

I caught his gaze from the corner of his eye.

"What is it?" he asked.

"Your kind…where did you land?" Even as I said those words, I desperately did not want to know the answer.

"Here." He was gruff, as if not wanting to say too much.

Dammit. I guess I'd have to be more direct.

"This country? This continent? The entire planet?"

He frowned. "Does it matter?"

I turned on him, the emotion in my voice palpable. "It does to me!"

Tears threatened to fall, and I swallowed them back.

"Emilia." He came to my side, wrapping his arms around me.

"No! Levi…please…" I hiccupped, my shoulders shaking.

He leaned back, cupping my chin in his hand, with the other securely pressing my waist closer to him. "You have people you care about. You worry if they are in danger."

I nodded in his grip the best I could.

Tilting my chin upward, I found I couldn't look away, couldn't think as his eyes gripped mine. He was Jupiter, and I was Juno. His gravitational pull kept me trapped.

"This country was the one who found our signal and responded."

"How did we get your message and not NASA or the European Space Agency?" No offense to the other space agencies, but I honestly knew very little about space. Plus, those two agencies reported the incoming meteor shower to the news stations.

"Those names are familiar. But I had little to do with the ordeal or the treaty."

My takeaway from his words was that only Austria was affected. It finally made sense why they told us to evacuate to Munich. But my blood ran cold as I remembered the newscaster speaking through our staticky television in the classroom in Guggenthal. She had said Turkey, Slovakia, and Czechia weren't responding.

"How sure are you?"

Levi raised an eyebrow, the subtle shift of his features causing my stomach to flip. "Absolutely certain. Your people responded, offered us a deal, and thus we came here. We knew there were other humans spread across the planet, but they did not respond or offer any support."

I really wanted to believe him, but why wouldn't the superpowers be chomping at the bit for such an opportunity?

The United States, China, Russia—why would none of them want a slice of what the aliens had to offer? *Unless…*

"What did you offer in exchange?"

He frowned. "What do you mean?"

"I know my kind. We're selfish and egotistical. Surely, you didn't beg to be allowed to stay here without offering something."

Maybe he started to understand what I truly asked because his face fell.

"We offered nothing because we had nothing."

Nothing.

No one offered to help because they wouldn't benefit from them. No technology, no secrets of the universe. Levi's kind were refugees, and like on Earth, all the nations turned a blind eye. It boiled the blood beneath my skin, my heart raced with anger and rage.

"By chance, do you remember the name of whoever it was you contacted?"

"A man from a company called ASAP. That is all I know."

I swallowed down the nervousness. Felis said he worked for the ASAP, Austrian Space Applications Programme. *Did he know about this?*

Levi's fingers trailed upward, gently caressing my cheek. "There was only a single thing we could offer."

"And what was that?"

A fleeting shadow passed over his features. "A cure."

He dropped his hand from my face, returning his attention to the fire. Standing over him, I watched the wood splinter, consumed by the flames. I didn't need him to admit to me what it meant. There was only one thing it could mean, and it was the reason the military had collected every corpse, ferreting them away to a facility headed by a scientist.

"Your blood…is there something in your physiology that is different from ours? A reason why…" I hesitated to say this word, "…experimenting on your kind would be beneficial?"

His shoulders sagged forward, and I knew the answer. "Your kind is predisposed to a myriad of conditions. Your own bodies plot against you, a ticking time bomb, as some might say."

"Your kind don't succumb to disease or old age?" *What are they, gods?*

Levi sighed. "No. I am sure you saw the pods we traveled in?"

"Yes."

"We only need to…recharge every now and again." He stared out toward the patio, where the hot tub sat under a pile of snow. "It's why there are so few of us."

"So, you don't have children?"

I could see the hint of a smile on his lips. "I don't. My kind procreates, but children are rare and hard to conceive. And such a thing is unheard of if you are not under the influence of The Link."

The Link.

I had so many questions, but I grappled with which should come first. But personal curiosity won out.

"When did you know?" He eyed me warily as if he wasn't entirely sure what I was asking. "About The Link."

His face fell, and I knew he was hoping I wouldn't inquire about it, that I'd drop it. But you couldn't reveal something like that and not expect questions.

He stood, turning to face me. We stared into each other's

eyes, and some unknown force compelled us to raise our hands at the same time—one of his cupped my face, the other resting on my waist. My hands went to his arms, gripping him gently.

"I knew the moment you threw yourself at me, plunging us off the cliff." He rested his forehead against mine. "I knew it was you unconscious in the snow, injured. All I could see was your beauty, your bravery, your selflessness. I knew what you did and why you did it. But my kind are hard to kill, and for a heartbreaking moment as I watched your chest rise and fall, I thought it would stop," he confessed. "I thought I would blink, and you would be gone." His voice cracked, and my grip tightened.

That entire time, while I plotted ways to escape, to kill him, he only saw the one person who meant the world to him. I saw a monster, and he saw salvation. I couldn't begin to understand how painful and confusing it must have been for Levi to look upon his enemy, someone who had betrayed him and hunted him down, the very person who had flung him off a cliff, and know that person was who he was meant to be with.

"I never asked for this," he whispered, his tone filled with equal parts fear and joy.

His face lowered, his lips coming closer and closer. His breath mingled with mine, and the world melted away. I could see nothing, hear nothing, feel nothing except Levi. It was like a puppet master plucked at our strings, bringing us closer and closer.

I found my voice. "We have a word for The Link between humans too."

He seemed surprised to learn this. "What do you call it?"

"We call them soulmates." It felt odd for that word to roll off my tongue so easily. I'd like to think I was scaring myself, but with his hands on me and his lips so close, I didn't care.

"Soulmates." He tested the word on his tongue, and the smile on his face grew.

This time when I saw the bony wings protruding from his back like blades, I didn't shy from the sight of them. They alighted around me, enveloping us together in a cage of bone.

"Emilia," he whispered my name against my lips, and goddamn, I could not help the slight gasp that escaped me.

I leaned in, but my eyes had barely closed when the darkness around us brightened in a fiery ball of white. I shuttered my eyes against the pain, crying out. Levi gathered me close in his arms, growling.

"Move." He ushered me away from the warmth of the fire as an acrid stench filled my nose and drowned my lungs. When my eyes finally adjusted to the brightness, I found us struggling down the length of the building toward the entrance as thick gray smoke filled the vast void of the barn.

Did the fireplace explode?

Even as the thought entered my mind, I knew that wasn't the case. Levi dragged me the few final steps, throwing open the doors before I could put the pieces together, and I knew he had walked us right into a trap.

The wind caught the door, ripping it wide open. Lights, shining with what felt like the intensity of a thousand suns, blinded us long enough to pause in our steps at the entrance. We were sitting ducks. I knew that, and Levi knew that. But his grip did not falter, and he did not leave my side.

This was his one chance. He could have escaped and saved himself, but what he did was incredibly brave and incredibly foolish. He put me behind him, and in his black outline in those garish lights, I saw his wings expand to their full size and heard a mighty earth-shattering screech escape him. My hands flew to my ears, desperate to block out the noise that seemed to rattle my brain. It must have startled whoever stood outside, too, because, in an instant, Levi was no longer at my side. He had launched himself into the garden, and after my eyes adjusted, I saw the figures of dozens of soldiers outfitted in riot gear with weapons raised, waiting for him.

"No!" I screamed out into the void.

A familiar voice answered me from that mass of highly-trained soldiers. It called my name, and as much as it disarmed me, it distracted Levi too. And that's all it took for the guns to fire, peppering his body. I heard the thuds—one, two, three—and suddenly he was sinking to his knees.

"NO!" I screeched, running forward.

The soldiers immediately collapsed onto him, dragging him away. I didn't stop to think, I ran and ran until I was upon them, but then I couldn't move. Powerful arms wrapped around me, dragging me away from him. Levi's body was moved further and further away, and I turned on my assailant, ready and willing to fight, until I saw the bright brown eyes and short brown hair of the soldier from Guggenthal.

"Lukas." I breathed, not quite believing what I was seeing. *He's alive.*

"Emilia, come, you're safe now," he said, gently turning me away from where Levi was being loaded into the back of a truck.

I heard his words, but I didn't care. I struggled against his grasp, desperately clawing at his fingers to release me.

"Levi, Levi," I whispered over and over.

A soldier appeared beside us, but I didn't know what he was doing or even who he was talking to when he said in German, "Need a little?"

Lukas' grip on my arm tightened, and I cried out at his vice-like grip.

"Emilia, stop. You're going to hurt yourself."

"No!" I cried out, watching them aggressively drag Levi up a ramp, his head lolling to the side.

Lukas' voice was a distant buzz in my ear. "Yeah, give me."

"Stop!" I yelled, twisting myself enough for Lukas' grip to give a little. But I gained nothing, as I felt something sharp prick my skin. I whirled on Lukas, ready to lash out. But my tongue felt heavy, my vision blurring slightly at the edges.

I mumbled something, but I don't know if it escaped my lips or was just in my head. My world spun, and I found myself falling, but Lukas was there to catch me and carry me in his arms like a child. My eyes zeroed in on the trucks as we drew closer, and the last thing I saw before darkness took me was a jagged bony wing tip illuminated by a soldier's flashlight.

Chapter 19

Wherever I was, it was cold. Not the raw cold of nature. It was the stark, unyielding cold of humanity. I was in a room, possibly lined with tile or stone, but I barely had the energy to open my eyes, let alone move to touch the wall I sensed was close enough to reach. But I didn't want to touch it, didn't want to see it. Because if I did, that meant everything I remembered was true, Levi was dead, and it was all Lukas' fault.

Lukas.

The spark of his name in my mind was enough to send flames coursing through my blood. It was his fault I was here and his fault Levi was now dead. I didn't know what he used on me, what pricked my skin and lulled me into an impossible slumber where I did not dream, but he didn't hesitate. I remembered that in my rage.

My eyes opened to white. But it wasn't the white of the snowy fields I had grown accustomed to over the last few days. It was the stark white of floor-to-ceiling tiles. On the furthest wall from the dinky cot I lay across sat a metal door with no visual way to open or close it. An odd square of tile sat in the wall beside it like it had some significance I couldn't quite gather, and of course, the door itself had a small sliver in it where I supposed food, water, and the like were inserted.

It was a cell.

I was in a prison.

My attention went to the wall the bed was against. Halfway up, a blacked-out window was set ominously within the tile. The blood in my veins chilled. I knew I was being watched.

I gathered the thin excuse for a blanket I was given and wrapped it around myself. I was still dressed in my black thermal leggings and a long-sleeved shirt. I was grateful for that, at least. They fought off a pinch of the room's cold bite.

Raising my hand, I knocked once on the glass. I waited, listening, even though everything told me it was likely soundproofed from their end, not mine. They could see and hear everything I did, but I'd never know if I had an audience or was screaming into the void. I knocked again, a little harder this time. When I received no response, I banged my fist against the glass and called out. But like before, only silence and the dying echo of my hello answered me.

I raised my fist again and again and again. I pounded on that stupid one-way glass, called until my voice was hoarse and my tears ran dry. Until my cheeks stung more than my fist, and I could no longer feel anything.

I didn't even know I'd gone too far, for too long, until I saw the smear of blood across the glass. I drew my fist back, wincing as I straightened my hand. The skin across the knuckles of my right hand was split, broken, and bloodied. I slid from the window, huddling beneath the blanket on the cot, wondering if this was how I'd die—a nobody in no place, with nothing.

Levi.

Even though I had no more tears to shed, my throat closed, and I coughed out a choked sob.

Then, since the first time I'd been awake, I heard something. Out in the hallway beyond my door, the rhythmic thumping of boots came and stopped right outside. I swallowed, listening, then something beeped before a lock slid open, and the door squeaked. Pulling the blanket down from my eyes, I stared at the intruder who stood in the doorway, and the number of emotions rolling over me froze like a deer in headlights.

"Hello." I couldn't say I ever paid much attention to the stark blue of his eyes and the way his dyed blond bangs brushed his bushy eyebrows. But I could never forget that face or his smooth German accent.

Except now there was no German accent. He sounded more like Lukas, like someone from Germany who had a British lilt because of their upbringing. But I pushed it from my mind, happy to see a friendly face.

"Felis." I choked out his name.

He flashed me a brilliant smile, but it didn't melt away my confusion. I leaned forward, clutching the blanket to my chest like it could somehow protect me. Felis crossed the room, and the moment he abandoned the doorway, I saw a flash of military outfits in the hallway.

Felis had brought guards.

Dashing any small hope of escaping I had conjured up at the sight of him, I turned to the man who had helped me escape the onslaught of Salzburg.

"Emilia. You're awake," he stated with no hint of relief in his voice. It was a fact from a scientist, not concern from a friend.

His eyes slid to my hand, the knuckles still cracked and bleeding, cradled in my lap.

"Were you there that entire time?"

There was no hesitation in him as he said in his posh voice, "I never left your side."

My eyes strayed from him to the blackened windows, which still refused to surrender their secrets to me.

"Why didn't you come sooner?" My voice cracked, more from anger than fear. But I don't think he knew that.

Felis sat beside me, coaxing me to let him see my hand. After a moment's deliberation, I placed my palm in his, and he looked over the cracked skin. Dried blood began to flake away at his touch.

"There are protocols we must adhere to. I'm sorry for any unpleasantness you have experienced."

"What protocols?" *What could possibly stop you from making sure a friend didn't hurt themselves?*

He sucked in a breath. "You were found following prolonged close proximity to one of the creatures. Your behavior led us to believe you had been influenced in some way, and we needed to keep you separated for observation."

"And?"

"The observation period has ended, and I don't believe you're a threat to yourself or others."

Even after I beat myself bloody?

"So, does that mean I can leave?"

He offered me a quick smile. "Of course, perhaps you'd like something to eat."

I declined his offer to help me stand, holding the blanket closer around me like a shawl before letting him lead me into the hallway. The two soldiers at the door stood at attention then followed us at a leisurely pace. Or, I guess, the most leisurely pace a guard could walk.

"I have some questions—" My voice echoed off the walls.

"Food first," he interjected.

I followed him blindly, like a lamb to its shepherd. Or, in this case, to the butcher. The corridors we walked along were no different than the room I had woken up in. Bland with no distinguishing features. They were hollow, lifeless, and built for the sole purpose of walking through and nothing else. But I guess that was the only purpose corridors served in a jail—transit.

"Can I ask where we are?"

For a moment, I thought he would say I needed sustenance first, but he cleared his throat. "A facility in Southern Germany."

I tried not to react, to give him any indication I knew exactly where we were. Or at least, I had a pretty good idea the facility Levi and I spied on was the same one I now found myself within. My heart ached as his name crossed my mind. Felis glanced at me, and I knew he could see the pain written on my face.

"Does your hand hurt?"

Oh good, that's all he thinks it is.

"Yeah." I played it up, holding my hand up to look at it. He thought Levi had influenced me somehow, and the longer I let him believe that, the better.

"I'll get you something for it."

The corridor ended abruptly. On our left sat double doors, and on our right, another corridor stretched onward beyond a barred gate. A small room, not much bigger than a storage closet, sat on the other side of the metal bars. However, from our vantage point, I saw a soldier sitting in an office chair, watching a panel of monitors.

It was a guard post. I took note of its position in relation to my room. Stifling a dramatic yawn, I cast my gaze slyly back the way we had come, eyeing the corners of the walls. A single camera seemed to cover the corridor from the guard room to my room. The knowledge did little for me now, but it could be handy later.

Felis muttered something in German to the guard behind the barred gate, and he pressed a button. The double doors illuminated neon green, and Felis pushed them open. We stepped into a wide hall that did not remind me of a cafeteria in the slightest.

"W-what is this place?" I was awestruck. It reminded me of the concept art you'd see in galleries for what popular city spaces could become. Someone had obviously taken that concept and brought it to life.

Felis led me across the now-familiar white tile, past crescent-shaped booths shrouded by wooden panels with gentle, mellowed lighting and edged with twisting topiaries and swaying reeds. A light breeze drifted down from vents set high in a ceiling that curved like waves at the beach. The mood, setting, and architecture all screamed the characteristics of futuristic design. Eccentric and asymmetric. If I didn't feel like a prisoner, I would almost say I felt at home among the crisp order the style shouted at me. I may have been fond of the classical era in dance and music, but I sometimes found it refreshing to set my sights on the future instead of the past.

Felis paused at a booth at the far end of the hall, sweeping his hand toward it. "If you take a seat here, I'll return shortly with a first-aid kit."

I nodded, distracted by the hard shells of bamboo and feathery tops of reed grass that swayed beside me. I was disappointed when the guards stood at either end of my booth, avoiding eye contact. From my vantage point, I could see other booths and sometimes glimpsed the top of someone's head. But if it weren't for the low drone of conversation in the background, I would have thought we were the only ones there.

Leaning back into the cushion, I eyed the nearest guard. "So, been here long?"

He did not move or speak.

Pursing my lips, I turned my attention to the other guard.

I swear I didn't even see his chest rise for a breath.

What is this place, an outlet for Buckingham Palace's extra guards?

Boots slapped against the tiles nearby, and a head poked around the guard.

"Emilia?"

I whipped my head around, staring down the traitor who caused all this.

Lukas raised his hands. "Emilia…I thought I heard your voice."

"I don't want to talk to you."

He glanced between the guard and me before holding up a finger. "Wait a second."

The sound of his boots bouncing off the tile as he departed sent an unusual amount of joy through me. I didn't want to see him, let alone talk to him. Levi was dead, and I was imprisoned here, all because he had found me.

He returned a moment later with a tray of food in his hands. Sliding it across the table toward me, he slid into the booth opposite me.

Sure, take a seat.

"I thought you might be hungry, and I didn't know what you're in the mood for, so I grabbed you a little of everything." He flashed me a smile that set a weight in my belly.

I didn't even bother to glance at what sat on the tray.

"How did you find me, Lukas?"

His mouth twisted. "A group of civilians made contact with our entry guard."

I blanched. That group of men and women at the barn, the ones I begged Levi to spare.

Tears streamed across my cheeks, blazing trails of warmth that pooled at the crook of my neck, soaking into the collar of my thermal. It was nobody's fault Levi was dead, except my own.

"Hey." Lukas slid across the booth toward me. "It's okay. You're safe now."

When the tears stopped coming, and I managed to clear the thickness from my throat, I put distance between Lukas and me. Even just an extra inch of space calmed me.

"Where are my friends?"

Something shifted in his demeanor, and I didn't miss the glance at the soldiers.

"How about you eat first?" he offered, sliding the tray closer.

"Lukas," I warned him.

His eyes slithered from the tray of food to my hands in my lap, and a shadow crossed over his face.

"Who hurt you?" His tone was deathly.

I turned on him. "Why do you care?"

In other circumstances, the hurt on his face would have caused an ache in my chest. But, right then, I didn't care if I hurt him.

"Emi, come on. How could you say something like that?"

I clenched my fists in my lap. "Stop."

His brow furrowed, "What's wrong, Emi?"

"You have *no* right to call me that," I spat at him. The blood that coursed through my veins felt like fire.

Only one person in the entire world called me Emi, and that was Theresa.

"I didn't mean anything—"

"Where are my friends?" I was on the edge of my seat, literally moments from exploding at him. I didn't care about food, I didn't care about his feelings, and I certainly didn't care about hearing what he had to say. I wanted to see Theresa, and I wanted to see Osman.

"Ah, I see you have found one another," interrupted Felis. I hadn't noticed him standing there.

He placed a white and red first-aid kit on the table. Flipping open the lid, he ignored the heavy blanket of silence between us. Fishing out a single-use alcohol wipe, he reached forward.

"May I?"

At least he asked. I held my hand out for him, wincing when he ran the wipe across the broken skin. I caught Lukas watching us out of the corner of my eye, and I swear a twinge of a familiar emotion settled on his face, almost like jealousy.

"Looks good," Felis said, shoving the dirty wipe into a small bag. Securing the lid of the kit, he held it under his arm before looking at the tray. "You really should eat."

"You said you would answer my questions," I said firmly.

He smiled. "Ah, I believe I said I would after you ate."

I glowered, tugging the tray closer to me. Finally, I allowed myself a moment to review what it held. When Lukas said he had collected an assortment, he wasn't joking. Spread across metal pots, plates, and bowls were fresh fruits, broiled vegetables, steamed or cured meats, and sugary breads. If I had to hazard a guess, I'd say he had grabbed one of everything available.

Mindful of Felis' stipulations, I picked up the fork and speared a broccoli floret. Eyeing the shine of salt and black pepper on it, I opened my mouth and shoved it in. Compared to what I'd eaten recently, that single piece of broccoli had me gripped with euphoria. I shamefully shoveled another few pieces in my mouth before I returned my attention to Felis.

"My questions," I said simply.

"Of course." He leaned against the booth. "What is it you'd like to know?"

Even I knew it was obvious they didn't want to tell me where my friends were. Nevertheless, I thought perhaps I could warm them up first to lessen their apprehension. Something easy to start with.

"How long was I out for?"

I could see his shoulders sag in relief. "A few days."

A few *days.*

"What did you dose me with?" I supposed that was a question for Lukas. He seemed to think so, too, as he shrank further into the cushion beside me.

Felis gave me an apologetic look. "Aah, yes. I'm sorry we had to resort to such measures. But rest assured, the proprietary cocktail I administered will have no lasting effects."

I bit my tongue, trying not to look either of them in the eye. Focusing my gaze on my food, I pushed a few pieces of green beans around in their bath of cheesy sauce.

"Am I a prisoner?"

Felis raised his hands as if somehow that would assure me of his sincerity. "Of course not. The cell was just a precaution."

"So, I can leave?"

He nodded.

"Can I see Theresa and Osman?" I asked with a note of hopefulness in my voice.

Lukas stilled, and for a moment, I saw his eyes on me. But I ignored the expression he was desperate for me to see. Felis looked down the hall, and I heard boots approaching us.

A man in a lab coat appeared beside the booth, a tablet clutched in his hands. He motioned to Felis with a nod.

"Pardon me," Felis excused himself, pushing off the seat to accompany his new companion.

"Felis…" I moved to rise, to follow him, but Lukas pulled me back into the booth.

"Emilia," he cautioned me.

I glared at him. "What?"

"Stop asking." His hand reached under the table to squeeze mine. I winced when his fingers brushed over the fresh wounds on my knuckles.

I rolled my eyes. "Or what, Lukas?"

What more could you possibly do to me?

His gaze hardened. "Or you'll find out what really happens here."

Chapter 20

Twirling the white keycard in my hands, I sat in my room. Felis had said I wasn't a prisoner, and the first thing he did to prove it was hand me a keycard and upgrade me to a nicer room. This one had a framed bed with a memory foam mattress and a fluffy duvet. There was a bedside table and a desk with a matching chair. An assistant came in while Felis was dutifully outlining my new room to look over my leg. She was quick to announce it was nothing more than a pulled muscle before shoving a few pills in my hand and promptly disappearing. I was hesitant to agree with her, but I noticed after resting for a while the pain was no more than a nuisance in the back of my mind.

But like the cell, everything was stark white. Everything except the bouquet of wildflowers set on the side table, that was. I learned those were courtesy of Lukas, which somehow made it far worse.

My skin prickled. His words played on an infinite loop in my mind.

"Stop asking…or you'll find out what really happens here."

I didn't know if Lukas was personally threatening me, but I got the hint there was more to Felis than met the eye. He had claimed he worked in communications and was a simple low-tier employee. But the more days that went by, the more I knew he had omitted a lot from me.

I'd spent three days avoiding both of them, which turned out to be a lot easier than I thought it would be. Whenever I inquired as to their whereabouts, my personal liaison would say that Felis was in the lab or that Lukas was out on assignment. I assumed that meant he was patrolling the areas around the facility for any more monsters to destroy.

My heart ached. Sometimes I thought I could still feel him—my own personal monster—the warmth of his hand on mine or hear my name on his tongue. But I squashed down the notion as soon as it appeared. It would do no good to obsess over the dead, especially since the dead was a universally hated invader, at least in the eyes of the public.

I tried not to think about him or my friends while I prepared for another day of exploration. Luckily, this room also had its own shower and toilet.

The very first day, I'd made use of the shower by sitting under the hot water until it ran deathly cold.

I glimpsed myself in the mirror as I made to leave my room. Felis had insisted I wear the neutral, cold-toned clothing of a business associate he provided. With long-sleeved dresses that never rose a hair above the knee and blocky blazers, the uniform reminded me of a 1980s catalog model. Part of me despised the offerings that appeared at my door on the third day with a note from Lukas. He had filled a box with assorted comfortable, although still neutral-toned pants, sweaters, and shirts. I wore the ones that felt like they would come in handy if I had to run suddenly—a pair of white sneakers, black capri pants, and a baggy white shirt I tucked into the front of the pants.

Like always, the moment I stepped foot outside my domicile, my guard was ready to go. I had to be content with being delegated to only a single shepherd. He was attentive, but unlike when there were two, I found I could observe more as I moved about the facility with one guard. By lunchtime, I had ventured through every part of the facility that wasn't designated as off-limits.

My adventures served more than an escape from realizing my freedom meant I was stuck here. It let me map out the facility, at least all the areas my keycard gave me access to. I had toured from the corridors of the living quarters where my room was, with their painfully white tiled walls, to the curvy cafeteria and its oddly placed booths. I had found a hydro farm with stacks of trays growing vegetables and fruits and a menagerie of animals in equally small-sized cages meant to optimize space.

I couldn't spend much time there, even though I loved animals. It made me sad and angry, almost as much as the chickens, fish, rats, rabbits, and guinea pigs inside.

I was grateful most of the facility seemed empty, but I knew I was being watched. I counted the cameras in the corners, and every now and then, when I passed the guard room with the monitors, I'd pretend to need to sneeze or adjust my shoelaces to see how much coverage each camera gave on the screens. There were blind spots, some would be easier to navigate around than others, but I wouldn't let myself forget where they were, just in case.

Considering my options for the day, I decided I was content with wasting time in the library. The library had a futuristic theme similar to the cafeteria, with white tiled floors and walls. Considerably smaller than the cafeteria, there was little room to hide here. Circular in shape, a dais rose in the middle of the room, and from the entryway, it reminded me of the whorl of a snail's shell. The walls were stacked with freshly printed books, most of them untouched. The spines had no crinkling, and the pages remained dog-ear-free. I wanted to applaud their dedication to preserving literature, but the bitchy part of me thought it was simply because no one came here. At least, every time I had gone, which had only been three times, I had never seen anyone coming or going or even sitting inside. Even my guard grew bored, opting to sit in a chair and stare listlessly at the white walls rather than pick up a book.

Resisting the urge to utter a sarcastic remark, I crossed the room to the very center, where the comfiest couches were. My book from the first day was still there, lying on the cushion, as I had left it. Picking it up, I ran my fingers over the leveled words, marveling at how beautiful the leatherbound edition of *Frankenstein* was. Admittedly, I'd never read it before. I hadn't even watched the movie, but I knew the general premise behind it. But now I was halfway through, I was addicted to discovering what would happen next. I supposed I could have taken the book to my room to finish, but I enjoyed having all that space to myself. Besides, it gave me the perfect excuse to meander through the halls since the library took me past the cafeteria and guard room.

The familiar sound of the door to the library sliding open interrupted the silence, and for a single second, my heart skipped a beat, thinking my guard had left me alone. However, my hopes were dashed a moment later when the boots that thudded against the tile toward me produced an undesirable sight.

"So, this is where you've been hiding." Lukas flashed me a smile.

My eyes didn't deviate from the page, even though I could no longer concentrate on the words.

"Yup."

"You look beautiful," he whispered. I tried not to show my disgust outwardly, bottling it up behind the patchwork dam in my mind. He tried again, "Did you get my flowers?"

Closing the book, I sat up, placing it on the seat beside me.

"Why are you here, Lukas? Surely, it is not for small talk."

He smirked, placing a finger against his mouth.

"Wha—"

A siren came to life, a piercing wail that echoed deafeningly off the tiled walls and floor. It filled the space, and I couldn't help but wince at its strength. My guard appeared at the edge of the dais, looking between us.

"Time to go," he growled in broken English to me.

Lukas looked at him, "I've got this."

His eyes narrowed, and he switched to German. "Bist du dir sicher?" <Are you sure?>

Lukas waved him off. "Ja klar." <Of course.>

"Ich bin gleich wieder da," <I'll be right back,> he called out to Lukas in German before disappearing.

The moment the door shut, the lights around the library flickered, then vanished, replaced by the gentle blue and red strip lights that seemed to edge every wall and step. Lukas reached forward, holding his hand out for me.

"What's going on?" I asked, unsure.

The siren lowered in volume but not intensity. It sang in the background, reminding everyone that all was not well.

"We only have a short amount of time."

Was he helping me escape?

I placed my hand in his, letting him lead me from the library into the corridor. The tiny red dot that usually blinked on the cameras was gone, and the corridors were only illuminated by the strip lights along the bottom of the walls. Soldiers ran to and fro, but not even one glanced at us. Whatever was happening was far more important than Lukas and me.

He led us past the hydro farm and gardens, through a corridor connecting the living quarters to the cafeteria, and up a flight of stairs down the hall from the guard room. He paused there, glancing left and right. Placing a finger to his mouth, he fiddled with something in his coat pocket. He produced a black keycard and pressed it against the obscenely white tiled wall beside us. I was about to open my mouth, my brows furrowed in confusion, when the wall slid open with an audible click, revealing a hidden corridor. He ushered me through before the door shut, and we hurried through the hall to an archway at the end that deposited us in a waiting room with multiple doorways. He chose a door on the left, swiping the card at the panel next to it, and led us through. This corridor did not have tiled walls or flooring. It was built of solid concrete.

At the very end was another door with another panel. It slid open with a swipe, revealing a rotunda with a panel of windows and a box of small buttons beneath the respective windows. Each window gave a view of a different room. The rooms were identical—white walls, wall floors, and white ceilings, with a white cot in the very middle. All the same, except for one thing.

Who sat within.

My blood chilled in my veins, and an odd sound escaped my lips.

Lukas squeezed my hand. "If you press the button, she can hear you."

Tears welled in my eyes, and a sickening feeling settled low in my stomach when I raised a shaky hand to hover over the button.

Theresa.

It was her. I knew it in my very soul, yet this wasn't the Theresa I watched them load into the back of a truck in Guggenthal.

"What did you do to her?" My voice was deathly still.

Lukas dropped my hand.

"*I* didn't do anything, but Felis did." His voice darkened. "Felis and those damn scientists."

Pressing the button, I leaned forward to speak into the microphone in the middle of the button box.

I struggled to get her name to roll off my tongue. "Theresa."

She didn't move—a lump beneath a pale blanket, her flowing brown hair peeking out from beneath the covers.

"Theresa…it's me. It's Emilia." I choked on my own name.

But it worked. Theresa stirred, turned onto her back, and pulled the covers across her face.

"It can't be," came her cracked, hoarse response.

Tears rolled down my cheeks at the sight of her. "It is. It's me. It's Emi."

This wasn't the Theresa I remembered. There was no hope or joy on her face. Her once full, pink-tinged lips were chapped and drained of color. The pale, freckled skin that had never known the ravages of puberty was marked, mottled, as if she had a skin disease. I swallowed the bile that sat at the back of my throat.

Her thin arms shook with effort as she pushed herself upright. The blanket fell from her shoulders to reveal patches of bandages on her upper back. She wasn't a tiny ballerina of muscle anymore. She was a skeleton.

How had she deteriorated so fast?

It'd only been maybe two weeks since I'd seen her. She dragged her legs to dangle over the edge of the bed and stared listlessly at the wall.

"Emi?" she called, her voice sounding so far away.

I pressed the button. "I'm here, Theresa. I haven't left."

"Can she see me?" I asked Lukas, not taking my eyes off my friend.

He sighed. "No."

She craned her head, staring right at me. The words she said next broke something within me.

"You should."

Choking back a sob, I tried to compose myself enough to be coherent. "I'm not leaving you, not again." I wouldn't ever make that mistake again.

Lukas shifted beside me, but I didn't have time for him. Theresa was what mattered.

Theresa's once bright green eyes lowered to the floor,

to her bare feet with her signature crimson toenail polish. Although now they were chipped. "Leave, Emi."

"No." I stood my ground, looking for a way inside.

"Emi, please," Theresa tried to argue, but her voice was so small, so delicate. So *weak*.

Fuck.

"We're out of time," Lukas said solemnly.

"No!" I shoved him aside, looking around the rotunda for a door, or slot, or some way to get into the room.

"The cameras will be back on soon." His eyes slid to the cameras sitting in the corners.

"I don't care," I spat, pressing my hands against the walls, hoping one would open a hidden door.

"We'll come back." Why would he possibly think that's what I'd want? I didn't want to go back there. It was a now-or-never moment. I was leaving there with Theresa, or I wasn't leaving at all.

I banged my hands against the window, thinking I could somehow force my way in.

"Emilia," Lukas warned. He grabbed my hands, pulling me back from the windows.

I kicked outward, struggling against him. "Let me go!"

His lips growled in my ear, "If you don't leave now, you'll condemn her and the others to death."

The others.

My eyes slid across the rotunda to the other windows. I didn't want to leave Theresa, but I had to see them. I had to know. Dragging my feet across the floor to the next window, I readied myself for what I'd see. But I didn't expect what I found. Osman sat upright on the bed, staring at the light above his head. His skin was far worse than Theresa's.

Pockmarked and bruised, bandages wrapped his arms and shoulders, some discolored by wounds beneath them. Tearing my eyes from him, I moved to the next window, and my heart fell. Lying in the cot, unmoving, was Oliver.

"What happened to them?" Part of me didn't want to know.

"They're guinea pigs for the cure." Lukas sounded as disgusted as I felt.

What Levi had said long ago made sense now. His kind lived long lives, void of illness. Of course, they'd need humans to test on after they butchered the aliens for whatever was in their blood.

"Felis would do this to Oliver?" I could barely accept a human would do this to another, let alone to someone they supposedly loved.

I returned to Osman's window, watching him run a hand through his oily hair. Did they know how close they were to one another? I should tell Theresa and Osman, but what would I tell them? *That they were both suffering the same fate?*

"We have to do something."

Lukas appeared at my side. "We will. But not here, and not right now."

I turned my icy gaze on him. "Promise me."

"We will save them, Emilia. I promise you."

Returning to Theresa's panel, I pressed the button once more.

"I'll be back for you, Theresa, I promise. Please, just hold on a little longer."

She didn't speak, just nodded slowly. I could see she was exhausted, possibly even drugged.

"I love you, Theresa."

Theresa looked toward the one-way window. "I love you too."

Before I bowed to Lukas' insistence on leaving, I cast one last gaze at the three of them, going from window to window to window. Theresa, Osman, Oliver. Humanity didn't deserve the cure at the expense of anyone, let alone the unwilling. If they couldn't seek revenge, I would gain it for them.

As Lukas led me back through the corridors, only a single thing was on my mind. He had promised we'd free them, that we'd be back. But I didn't want to simply free my friends.

I wanted to burn the entire place to the ground.

Chapter 21

A FEW MORE DAYS PASSED, BUT I DIDN'T WANT TO LEAVE my room. I didn't go to the cafeteria to eat. I didn't venture through the hydro farm to sniff the fresh fruits or along the boardwalk in the menagerie to see the languishing livestock. I didn't even go to the library to finish *Frankenstein*. Instead, I waited patiently for Lukas to return.

He was rostered for patrol for a few days after he brought down the cameras, and during that time, I couldn't bring myself to leave my room. I knew if I saw any of the people who worked there smiling and joking around, I wouldn't be able to contain myself, especially if Felis walked into my room and gave me his fake smile. I didn't have much of a plan except to rescue my friends. Lukas promised he'd think it through, and we could mull it over together when he returned.

On the day he was due back, I dragged myself from bed at the crack of dawn. I quickly showered and changed into another capris and shirt ensemble, black and white, of course. Then, sitting on the edge of my bed, I pulled on my shoes and sat, staring at the desk across from me. I didn't want to do anything, yet I despised myself for knowing there was nothing I could do. Without help, I could not get into the hidden corridor, let alone get in there unseen. Whatever Lukas had done to buy me those few precious moments with my friends, I'd have to rely on it again to free them.

There were footsteps outside my door, and I heard a familiar voice before an enthusiastic knock sounded on my door.

Please don't let it be Felis.

"Come in," I hollered.

The door slid open, revealing a smiling Lukas. He joked in German with the guard, who couldn't help but chuckle at whatever he had said. But the moment the door slid closed, his demeanor changed. His face fell, and a shadow crossed his eyes.

"Lukas."

He put a finger up to his mouth.

"Hey, Emilia, how are you feeling?" he asked with forced enthusiasm.

My eyes narrowed. He was acting odd.

"Good…" I tested the waters.

He tapped his ear, and I understood. There was a device somewhere letting them hear whatever we'd say.

"I heard you haven't left your room for a few days."

I shrugged. "I didn't really feel like it."

"Perhaps you'd be up for a walk?"

Letting out an audible sigh, I stood to my feet. "I guess."

When we emerged into the corridor, I was grateful my guard was nowhere to be seen. I wanted to thank Lukas, but he continued to act distant, and I assumed that was a cue to keep my mouth shut.

The dynamic had changed since I'd last left my room. An uncomfortable weight had settled into the tiles of the facility. The men and women, scientists and soldiers, went about their normal day-to-day activities, but there was less laughing and joking. The smiles were forced, and shadows had settled into their eyes. I could tell it wasn't solely because they worked long, grueling shifts.

Lukas led me to the library, and like always, on the way there and within, it was devoid of any life. *Frankenstein* still sat on the sofa, waiting for me to pick it up and resume the tale from where I'd left off. He motioned for me to sit but stayed standing and picked a random book from the shelf before standing over me.

"Do not speak. Only listen." His eyes slid to the leatherbound classic beside me.

I plucked the book from its resting place and pretended to flip through it.

He flipped a page. "They found out what I did—" He noticed my eyes widen and quickly finished, "Don't worry, though. They have no idea it was me. But since then, I haven't been able to get back into the system."

"And what does that mean—"

Cutting me off, he said, "Don't speak. The cameras can see your mouth from here but not mine."

I resisted the urge to peek at the corners of the room where I knew they were.

"It means I can't pull that stunt again."

My rage bubbled to the surface, and I fought to keep it from showing. "So, that's it? My friends must suffer?"

Lukas flipped another page, and I mirrored him. "No, I have an idea. It's a long shot, but it might work."

I eyed him suspiciously.

"Do you remember the guard room by the cafeteria?"

I nodded. Of course, I did. It was hard to miss the room filled with screens showing the camera feeds for the entire facility.

"If I can get in there, I can control everything."

It was a long shot. I couldn't say I had much faith, but I listened to every word. By the time he had finished, I had acquired some faith in the plan, although it was a minuscule amount. Although only half an hour had passed, he was eager to return me to my room to keep up the façade.

The panic began to set in the moment the door began to slide closed.

"Three days," he murmured before the door clanked shut.

Three days.

Easy.

Those three days passed in the blink of an eye. I kept my noises to a minimum, intimately aware I was most likely heavily monitored. Somewhere around noon on the third day, there was a commotion outside the door and the familiar voice of Lukas.

He was switching places with the guard. I tried to contain my excitement as I snuggled further under the blanket and turned to face the wall. An hour passed before I heard three light taps against my door, telling me to be ready. Not even five minutes later, I heard Lukas conversing with someone, followed by a louder knock and the door sliding open. I gripped the keycard tightly, trying to keep my breathing under control.

I spied the top of Felis' head above the edge of my blanket. He was standing in the doorway. He came to the side of the bed, and the door slid shut.

"Are you awake, Emilia?"

I took a moment to prepare a very shaky. "Yes."

"That's good. I've been told you haven't left your room in a while. I am worried about you."

To his credit, he genuinely sounded concerned. But I couldn't care less how he felt or what emotions he showed, genuine or otherwise. This man, although maybe not directly involved in it, expressly knew about the experiments being run on Theresa and Osman. And his own boyfriend, at that.

How could anyone do that? *What sort of psychopath…*

I shook the anger from my mind. It would do me no good here. After all, I had one job. A simple but extremely delicate job. If I failed, everything would be lost.

"I thought perhaps you'd like to have lunch with me today?" I hated how kind and soft his voice was at this moment. But it gave me that extra push I needed to go through with this and feel no guilt. He deserved everything that was about to happen and more. I only wished I could be there to see it unravel.

I beckoned him closer, and he sat on the bed beside me.

I sat up, hugging the blanket tighter around me. "I don't know if I'm hungry right now."

He pursed his lips. "Perhaps I could bring you something?"

He moved to leave, so I quickly interjected, "Maybe we could talk…for a little while?"

As I settled back on the bed, I saw the muscles in his shoulders and face tighten with apprehension.

"Do you think things will ever return to normal?" I asked.

The tension in his shoulders softened, and he stared at the desk. "I don't think things can ever return to the normal we remember. Things will be different. Life will be different. We'll have to make a new normal."

"Is that what you're doing here? Making a new normal?"

He let out a sigh. "I'm trying. We all are. But nothing is ever easy, and progress is frustratingly slow."

How dare you.

I reeled back the anger, but I was a fuse ignited by rage, and I was getting closer and closer to exploding.

"I hope my parents are okay." My voice wavered, and I was grateful it was with sadness and not anger.

Every time I spoke, his eyes darted away, and I moved a little bit closer.

"They're in Australia, right?"

Did I ever tell him where my parents were?

"Yeah, that's right."

I inched closer.

"If it helps, I don't think Australia has been affected."

"How can you be so sure?"

He cleared his throat, his eyes darting to a corner of the room.

Is that where the microphone is?

He ran his hand through his thick hair. "Communication from overseas hasn't halted."

If I had to be honest, his admission lifted a great weight off my shoulders. Not because I trusted him but because it confirmed what Levi had told me. His kind only landed in Austria, and Felis was careful not to reveal that.

"I hope I'll see them again one day." I was grasping at straws now. He was still so far away.

He cleared his throat, standing up. "I'm sure you will. Have you changed your mind about food yet?

Shit. He was trying to make an exit. *It was now or never.*

"I know this is a weird request, but…can I have a hug?" I squirmed, even thinking about receiving such intimate contact from him, but it was the only thing I could come up with on short notice.

He seemed taken aback, his brows furrowing, his lips parting. But he quickly recovered, flashing me a smile and opening his arms. "Of course."

Drawing back the covers, I eyed the keycard hanging from his lab coat pocket. As he wrapped his arms around me, I slid one around his back and unclipped his keycard, slipping it into my pocket before wrapping my other arm around him.

I pulled back. "You know, maybe I will join you. But do you mind if I take a quick shower first? I can meet you in the cafeteria."

He flashed me a smile. "I'll meet you there."

Good. I've bought myself the time I needed.

The moment the door closed, I changed into a pair of black cargo pants, pulled on a cream-colored knit sweater, and slipped into my sneakers. Crossing the room, I made the audible noises of someone preparing for a shower would do. When I heard the faintest of taps on my door, I turned the shower on full blast to disguise the sound of the door sliding open and me following Lukas into the hallway.

We knew we were on a timer, and right then, as we walked down the corridor toward the cafeteria, we were also in full view of the cameras. Lukas walked behind me, staring blankly ahead like a good guard. I kept my eyes down, trying not to draw undue attention. The cafeteria doors reared into view on our right, as did the barred metal door leading to the guard room that held the screens for the cameras. A single spot in the corner where the cafeteria doors met the barred metal held a small pocket of space the cameras could not see.

We stood in the shadow, huddled against the cold tiled wall. Lukas' hand met mine, and I slipped him the black keycard. He swiped it against the panel, the gate slid open, and Lukas snuck inside. I waited by the gate, anxiety causing my heart to race in my ears. I knew what would happen next, and I didn't want to hear any of it, let alone see it.

Looking down both corridors and listening for commotion on the other side of the cafeteria doors, I snapped my fingers and watched Lukas surge into the guard room.

I heard the shuffling, the grunting, and the strangled gasps. Swallowing down the bile at the back of my throat, I desperately tried not to lose what little composure I had left. A few moments passed before I felt a tug on my shoulder. Lukas passed the black keycard to me, blood dribbling from a cut on his lip.

"Lukas?"

He waved me on. "Stick to the plan, Emilia."

I nodded.

He disappeared back into the guard room, and the gate behind me snapped shut. My eyes wavered on the camera above my head, that red dot holding strong. Until it suddenly disappeared, and I made a run for it. I followed the path we had taken three days ago, and I found myself standing at the inconspicuous wall. Raising the black keycard against an unseen panel Lukas assured me existed, I waited with bated breath. Then, a click sounded, and the door slid open, revealing the long hallway. I bounded down it to the room with the chairs. Part of me anticipated seeing someone, anyone. This entire plan hinged on me not bumping into anyone, and other than hearing someone's footsteps, I didn't encounter a soul.

The camera in the corner of each room sat like a ghost, and I hoped with every ounce of my being that Lukas had lived up to his promise. Even though I'd only been there once, I seemed to know where I was going without paying attention. I found myself at the rotunda with no soul in sight. That is, none except Theresa, Osman, and Oliver.

I smashed my hand against the button and called out her name.

"Theresa! I'm here!"

Theresa stirred, throwing back the covers and looking toward me.

"Emi? What's going on?"

The hope in her voice stirred tears in my eyes. "I'm here to free you."

"H-how…"

I looked around the rotunda. Other than the door I came through and the windows and button panels, there seemed to be no way into the rooms.

"Do you know how I can get in there? I don't see a door."

She squinted in the harshness of the light, thinking. After

a moment, she pointed to the wall opposite the window. "The door opens here, but I don't know how you'd get to it."

Damn.

"Okay, hold on," I said, doubling back the way I had come to the room with the chairs.

There were other doors, and I only had a few seconds to guess which one it was. I chose the next closest, and it opened into a corridor with a grated floor suspended over a laboratory. I followed it to the end, where it snaked past several nearly invisible doors.

This has to be it.

Hoping whatever god there was would show pity in the moment, I pressed the keycard against the first door and watched it slide open. But this room wasn't stark white and tiled with a cot in the center, and it wasn't Theresa waiting to greet me.

The room had blackened walls and grated flooring, and in the middle, on a dais suspended by tubes and chains, sat an alien. He lifted his head at the gasp that escaped me. The world spun around me, yet time seemed to simultaneously stand still.

"Emilia."

My name on his lips stirred me to life, and tears rolled across my cheeks.

"Levi."

Chapter 22

NOT SURE WHAT TO DO, I DASHED TO HIS SIDE, MY hands hovering over him. Needles attached to tubes leading to sacks suspended from the ceiling pierced his pale gray skin, pumping him full of clear liquid. Electrodes and wires were attached to him with pale medical tape, feeding into machines on the wall. The consistency of the droning reminded me of a hospital, but this was far from it. This was a prison, and he was not being saved.

I had to help him. I must release him.

"Tell me what to do," I pleaded.

His head hung limply to the side, his long dark hair shadowing half his face. There was bruising on his skin, and cuts marred the beautiful runes that skittered across his bare flesh. He was strung up like a naked puppet, waiting for its master to return.

My throat thick, and my voice heavy with anguish, I

collapsed at his feet, resting my head against his knee. "I'm sorry, I'm so sorry."

He was here because of me, and because I thought he was dead, I didn't bother to look for him.

It's all my fault.

"Emilia." His voice sounded so far away.

I gripped his leg, my eyes wandering to his crimson irises that looked upon me with such a fierceness I found myself lost in them.

"It is you," he whispered, stirring from an obviously drug-induced stupor.

Rising to my feet, I cupped his face, nearly recoiling at how cold he felt. "It is. It's me. I'm here."

He moved his head against my hand, his lips brushing against my palm. "I never thought I'd see you again."

My eyes strayed to a panel on the far wall, where an array of buttons and a screen detailed the medical information they were getting from him.

"Tell me what I can do." My heart broke watching him struggle to stay awake.

He nodded toward the panel. "There is a liquid they're pumping through my veins…"

Gently releasing his face, I crossed the room, staring blankly at the panel. There were terms and symbols that meant nothing to me. I had no idea what I was looking for, but I started pressing buttons, and a small pop-up flashed across the screen, asking me to log in.

Fuck.

Digging the black keycard out of my pocket, I swiped it against a pad beside the panel, and the pop-up glowed green before disappearing to display an array of tabs and buttons.

Breathing a sigh of relief, I looked through the information on the screen, but nothing became any clearer. The complicated words could be names of drugs, procedures, or hell, even a scientist. Knowing time wasn't on my side, I did something drastic. I pressed every red button I could see. The panel lit up, and odd noises sounded around the room. An anxiety-riddled moment later, the tubes attached to his arms ran dry.

Darting to his side once more, I looked for a way to remove the chains and shackles around his wrists and ankles. But they obviously needed keys, which I didn't remember Felis having. Gripping the shackle on his wrist, I pulled and pulled to no avail.

I don't know why I thought it would work.

He stirred. "Emilia."

I stopped. "Am I hurting you? I'm sorry—"

"Lever…behind me."

My eyes strayed to the abyss of the black wall, and sure enough, hidden in the darkness was another panel. I literally ran across the room, sliding to a stop before the panel. There were no labels or information, just a simple lever in the up position. Wrapping my hand around it, I pulled it down, and an audible clank echoed off the walls. Above me, a small platform lowered from the ceiling, where the chains were attached to it.

Returning to Levi's side, I gathered him in my arms, and we sat on the grated floor. His bony wings wrapped around me, pulling me close. Heartbreaking minutes passed, and I knew time was running out. If Lukas hadn't been caught yet, he surely would be soon. I was certain Felis would return to my room at any moment, and there was no way he'd pass by and not notice Lukas missing and my room empty.

And then, by some miracle, Levi stirred in my arms. His crimson eyes flashed bright, the fog fading from his features.

"Levi?" I choked on his name, bringing him closer.

He reached out a shaky hand to cup my cheek. "You saved me."

Leaning forward, I pressed my forehead to his, our lips a breath apart. "We didn't get the chance to do this before, and I won't let us miss it this time."

I pressed my lips against his, and for a moment, he did nothing. He didn't react—didn't move—as if he was stunned I would do such a thing. But then, emotion overcame him. He threaded his fingers through my hair, pulling me close. Our lips parted, and I could taste him on my tongue, feel his tongue moving amongst mine, our bodies pressed as close together as they possibly could. Where my fingers brushed the runes on his shoulders, sights, sounds, and smells flooded into my being, overwhelming me with trickles of emotions. He stirred beneath me, pulling me into his lap where I could feel his hunger for me pressed against my thigh.

It wasn't enough for me. I wanted more. I needed more. And my heart hated me for pulling out of the embrace, breaking that moment. He looked confused and wary, but mostly, I saw the hunger in his eyes. I wasn't the only one who wanted more.

"We don't have much time." My eyes darted to the door, which I expected to slide open any minute to reveal men with guns.

"Then let's move."

He rose from my arms to his full height and stretched out his wings. With blindingly fast reflexes, he almost seemed to shift away from me, and the sound of the chains snapping alerted me to his freedom. The shackles still clung to his wrists and ankles, but he was no longer restrained by the chains. He stood before me in his naked glory, and I couldn't help but let my eyes wander over his form.

As I pressed the keycard against the panel on the door, it slid back, revealing an empty corridor. Levi paused in the blindingly white corridor, eyeing the next barely visible door.

"What is it?"

His crimson eyes narrowed. "My people languish behind here. I cannot leave them."

"Alive?" *It wasn't just him…*

"Please." The single word held so much emotion I didn't waste time running to each door.

Within were rooms identical to Levi's, each with an alien attached to chains, tubes, and wires. I deactivated the panels and lowered the levers, and Levi stirred his brethren back to life. They were not nearly as quick to stir as he was. Upon opening his eyes, the first alien lashed out. Levi called to him in an oddly lyrical language that brought the light back to the alien's eyes. He glanced at me but did not say a word, quietly following Levi and me to the next room. We did this four times but paused at the fifth door.

There, when the door slid back, revealing a room like all the others, I stifled a surprised gasp. The alien propped up within differed from the others around me. This one was female.

I worked the panel and the lever and turned to watch Levi cross the room.

He stood over her. "Arise, Tress."

The other aliens had fanned out around the room, waiting patiently.

Her golden hair cascaded across her shoulders and over her breasts, and the runes speckled across her turquoise skin came to life, glittering in the harsh light like glass on asphalt in the midday sun. She raised her head, bright purple eyes staring up at Levi.

She said something to him in their tongue, her voice holding a beautiful, mythical lilt, like an angel's. But when I saw her bony wings, my heart lurched. There were red lines carved into every inch of her wings. The tips were seemingly dipped in gold. She looked beautiful but deadly—a black widow.

Her eyes snapped to me, brow furrowing. Levi said a single word, and a slow smile crept along her face. Two others ran forward to support her from the room when she hauled herself to her feet. I led them from room to room until every single one in the corridor was empty.

When we were finished, I stood with thirteen aliens at the end of the corridor, standing by the walkway that hovered over the laboratory.

Levi stood at my back. "Lead us, Emilia."

"My friends." I had saved his people, but mine still languished as prisoners.

"Show me."

They followed me through the corridors to the rotunda without a word. The only noise was the rustling of their wings as they stretched and closed in anticipation. I could feel the tension in the air, and the silence of it weighed heavier than the frantic beating of my heart. Chaos was on the horizon, and I was the harbinger.

The air in the rotunda stood still, as time did when I looked between Theresa, Osman, and Oliver. I had warned each of them and begged them to hold tight for a little bit longer. I saw their faces light up with hope, and it pained me to know it would quickly fade when I admitted I couldn't find the corridor leading to the doors of their prisons.

I turned to Levi, my throat thick with worry. "I don't know how to free them."

His kind had been sedated and held in chains, yet they proved far easier to free than humans stricken with illness and pain. The sorrow I felt at seeing my friends burned hotter than the rage.

Levi's gaze wandered across the rotunda from the panels and windows to the floor and ceiling before returning to me.

"Tell them to get as far from the windows as they can and to shield their faces."

My skin prickled. "What?"

"Do you trust me?"

From the corner of my eye, I saw the other aliens watching us curiously, except the female, Tress. She had a smile on her face, and her lavender eyes glowed.

"Yes."

Levi nodded at me, waving his hand at the other windows. Two aliens broke off to stand before the windows, and I ran between each microphone, warning Theresa, Osman, and Oliver to stand as far back as possible and cover their faces. The moment they did as I had asked, Levi led the charge, leaning back and pushing his entire weight into the glass. At first, the glass didn't so much as creak. But as he reared back and did it again, there was an audible crack, and a line formed across the window. The other two aliens followed suit, and soon enough, each window was fractured with hundreds of cracks. In one fell swoop, the aliens stepped back and surged forward, putting their entire weight into the rush. The windows popped from their frames, shattering when they hit the ground.

I heard my friends scream, their voices chilling the blood in my veins. The aliens retreated behind me, and I rushed forward, reaching my hand out to my friends. One by one, I eased them from their prisons to stand awkwardly in the rotunda.

They stood behind me, their eyes wide, hands shaking.

"Emi…what's going on?" Theresa spoke first, her eyes darting between the aliens that stood ten feet away and me. Her cheeks heated at the sight of the naked aliens and the runes skittering across their skin like glittery tattoos.

In hindsight, maybe I should have warned my human friends about the naked aliens.

But I didn't care about their nakedness. I only cared for one thing. I ran to Theresa, pulling her into my arms.

"It's okay," I whispered in her hair.

Osman and Oliver took a tentative step forward.

"That's the one, isn't it?" Osman's eyes never left Levi.

Of course, he'd remember him. That was the last he'd seen of me before I fell from the cliff.

"He is."

Theresa pulled back from my embrace, more curiosity in her eyes than fear. "They saved us."

Osman tore his eyes from Levi, watching Theresa take a shaky step toward the aliens. Levi stood still, watching her.

She reached out a hand to him. "Thank you."

Levi's eyes went from her face to her hand before he reached out to awkwardly shake her hand.

"We don't have much time," I warned, ushering Osman and Oliver closer to the door.

Oliver stood at the back of the group as the aliens filed out into the corridor, led by Levi. Osman had gathered Theresa's hand in his own, putting space between her and the nearest alien. But that left me at the back of the pack. I turned to Oliver, extending my hand.

"It was Felis the entire time, wasn't it?" His voice wavered, and a part of me broke.

He had the haunted look of someone who had been betrayed, whose trust had been broken and could never be repaired. I didn't want to confirm it for him. I didn't want to be the one to have to tell him the truth. But if I didn't, who would?

"Yes."

He closed the distance between us, staring me in the eyes. "I want to destroy everything."

I offered him my hand, and he took it without hesitation. "Then let's get to it."

I led the charge through the laboratories, opening every door we saw. Fires were lit, solvents poured, beakers broken, and chairs thrown. Nothing was left untouched. I let them pour every ounce of anger, fear, pain, and regret into sacking that goddamn facility. If it burned to the ground in the end, I did not care. The aliens deserved their revenge and then some. I even watched Theresa, Osman, and Oliver move alongside the aliens, working together toward a common goal.

By the time we reached the darkened hallway that led to the main part of the facility, a rosy hue lit the passages behind us. The smoke would soon trigger the alarms, and whatever incredible advantage we'd had so far would be gone.

I noticed most of the aliens had found clothing in the

hidden part of the facility, most notably *their* clothing. The scientists must have kept them stored somewhere, and the aliens were quick to reclaim what was theirs. At least Theresa no longer squirmed uncomfortably at the sight of them.

As I pressed the keycard against the hidden panel, the door slid open, and a man in a soldier's uniform paused to look at me with a questioning gaze. But his expression changed the moment he saw what stood behind me.

He jerked forward, his lips parting, and a soft gasp escaped. Something wet splattered against my face, and my eyes drifted down to see the tip of a bony wing penetrating the young soldier's chest. Blood dripped across the bone and down his shirt, hitting the tiles at my feet. With a sickening realization, I knew the speckle of warmth on my cheek belonged to him.

His body sagged, the wing retreated with a sickening plop, and the soldier collapsed to the ground, the light already gone from his eyes. I cast my gaze down the corridor, but there was no one else. My eyes raised to the corner, and my heart stopped. A red light blinked below the camera aimed right at me.

Fuck. Did that mean Lukas had been caught?

It was too late now. It had already seen me. Taking a step out into the corridor, I stared the camera down, hoping, by some small miracle, Lukas was still there.

The lights in the corridor blinked, and the sound of doors unlocking echoed around me. Every door slid open, revealing the rooms within. A moment later, an alarm sounded, and the sprinklers came to life. I smiled at the camera, mouthing a thank you, before leading everyone from the corridor. Some of the aliens broke off, sneaking into the rooms. I heard the destruction, breaking glass, shredding paper, and furniture being tossed.

Leaving them to their revenge, I led my friends to the metal bars of the guard room.

"Lukas?" I called into the darkness.

Lukas took a step forward, a solemn look on his face.

I greeted him with a smile. "We did it, Lukas."

Theresa, Osman, and Oliver stepped forward, greeting him with praise. He had saved them as much as Levi or I had.

"No. *We* didn't." His tone was as dark as the corridor he stood in.

The water from the sprinklers dripped across my face, and I swiped it from my eyes as best I could.

"What do you mean?"

His gaze hardened. "You were meant to save humanity, not destroy it."

And then I felt Levi take a step forward, and I understood.

Lukas thought I had betrayed us.

Chapter 23

"Emilia...how could you?" Lukas took a step back, shaking his head.

My face fell. "W-what?"

"I remember." He pointed at Levi. "You tried to kill it. You plummeted off a damn cliff, trying to take it down. And yet, here you stand so casually."

I didn't miss the way Lukas referred to Levi as *it*. That's all he saw them as—monsters. But he didn't know better. He didn't know who the real monsters were here.

"Lukas, it's not their fault."

He scoffed. "Really, Emilia? You want to believe that?"

"I've seen it, Lukas."

"So have I." His hands balled into fists. "I saw it when they came down in their fucking pods, destroying our cities. You don't do that in the name of peace."

"We promised them the world. Our government, our military, promised them peace. Then went back on their promises."

"Then why did they attack civilians as soon as they landed?"

I swallowed the bile at the back of my throat.

"I was front and center that day. I saw a little girl torn in half. I saw an elderly man ripped limb from limb. I saw it *all*, and I couldn't do anything because they were stronger than us, faster than us. It took an entire clip to bring one down, Emilia. So don't stand here and try to defend these things to me because I'll have none of it."

"Lukas—"

He held up his hand. "Stop. This is as far as I help you, Emilia."

No…*no*!

Lukas' eyes glittered with tears, but he did not let them fall in front of me. With one last sorrowful glance, he turned his back on me, returning to the guard room. A moment later, the doors to the cafeteria opened, and the lights went dark, leaving only the strips along the floor to guide us.

"Fuck!" I heard someone in front of me growl.

"Move!" I hollered to Theresa, Osman, and Oliver.

We dashed down the corridor toward the living quarters, whose doors were wide open, as several aliens surged into the cafeteria. Levi and Tress were behind us. Even in the darkness, I could feel the tension rolling off them.

The corridor ended in a fork, left and right, leading into darkness.

"Where do we go?" Levi asked at my side.

I ran my hand across my eyes, wiping away the water still streaming down from the fire sprinklers. Both corridors looked the same—dark and lined with strip lights and open rooms. *Was it all living quarters?*

"I-I don't know."

Fuck.

Oliver strode past me, walking calmly down the left corridor.

My gaze went to Theresa and Osman, but they simply shrugged, following him. Sighing, I followed them without a word. Several aliens joined us after a while, silently trailing behind Tress and Levi.

The corridor Oliver chose met a staircase. He wordlessly ascended it to the next level to a wide hall filled with cushioned benches and long desks. The sprinklers had not activated there, but the lights were still off, with only the guiding floor strips. At the front of the room, on a dais, was a notably nicer desk heaving with the weight of books and with a single armchair tucked under it.

This clearly served as a school of some type.

Oliver didn't glance around the room as he strode past the rows of desks to the door set on the left. Another dark, empty corridor greeted us, and at the very end sat a pair of doors like the ones to the cafeteria. Oliver led us confidently through them into a group of rooms that were cut like the stalls of a stable. Each stall was filled with crates, barrels, or boxes, all labeled in German. Most boasted innocuous labels like vegetable oil, bandages, or assorted lightbulbs. But the further we got into the storage area, the more dangerous the labels became. Some had toxic warnings or flammable or biohazard labels. But then, at the very end, before an archway heaving with plastic doors, sat a row of refrigerators locked in a room behind clear glass doors. We paused, reading the bright red warning label over the doors in German, and I felt everyone's mood shift.

Caution: Human Specimens.

Osman turned Theresa's attention away, hurrying her past the display. I felt dizzy and disgusted, my heart hardening. The experiments hadn't started with Theresa, Osman, and Oliver. But I would certainly make sure it ended with them.

Levi pressed a hand against my shoulder, steering me through the plastic doors after Theresa and Osman. Oliver once again regained the lead through the corridor to a small waiting room with wide metal doors set into the tiled walls. A panel of buttons sat to the right of the doors, and my heart skipped a beat.

"How did you know?"

Oliver turned to me, his face darkened by more than the lack of light. "Felis brought me here when we first arrived. He said if anything ever happened, to use this route to escape." He pressed the button on the elevator, and the doors slid open. "That was before he decided to include me in his experiments."

We filed into the elevator wordlessly, but the silence didn't last. We heard rustling from beyond the plastic doors. Then, suddenly, they burst open. The aliens who had broken off to hold back the people in the cafeteria arrived from the gloom like demons, barreling toward us. And they weren't alone. Hot on their tails were soldiers armed to the teeth. Their shouts echoed off the walls, and the flash of their weapons in the strip lights caused panic to rise within me.

Levi shouted something to his brethren. They turned to nod at him before returning their attention to the soldiers. Only two more aliens joined us. Three stayed behind, rushing into the line of fire. We heard the crackle of guns and bullets ricocheting off the tiled walls and floors. Oliver leaned forward and pressed the button in the elevator. The doors slid shut on the brave aliens who stayed behind to ensure our escape.

In the gloom, I waited as the elevator roared to life and thanked whoever was listening for letting the elevator still operate. It jolted slightly before carrying us upward. Everyone stood, unmoving, the sounds of our hearts keeping us plenty company.

Tress stepped forward, leaning in to whisper to Levi. A smirk lit his lips, and he nodded in response. She went between the aliens, whispering to them in their lyrical tongue. Once clouded in pain and desperation, their faces seemed to ease into relaxation. Whatever she told them, they grasped it firmly. The aliens stirred to life, moving around the elevator. It took me only a moment to realize they formed a crescent shape around the humans, hugging the walls and leaving the space by the door open. I looked to Levi with panic in my eyes, and he reached out a hand to grasp mine, those crimson eyes alight.

Several minutes passed before the elevator rolled to a stop, a ding echoed around us, and the doors stuttered open. A cold breeze smacked into us, and I let out a shaking breath, steam curling into the sky.

"Fancy meeting you here," came a voice from the snowy void.

Standing before us, surrounded by soldiers clad in black and holding assault weapons, was Felis. He took a step forward, a smile on his face. "I believe you said you were going to meet me in the cafeteria?"

I swallowed the dread that was rising. "Enough, Felis. It ends here."

"Which is most unfortunate. I wish you hadn't done that because now you will all have to die."

The soldiers raised their weapons, each aiming at a different target. I'd like to think we easily outnumbered them and stood a chance. But I already knew the answer. *We* didn't stand a chance—Theresa, Osman, Oliver, and I. The aliens would no doubt eviscerate them, but us humans? We were made of soft, vulnerable flesh, perfect for being shredded to pieces by bullets.

An odd sound filled the void left following Felis' announcement. His gaze shifted to behind me, his brows furrowing. With a start, I realized it was a laugh.

Someone was laughing.

Turning my gaze, I watched Levi step forward, his lips parted in amusement.

Felis cocked his head sideways. "Something funny?"

Levi stared him down. "For someone so smart, you are incredibly stupid."

Felis rolled his eyes. "Coming from the monster staring down a dozen barrels."

Levi raised his hand and snapped his fingers, and after an anxiety-rising minute…nothing happened.

The soldiers snickered. Felis raised a hand, silencing them.

"Well, I'm growing tired, and you are of far more use to me dead. I have everything I need and then some." He motioned to the tarmac behind him, where soldiers were loading black boxes into the backs of vehicles.

When he made to leave, Levi took another step forward, drawing the soldiers' attention.

"I wouldn't leave so soon. You'll miss the party," Levi taunted.

Felis cast a gaze over his shoulder, raising his eyebrows. "I've seen enough." His gaze settled on Oliver for a split second before he turned his back.

The soldiers raised their guns, aiming for our hearts. With their fingers hovering over the triggers, I closed my eyes and reached out to grasp Theresa's hand. But nothing happened. I heard static popping in front of us, followed by muffled screams and shouting. I opened my eyes to the soldiers wavering, looking at one another. Their headsets were alive with the sounds of death and destruction, and their expressions were as clear as day. Somewhere, people were dying.

Felis turned to the nearest soldier, taking his headset and shouting in German. The only reply was screams.

"What the f—" Then chaos exploded around us.

The ground shook beneath our feet, and a vehicle on the tarmac exploded into a bright fireball. Soldiers ran between them, ducking from flying debris, desperately searching for a weapon. The soldiers in front of us turned toward the chaos, and the aliens surged forward, ripping them limb from limb. Theresa screamed beside me, and Osman pulled her out of the elevator and to the left, toward the fences. I made to run after her, but I was entranced, unable to move, as Oliver crossed the distance to where Felis stood among the blood of the fallen soldiers. At the same time, aliens had dispersed, running along the tarmac toward the soldiers desperate to escape.

Oliver took a few steps forward, staring down the man he thought loved him. "You told me when you first hooked me up to those machines I wouldn't suffer. But right here, right now, I come to you hoping you will."

In the distance, a surge of aliens had breached the facility's perimeter. They were racing across the tarmac and destroying everything in their path. Leading the pack was an alien with deathly white hair and pale yellow eyes—Raak. The alien Levi and I had met in Berchtesgaden.

I took a step forward, gripping Oliver's arm. "It's time to go."

Oliver left Felis standing amongst the chaos, his eyes wide, hands shaking, as he watched everything he had built be destroyed.

Tress raced ahead to help Theresa and Osman. As we caught up, another alien appeared from a hangar nearby, saying something to her. She nodded, and we followed him to a part of the fence behind the hangar where a tree had fallen, breaking the fence in half. Tress and the other alien helped us through the gap, and we escaped into the surrounding forest.

The snow bit at our ankles, and the cold cut into our exposed flesh, but in the heat of the moment, fueled by adrenaline and the thirst for freedom, we didn't care.

We climbed the rocky hill through the forest, finding ourselves overlooking the facility in the valley. We were on a plateau not unlike the rocky outcrop Levi and I had stood on what seemed to be so long ago. From there, we paused to watch the smoke rise above the black and white buildings. Fires, although slow, devoured everything in their paths, not even letting snow hamper their destructive natures. Intermittent gunfire sang in the distance, followed by shouting, explosions, and vehicles revving. It was hard to tell the difference between friend and foe, alien and man.

And above it all was a sky alive with the touch of the coming sunset. Streaked with marigold and magenta, violet and azure, even the peppering of gray clouds pregnant with a fresh fall of snow could do little to mar the beauty of nature.

Tress took a step forward. "The humans tire. We must find shelter for the coming night."

I nodded. "Can you do me one thing?" Her lavender eyes swirled. "Can you take care of them?"

She nodded.

Theresa took a step forward, worry etched on her face. "Emi, where are you going?"

"I have to find Levi." I knew he could handle himself, I knew it, but I couldn't leave him.

Not again.

"He'll be fine." Her voice wavered, and it wasn't the cold that shook her.

"Theresa…"

She broke free of Osman's grip, wrapping her arms around me. "Promise me you'll return. Promise me you'll find us."

I pulled out of her embrace, giving her a soft smile. "Theresa."

Osman gathered her into his arms. "She'll be fine, Theresa."

"Promise me," she whispered, her voice breaking.

An explosion sounded in the background. But I had set my resolve. "I promise."

With one last glance at my friends, I trekked back the way we had come.

Chapter 24

Spurred on by the knowledge I couldn't leave Levi, it didn't matter I had no idea where I was going. Although I knew he was more than capable of taking care of himself, after everything we'd been through, I couldn't let him out of my sight again. I didn't think I could survive, thinking I'd lost him again.

After twenty minutes of stumbling through calf-deep snow, I found myself in a small glade between the mountains in the forest leading to the facility. I could still smell the smoke and the acrid scent of a chemical spill. I didn't want to imagine what horrors were being released to soak into the water table, but that was an issue for another time. Right then, all I had on my mind was finding Levi.

Shouts echoed through the glade, drawing my attention to its edge, where a puff of steady smoke curled into the air above the evergreens. The sky was darkening with the advance of twilight, and stars appeared like little balls of light at the edge of the marigold and magenta ribbons of sunset.

Marching through the snow, the crunching nearly caused me to miss the boisterous laughter that roared out of the trees to my right. Somehow, I'd circled to where the smoke came from and found myself staring at a fire that roared in a haphazardly constructed pit. Beside it, several soldiers sat in the snow, drinking from canteens and joking with one another in German. But I didn't care about them. Instead, I cared about the slouched-over alien tied to a tree on the other side of the hungry flames. I'd barely noticed him, but the moment I did, all other trains of thought left my mind, and I found myself walking forward.

"Emilia?" One of the soldiers called out to me, scrambling to his feet to catch up to me. But I paid him no heed as my legs propelled me toward the alien.

His wings were mangled, cuts and bruises marred his beautiful pale gray skin, and the golden runes that skittered across him like fairy lights were dull and coated in blood. His familiar black leather clothes were ripped, and I swear they were burned in some places.

"Levi." My voice broke at the sight of him.

He opened his eyes, staring up at me, and tugged at the chains that bound him to the tree. I heard them rubbing against the wood, sending splinters flying into the surrounding snow.

What have they done to you?

I wanted to ask. I wanted to toss myself at him, but I found my voice unwilling to sound and my body unwilling to move. Hands gripped my arms, pulling me backward, away from him. I kicked out, screaming and shouting until those hands twisted me around, and a familiar face loomed into view.

"What are you doing here?" Lukas' eyes searched mine.

I craned my neck around to see Levi, but Lukas' grip was firm, and I didn't miss the aggressive way he whipped me back around to keep my eyes on him.

"Emilia, answer me. What are you doing here?"

I shook the surprise of finding them both there from my mind, my gaze narrowing. "I came to find *him*."

Apparently, that was the wrong answer. Lukas' gaze went cold, his fingers digging into my arms.

"Lukas—" I tried to warn him he was hurting me, but his nose crinkled, disgust written across his face.

"You came back…for *him*." He looked me over, his eyes roaming behind my neck and down my arms.

"What are you doing?" I squirmed in his embrace, my skin prickling with warning.

Something, my self-conscious perhaps, was telling me I had made a grave mistake. I shouldn't have burst into the soldier's little camp. But I hushed the warnings. This was Lukas. He wouldn't let anything bad happen to me.

"I helped you, Emilia. This entire time, I put my life on the line, and after everything you did, you left me down there. You set fire to the entire facility, and you fucking *left* me." There were tears in his eyes as his tone darkened.

The soldiers sat uncomfortably where I had walked past them. Some eyed us while others kept their focus on their canteens.

"Why, Emilia?" His voice broke, and it dawned on me. *He felt…betrayed.*

"Lukas…it was your choice." He had the chance to come

with us, and at the very end, he said he wouldn't help me any further.

He stood there speechless.

"You stayed behind. I wanted you to come with me," I pleaded with him.

His grip tightened, and I swear I felt his fingers bruising my arms. "No, you wanted me to betray my own people for *them*."

"You had no problem betraying humanity for my friends. Why is it any different for his kind?"

A shadow crossed over his face. "Aah, *his*."

My stare didn't falter. Lukas couldn't see past their differences. To him, Levi and his kind would never be our equals.

"What did he do to you, Emilia?" Lukas shook me, and a gasp escaped from between my lips.

"Lukas, stop. You're hurting me." I hated how weak I sounded, how my voice broke in the middle, and how tears glistened in my eyes. Chains clinked behind me, and I knew Levi had been stirred by my cry.

Lukas turned his gaze behind me to where Levi sat, chained to the tree like some monster. "What did you do to her?"

I heard a hiss in response.

He turned his gaze back to me. "He did something to you."

I scoffed. "No, Lukas. It was my decision."

He shook his head. "No, it wasn't. Because if it was, you would have left the facility with me, not with *him*."

"Lukas…"

He closed his eyes, and before I could comprehend what was happening, he leaned forward, pressing his lips against mine. I stood stunned, unable to react.

Lukas was *kissing me*.

But several seconds passed, and suddenly it wasn't a simple kiss. He pressed harder, his lips insistent, his grip on my arms increasing. I pulled back from him with a cry.

"Lukas, what are you doing?"

He didn't say a word, just pulled me into him and pressed his lips against mine once again. I struggled in his grasp, but he was too strong, too insistent, and I shook as fear flooded over me.

Why was he doing this?

"Please…stop…" I murmured between his lips, but he didn't give an inch.

The laughter of his friends caused the tears to fall from my eyes. But Lukas didn't seem to notice, or if he did, he didn't care.

His tongue wormed its way between my lips, into my mouth, and I saw red. I lashed out with my foot, driving it into his shin. He growled into my mouth, pushing me backward. A jolt of pain crept from my backside up my spine as I fell to the ground, and I cried out.

Lukas stood over me, the light from the fire casting him in silhouette. "You want this, don't tell me you don't."

A chill ran through me that had nothing to do with the cold breeze or the snow I sat in.

"No," I said firmly.

The soldiers behind him snickered.

Lukas kneeled beside me, reaching out to cup the side of my face, but I batted his hand away. The sound of the slap echoed around the camp. Their snickering intensified.

"I don't know what has gotten into you, but you're not the Lukas I met in Guggenthal or the one who helped save my friends in the facility."

The hurt on his face was quickly replaced by anger. "Don't tell me you're *sleeping* with this thing?" He growled, his hands balling into fists, eyes narrowing.

I balked. "No. And even if I was, that's none of your concern."

He spat on the ground. "You're a fucking traitor."

I gathered myself into a seated position, staring him down. "The only traitor I see here is you."

I felt and heard it, but I never saw Lukas reach out to strike me across the face. The pain was blinding and radiated from my cheek to my jaw. Tears that had never stopped flowing streamed freely across my cheeks, blazing trails of warmth that paled in comparison to the searing heat his handprint left behind.

With my gaze blinded by tears, I raised my eyes to his. "Fuck you, Lukas."

He lunged at me, knocking me back into the snow and straddling my waist. His hands gripped my wrists, pinning them on either side of my face.

This couldn't be happening.

"L-Lukas…don't do this."

He released my wrist long enough to strike me across the face again, and I whimpered.

An earth-shattering snarl sounded nearby, and I heard the chains rattling and wood splintering again.

Lukas laughed, a nasty maniacal noise that haunted me. "Your boyfriend doesn't approve."

"Please, just let me go," I pleaded.

He chuckled. "Nah. If you want to lay with beasts, I will treat you like one."

His hand gripped my throat, and I clutched uselessly

at his wrists. I gasped, desperate to draw fresh air into my lungs, desperate for even a single breath. Panic built in me, and a strangled gasp escaped.

Digging my nails into the flesh at his wrists, blood streaked across my fingers, trapping itself beneath my nails. No matter how hard I fought, he didn't budge.

"He can watch you die, and then I'll burn him alive." Lukas cackled, a sneer marring what I once thought was a handsome face.

But I couldn't focus on his words or his malice. All I could focus on was taking one breath, fighting for a single lungful of air. Still, I couldn't focus, and as the light of the fire faded from view, so did Lukas, and I knew I had lost. I was sitting at death's door, and a shadow moved behind it.

I managed to squeeze out a single word.

"Levi."

A shriek shattered my consciousness, echoing around me like in a metal hall. I felt, rather than saw, a flurry of snowflakes wisp around me, holding me like a cocoon, and the sound of something snapping. It took me a moment to realize that the hands around my neck were gone, and I was gulping air like a fish out of water. My head swam, my throat hurt, and finally, my sight returned. Only, I wish it hadn't.

I'd heard the screaming. The horrible choked cries of men with blood filling their lungs and the sound of their limbs torn from their bodies, thudding into the snow. I heard the squelching, the squishing, and the cracking and breaking.

There was no gunfire, no evidence of fighting. It was a slaughter, and the dark streaks in the snow confirmed that.

There was a whimpering, a fluttering of someone scared nearby, and I squinted past the dying flames that struggled against the snow and the blood that fought to smother it. On the other side, I saw bony wings spread wide and blackness that dripped off them into the surrounding snow.

Two shadows grappled with one another

"Stop him," Lukas begged, clawing at Levi's hand around his neck. "Mercy, please…"

Levi turned his crimson eyes on me, waiting. He was waiting for me to decide his fate. After everything Lukas had done, Levi waited for my decision. But I knew what had to be done, even if it caused my chest to ache.

"Where was your mercy when his kind was being slaughtered? Where was your mercy when you had me pinned in the snow?" I turned from them, my eyes falling to my hands, gathered in my lap.

The crack that followed a moment later told me Lukas was gone.

Boots stomped toward me, and a blood-specked hand appeared in my view. Wordlessly, I took Levi's hand, letting him drag me to my feet. We walked around the mangled corpses into the clearing, hand in hand.

The darkness was near absolute. The gray clouds that had hung above the facility were over our heads now, and the first snowflakes had begun to fly around us. I shivered uncontrollably, my adrenaline no longer feeding me the energy to ignore the frigid air and the random pains. Levi seemed unaffected by the cold and whatever injuries he had, or perhaps he was simply trying to be brave. But I didn't miss the sidelong glances or how he'd squeeze my hand when I faltered or slowed.

"I can't feel my toes," I whispered, knowing full well the dangers of frostbite. I was sure I'd lose a few toes before succumbing to hypothermia, and Levi would continue onward, unaffected.

But he paused long enough to bend down and sweep me into his arms, cradling me to his chest.

"T-thank you," I murmured, resting my head against his chest. I tried to ignore the tangy metallic scent of blood and sweat.

He pressed his lips against my forehead. "Look in the distance."

Rising from between the dark tree trunks aligned like a picket fence was a lazy mist that hung close to the ground. But it was what hovered above that had caught my attention.

"I-is that—"

"A hot spring," he murmured with a smile.

We struggled up the steep bank packed with snow. A hedge that had outgrown whatever shape it was intended to keep towered above our heads. An archway that no doubt once held flowering vines rose to greet us, and we passed beneath it into a courtyard of flowerbeds and topiaries. Or at least, that was the shape the clumps of snow gave me the impression of.

Levi held me over the gently bubbling water, letting the steam rise to meet our cold faces. It was a natural hot spring sitting at the foot of a clearly abandoned lodge, and we were the only ones there.

"Levi—" Before I could finish my sentence, Levi took

a step into the spring. Then another and another until the water was lapping at his knees, then his thighs.

He didn't care about our clothing or shoes as he sat, submerging us both to our shoulders.

I rested in his lap, with my arms around his neck and his moving to encircle my waist. There was no care then for my soaked clothing, my ragged hair, or the warmth of the pool heating my skin. At least, I wanted to tell myself that was why my cheeks warmed.

I raised my eyes to his and nearly lost myself. His crimson eyes smoldered as he bent his head toward me. I didn't pause, didn't think about it. I pressed my lips against his.

The passion and emotions at that moment filled me—the fear, anger, hate, and overwhelming desire—also coursed through him. I wanted this, needed this, and I wouldn't let anything stop me. I ran my hand through his hair, and he mirrored my action and pulled me closer as his free hand gripped my waist, drawing me into him.

Straddling his waist, I gently pulled his hair back and sighed deeply, running my tongue along his bottom lip. He groaned, taking my mouth with his. When his lips parted, mine did the same, our tongues dancing as we hungrily devoured one another. Time stood still, a meaningless phantom that operated in the background. Not even the flurrying snow could pull us from one another, and I let myself become lost in him—lost in those crimson eyes, the firmness of his muscles against my body, and the taste of his lips on my tongue. Even his wings wrapped around me did not bother me.

As our kisses deepened, our hands drifted, and I could no longer ignore the feeling of him pressing against my inner thigh. I could feel his eagerness in the urgency of his hands drawing lines from my backside and along my thighs. But he wouldn't go any further. He wouldn't make the first move, and I knew that meant I would have to. It wasn't my first time, yet, I had no idea what the protocol was here.

Did his kind do things differently? Did I care?

No.

Distracting him with a deep kiss, I pulled back, fumbling with the hem of his shirt. He understood and helped me remove it. I tossed it into the snow, my eyes roaming over his exposed chest. The runes on his chest glittered, the only light in the near-total dark. I raised my hand, but his hand met mine, drawing it back in the water. I eyed him, waiting for clarification when his hands moved to the hem of my shirt, and I understood. I helped him lift the shirt above my head, and with a wet plop, it collided with the snow beside his shirt. He moved to fumble with my bra, but I took control, unhooking it and throwing it aside. With my breasts bare to the coldness of the night, I shivered slightly at his touch as his hands slid up my waist to cup my breasts. I gasped softly at his touch, unable to control myself.

When I ran my fingers from his shoulder, across his chest, and down his stomach, a reel of memories played in my mind. *His memories.* All the sights and sounds, emotions that ran through him in every moment now coursed through me, and I lived every single one beside him until I paused at the runes that barely peeked out of his waistband.

His crimson eyes smoldered, darkening, his lips parting as if he wanted to ask me, *beg* me, to continue.

Hooking my finger beneath his waistband, I tugged at the intricate knot that kept his pants in place until the strings were loose, floating in the water beside us. He shifted upward as I pulled his pants lower and lower, following the line of runes that seemed to run the full length of his body down to his feet. In the glow of the runes, I took in the fullness of him, and a soft noise escaped me.

Hunger glinted in his eyes as he fumbled with the buttons on my pants, and I pulled them down with his help. As I did, he hooked a finger around my underwear and tugged at them, also pulling them over my butt and down my legs until they floated in the pool beside his.

I straddled him, not quite letting more than our thighs touch. The hunger in his eyes matched my own, and his wings twitched in anticipation. Leaning forward, I cupped both sides of his face with my hands and drew him closer for a deep and painfully slow kiss. He planted one hand on my upper back and the other on my hip, drawing me into him until there was no mistaking his member pressing up against me.

I drew back from our kiss, and as he searched my eyes and I his, I slowly sank onto him. The moan that escaped his lips matched my own, and we were instantly moving to an unheard rhythm.

The world faded away. There were no snowflakes falling from a darkened sky, no chilly breeze sweeping down from the mountains, and no water lapping at our waists.

It was only us.

Chapter 25

Buried beneath a quilt, a duvet, and two luxuriously soft blankets, I woke and spied six pillows haphazardly thrown around the bedroom. Last night felt like a dream, and I never wanted it to end. And neither did he. I don't know how we made it inside the lodge, but I know we left our mark on the way to the nearest bedroom.

I hadn't left Levi's arms since he picked me up in the forest, which was as true now as it was last night.

He stirred beside me.

Twisting around in his arms, I smiled up at him. "Morning."

"Morning." He leaned forward, placing a kiss on my brow.

My arms around his back pulled him closer, and I rested my head on his chest. It would be so easy to let the gentle, calming beat of his heart lull me back to sleep, but we both knew today would be a different day.

We had to find Theresa, Osman, Oliver, and all the other aliens who had scattered into the woods after the facility was destroyed. I remembered still being able to smell the smoke last night and Levi pausing to stare out over the tops of the trees to where a plume of smoke curled high into the clouded sky.

We lay silently in one another's arms for another hour until sunlight filtered through the window, forcing me to accept the time to rest was over. Levi must have had the same idea as he pulled back the covers and swept me into his arms. I giggled, burying my face against the crook of his neck. He carried me across the room to the bathroom, where, by some luck, the plumbing still worked. I had a vague recollection of finding a generator last night. Still, I had assumed the abandonment of the lodge would have caused pipes to burst as the seasons changed. But so far, the only evidence of decay was the layer of dust across the furniture and a spot of mildew in the foyer.

Levi turned the shower on, waiting for the steam to fill the room before setting me on my feet. We stood in one another's arms, as naked as last night, letting the water run over our bodies. Grabbing a bottle of body soap, I squeezed a dollop of lavender rinse onto my hand before swiping it across Levi's chest. His answering smile stirred me, and I took it as an invitation to spread the soap across his shoulders and down his back and chest. He reached for the bottle, mirroring my actions, before drawing me close and smoothing the soap across my arms toward my chest and over my breasts. He paused halfway across my stomach before the mood shifted.

It started with the darkening of his eyes and the firmness of his grip on my waist. I answered in kind, moving close to him and moaning as he caressed my soapy breast with his hand, his fingers flicking across my nipple, causing it to harden. A moan escaped me, and that's all he needed to turn me around and push me against the wall, burying himself inside me. I sought his hand, entwining our fingers as he thrust into me. I didn't bother trying to be quiet, and neither did he. We let our moans fill the room, louder and louder, until we both reached our limits, climaxing as one before falling into each other's arms.

This time was different. Levi cradled me close, nuzzling my cheek with his nose and lips. When the water began to run cold, our bodies shivering and flesh pebbling, Levi turned off the tap. Together, we grabbed the towels on the rack to dry ourselves, barely keeping our eyes to ourselves.

The bedrooms didn't have any spare clothes, but they did come with complimentary full-length bathrobes. Levi's was a deep navy blue, and mine was a gentle creamy gold. We carried our old clothes out to a fireplace in the lodge foyer, where Levi was quick to get flames roaring. We hung our clothes across chairs that we dragged across the wooden floorboards to sit before the fireplace. We had no choice but to wait for them to dry before heading out, but the sun sat halfway to the highest point in the sky, and we knew we were losing valuable time. But there was nothing we could do about it.

Lounging across the sofa, entangled in one another's arms, we made ourselves comfortable with the silence.

"Emilia?" His honeyed tone still stirred me, the way he said my name causing warmth to spread across my cheeks.

"Yes?" I could barely spit the word out, distracted by the lazy circles his fingers drew across my hand.

He hesitated. "Do you think hope exists?"

"What makes you ask that?" I frowned.

"Perhaps it is because I have found myself in love with you."

I froze, and I was certain he did not miss it. Was he saying he *loved me?*

"Link or not, I have fallen for your charisma, strength and guile, and ability to care. You were the first to show me what a true act of heroism was, and if we can manage, then there is hope yet."

Now it was my turn to hesitate. "What happens now?"

He pondered the question. "We find our friends and forge our own path."

"I'm not even sure where we are." *How could we even begin our search?*

"Come. Let us have a look." He pulled me up with him, and a giggle escaped my lips.

I felt like a teenager in love, and that thought didn't bother me one bit. I was here with Levi, safe and sound. He loved me, and he had hope for us. I found myself realizing more and more our kinds weren't so different, not really.

He threw open the doors, walking out in the sunlight. His hair glistened in the sun, a light breeze ruffling it across his shoulders as he stared out over the garden and hot springs.

"Hey, Levi?" I called out to him.

Turning around, he returned to my side. I took him by the hand, marveling at the strength and firmness of his palm. He faced me with a curious gaze, and I bounded forward in his arms, staring up into those bright crimson irises of his.

"I love you too."

Our lips met, and this time the world truly did fade away. Euphoria filled my being, and I could see brightness. For us, for the future, and for a world that was ready to heal.

But he froze in my arms and pushed me behind him toward the doorway.

"What is it?"

"Quiet," he warned, his eyes scanning the woods.

He called out into the wood, his cry echoing between the trees and over the snow. Almost instantly, the woods came alive, a mass of arms and legs carrying a small army out from between the tree trunks. They spread out around the lodge, filling in the spaces.

Leading the pack, standing at the foot of the hot spring, was Raak, ivory hair tumbling across his bare chest, with his light blue skin marred by various open wounds. I could see the blood splattered against his flesh, but I didn't know if it was his or someone else's. Behind him roared an army of aliens, each one the same, yet different.

Their wild hair ranged from black to pink to blue to white to gold, and their flesh was an impossible rainbow spectrum. A particular alien drew my attention with her golden hair and small forms emerging from the woods behind her. There was Tress, and behind her followed Theresa and Osman hand in hand, and Oliver a foot back, eyeing us. I wanted to run forward and greet them, but some invisible force told me to wait. My gaze swept the lodge lands, and I became increasingly anxious.

There were so many aliens, their sharpened wingtips glistening in the morning sun. I didn't know how to feel until I watched Levi's shoulders sag in relief, and he strode forward to envelop Raak in a hug. They rested their heads against one another, whispering words I couldn't hear. When Levi pulled away, Raak nodded and took a step back to be in line with the rest of the aliens.

Levi turned to the assembled crowd, his spine straightening, shoulders back, and head held high.

"Brothers and sisters, I welcome you."

I realized he addressed them in English, and curiosity clawed at me.

The crowd stirred, and most expressions were of relief or gratitude, but there was plenty of fear and anger. Some had sustained more than cuts and bruises from whatever they had been through. Some had been crippled or maimed.

"I am grateful many of us survived the landing and what was to come. It hasn't been easy, and I'm here to let you know I see you, I hear you, and I feel you."

There were murmurings amongst the crowd, but not of discontent, just simple acceptance.

Raak strode forward again, standing before Levi.

"We sought you out across this world for one thing, brother," he spoke. Levi nodded, steeling himself. "It is clear our acceptance here was not only unannounced but unaccepted by the creatures that called this planet home. Many of us suffered at their hands, and many more lost their lives. We ask today you lead us toward the future."

Levi froze, clearly not prepared for such a thing. His people were asking him to lead them. My eyes scanned the crowd, and I realized one of the emotions I didn't recognize before, that twinkling in their eye. It was reverence.

He turned his attention to the crowd. "Is that what my people desire?"

Raak raised his fist to the sky. There was a moment of silence and trepidation before Tress raised her hand, then another alien—one I recognized from the laboratory—then another and another until the hundred-or-so-strong crowd echoed the movement in solidarity.

Levi mulled over the moment, no doubt struck by the turn of events. But he was quick to recover, his hand balling into a fist as he, too, raised it into the sky.

The crowd roared, chanting a word, or maybe a name, into the sky. It echoed around the lodge, through the trees, and even vibrated through my chest. The power behind it reverberated through my bones and into my soul.

A stranger strode forward, raising his voice above the crowd, who were quick to fall silent. "Brother, tell us. What do you plan to do about the human situation?"

Levi immediately cast his gaze over his shoulder at me. I shrunk under his eyes as the crowd followed his lead. Every alien had their eyes on me, and I felt like a deer in headlights.

He held his hand out and whispered, "Do not be afraid."

Swallowing my nervousness, I placed my hand in his and let him lead me before the assembly.

"There is no future for us without them in it. This world had survived before them, and it'll survive after them. But us? We are no different. We may live longer, but we still have much to learn that only humanity can teach us. The good and the bad. In order to survive, to thrive, we must work together. We must learn to co-exist."

Another alien walked forward and asked, "How can you be sure this is the right decision?"

He squeezed my hand, his crimson eyes on me. "Because The Link presented itself to me in this human, and I would not defy nor deny such a thing."

The crowd gasped, the whisperings accelerating into a roar. But there was no malice, more curiosity, with a twinge of fear. The Link was important to Levi's kind, something that could not be questioned, and as the realization dawned on each one, they raised their fists into the air once more.

Levi raised our hands together toward the sky, and the crowd erupted in cheers.

Theresa and Osman mirrored us, and after a moment of hesitation, I watched Oliver wordlessly raise his fist in response.

Their chanting echoed across the forests, the sun rising higher and higher. This was the beginning of something scary, something new. Humanity might not be ready for it, but with every breath I took, I'd make sure what had happened in Austria would never happen again. Levi was right.

The only future we had was one of peace.

Together.

I squeezed his hand in mine, our smiles matching.

This new world would be one I could be proud of, one I could nurture. And we would do it together, hand in hand.

Acknowledgments

A big thank you to my mother and sister for reading every story I've ever written and giving me the encouragement to keep going.

I would also like to thank my friends and the reading team for tirelessly sifting through the rough drafts and helping to turn them into diamonds. A special thank you to Yvonne and Andre for the German translations, Mary for her unquestioning support at deciphering the rough, rough drafts, and of course to my consort for unwavering devotion for which I would never have managed to make it this far without.

Your unending support is why there are many more stories to come!

About the Author

TONI MOBLEY was born in the United States and raised between the serene coastlines of Australia and the vibrant cities of Japan. A lifelong storyteller at heart, she draws inspiration from her multicultural upbringing and love for exploring the unknown. When she's not writing, Toni enjoys reading across genres, tending to her garden, experimenting in the kitchen, traveling to new places, and immersing herself in the worlds video games have to offer.

You can find more about her at *www.tonimobley.com*.